THE QUALITY *of* MERCY

THE QUALITY *of* MERCY

A MILAGRO MYSTERY

KATAYOUN MEDHAT

Leapfrog Press
Fredonia, New York

M
Medhat

The Quality of Mercy © 2017 by Katayoun Medhat

Published in 2017 in the United States by
Leapfrog Press LLC
PO Box 505
Fredonia, NY 14063
www.leapfrogpress.com

Printed in the United States of America

Distributed in the United States by
Consortium Book Sales and Distribution
St. Paul, Minnesota 55114
www.cbsd.com

First Edition

ISBN: 978-1-935248-95-8

Library of Congress Cataloging-in-Publication Data

Names: Medhat, Katayoun, author.
Title: The quality of mercy / Katayoun Medhat.
Description: Fredonia, NY : Leapfrog Press, 2017. | Series: The Milagro
mysteries
Identifiers: LCCN 2017017439 (print) | LCCN 2017030255 (ebook) | ISBN
9781935248965 (epub) | ISBN 9781935248958 (softcover : acid-free paper)
Subjects: LCSH: Murder--Investigation--Fiction. | Police--Fiction. | BISAC:
FICTION / Mystery & Detective / General. | FICTION / Crime. | FICTION /
Humorous. | GSAFD: Humorous fiction. | Mystery fiction.
Classification: LCC PR9110.9.M43 (ebook) | LCC PR9110.9.M43 Q35 2017 (print)
| DDC 823/.92--dc23
LC record available at https://lccn.loc.gov/2017017439

IN MEMORY

Lili Medhat née Pollak
1897-1979

Khosro "Punki" Medhat
1930-2016

WANDERERS and WONDERERS

CONTENTS

CHAPTER ONE

The man's body lay facedown in the shadows below Chimney Rock. His arms were pressed straight against his sides, his feet aligned, his toes touching the ground so that he looked as if he had been suspended swimming—as if his last act had been to dive in and swim into the dark and sheltered space, a nature-made crypt between rock and boulder. Above the dead man Chimney Rock towered like an outsized gravestone. Sagebrush growing out of porous rock face formed a dusty green canopy.

· · ·

"He moved!" Dom Benally's face was ashen, his eyes fixed on the body.

"Must be the light," said Sheriff Weismaker.

"Just now he moved," Benally insisted. He looked as if he had lost inches in height and gained decades since K had last seen him.

"He's dead, Dom," K said softly. "It's been a shock for you finding him."

Benally shook his head.

K walked over to the shadowy recess under Chimney Rock. The man lay as he had lain all this time, facedown, motionless, dressed in T-shirt, jeans and sneakers, neatly fitted into the narrow gap between the rocks and quite dead.

A small horned toad was making its way along the dead man's back.

"It's a lizard," K called over his shoulder. "What you saw move is a horned toad."

The horned toad had progressed to the dead man's neck where it now squatted resembling a scrofulous growth. K wasn't sure about forensic etiquette regarding trespassing reptiles. He clapped his hands and the little lizard scuttled off the body to seek safety in the shadows.

"Na'ashǫ́'ii dich'ízhii? A horny toad?" Benally looked even more shocked now. "On the person?"

K nodded.

"The horny toad is supposed to protect us," Benally whispered.

"Can you tell us how you found the body?" the sheriff asked gently.

"Morning run. . . . Today I took a different route."

"Any reason you took a different route today?"

"I hear this coyote." Benally's voice was hoarse. "When I hear the coyote I stay away. Avoid him, like you're supposed to. But today I feel somehow . . . it made me follow the call. I know something is wrong." Benally rubbed the back of his hand over his forehead. "When I see the shoe—could be somebody sleeping off a drunk, you know? But when I come closer I see . . . this. Can we go someplace else? I feel very bad to be here."

They took Dom Benally's statement in the patrol car, then sat waiting for Delgado Forensics, their silence interrupted occasionally by the croak of a raven and the screech of a red-tailed hawk. Above, turkey vultures circled languidly.

• • •

"Redwater want us over at Ridgeback," said Weismaker, putting away his cell. Around them the Delgado forensic team was getting busy securing the scene. The sheriff reversed and maneuvered the patrol car onto the dirt track.

K was surprised. "Redwater want us at Ridgeback?"

It was rare for the Navajo Nation police to call out cops from across the state line.

"That was Lewis King. They found three bodies by the old Ridgeback trading post," the sheriff said grimly. "They need backup until Window Rock get there."

• • •

They drove down Highway 288 South toward Ridgeback on the Navajo reservation, rumbling over potholes, cracked pavement, past the roadside crosses of victims of accidents adorned with garlands of plastic flowers and laminated tributes. The air was balmy, the sky deep blue.

North of Redwater they entered the perpetual fug zone created by the emissions of Needlerock Power Station. Sunlight morphed into a chrome-yellow haze that gave no warmth.

The sheriff took a left turn onto an ungraded road flanked on either side by petrified lava-flows rising to the Ridgeback crest beyond.

They drew up to the Navajo force patrol car parked next to a couple of long redundant fence posts.

"There's Lewis King," said K.

"And Ernie Tso," added Weismaker.

Lewis King had taken off his hat and was rubbing his forehead. Ernie Tso was leaning against the door frame of the abandoned trading post, hands in pockets.

"Thanks for coming. Appreciate it," said King. He shook hands, first with Weismaker, then with K. Tso nodded, spat out the piece of straw he had been chewing on and walked toward the weathered pickup parked behind the trading post. King looked at them and shrugged. They followed Tso.

The pickup stood in the shadow cast by the old store's crumbling structure. The windows were rolled down. The air was thick with buzzing flies. They moved closer and peered into the truck's dim interior.

On the backseat sat a young woman. Her long dark hair fell loosely around her shoulders. A turquoise pendant earring dangled from her ear and moved with the light breeze. Her jaw was slack. Her nose had the peaked shape particular to the dead. In her left temple was a bullet hole.

The driver, too, was young, his hair in a crew cut, a scar running from the corner of his eye to his nose. Blood had oozed from the bullet hole, trickled down his cheek and congealed on his T-shirt. He was staring straight ahead. The third person, the young man sitting next to the driver, was facing them. His body was tilted toward the driver, his mouth open in a final scream. The bullet had caught him in the middle of the forehead.

Weismaker cleared his throat. "Looks like he was the only one to see what was coming."

"He had it coming," Tso sneered.

"Pardon?" said K.

"Leroy Cuthair," said Tso, "one of those Utes coming down here to make trouble for us."

King chewed his lip.

"What about the others?" asked Weismaker neutrally. "Are they known?"

Tso shrugged. "Don't recall these two. Reckon they were looking for some quiet spot to make a deal."

"You think it's drugs?"

"I know it's drugs," said Tso. The sneer seemed to be permanently welded to his face. "I reckon we should be grateful to these guys for offing each other. Less work for us, true?"

K felt the rush of blood to his face. He sensed Weismaker's eyes on him, breathed in slowly and ground his teeth.

"Anything you want us to do?" asked the sheriff.

"Just hang around until the folks from Window Rock get here," said King.

"Could be hours, could be days. Lucky you," Tso sneered.

K was beginning to catch Tso's rhythm. Sneer. Shrug. Sneer. He wondered how Lewis King, a mild-mannered Navajo of the old school, coped with Tso.

Weismaker carefully waved away a fly that had settled on the dead girl's forehead. "She can't be older than 22," he said. "None of them are, I guess."

"The younger they die," Tso began.

"Enough!" said Lewis King. K observed that Tso neither sneered nor shrugged. Maybe Tso just needed to be shown some boundaries.

Through the hum of buzzing flies came the sound of distant rumbling. A convoy of approaching vehicles raised clouds of dust.

Lewis King looked at his watch: "Pretty good response time."

"Reckon we caught them on their way to lunch at the Taco Factory," Tso sneered.

Three patrol cars parked in single file along the erstwhile fence. Two officers got out of each of the cars, synchronously placed hats on their heads and advanced at a stately pace.

They shook hands ceremoniously, with Weismaker, with K, with King, with Tso, who was now standing to attention, eyes glazed with eager ambition.

Carlton Peshlakai, tall, broad-shouldered and carrying the kudos of a Window Rock official, was the first to approach the pickup. He squinted into the dim interior, then circled the truck.

"Whoever did this was a clean shot, for sure. Must've been real fast too," Peshlakai asserted. It sounded like a positive appraisal for the benefit of prospective hirers of hitmen. No one like a cop to appreciate the true craft of the consummate criminal.

"Would you like us to stick around?" Weismaker asked.

"I reckon we are good," Peshlakai said.

Weismaker and K made another round shaking hands.

"I'll walk you to your ride," Lewis King said. He leant into the car as the sheriff and K fastened their seatbelts. "I had some dealings with that Leroy Cuthair. He wasn't all bad, you know? Whatever happened he did not deserve this. None of them did."

"Don't get the impression Tso agrees with you," K said.

King shrugged apologetically. "That boy's a high-flyer. He can't afford not to be prejudiced."

"What do you think will happen now?"

Lewis King rubbed his chin. "I guess Ernie's got company. There's many that think any pusher killing another is doing God's work, you know? Could be another case going straight to cold case." King's eyes roamed the Ridgeback badlands before meeting K's. He waved away a fly. "Maybe we find some relatives and they decide to raise hell?"

"They are kids. They are bound to have relatives," said K.

"Yeah. But do they have relatives that care?" said King.

"Could be you have been in this job too long," K said.

"You think? Maybe . . . maybe." King looked crestfallen.

"No, actually," said K, "but I do think that anybody who doesn't feel that every case deserves solving and that every dead deserves respect has been in the job too long."

"I like the way you say 'actually,'" King said.

"How's Robbie Begay?" K asked.

"Working his way through a bunch of paperwork. Somebody's trying to teach him a lesson. You know how it is." King smiled ruefully. "I'll keep you posted. Ahehe."

On the way back they caught the lull between lunchtime traffic and afternoon rush. There were hardly any vehicles on Highway 288 East.

K watched the landscape drift by, the arid plain and the parched mesa, the road climbing toward the San Matteo range that would receive its first dusting of snow just a few weeks from now. He thought of the three young people, no, four young people, who would never see snow again, who had woken up, not knowing that this would be their last day on earth, who surely had relatives, somewhere. And he thought of all those who would be touched, hurt and changed by these deaths: parents, grandparents, siblings, friends, the descendants of anyone close to the victims for generations to come. Because that was what unnatural and violent deaths did—they tore into the fabric of life, ripped it to shreds, created runs that could go on forever.

"What's going on in there?" asked Weismaker.

So K told him.

14

They passed a roadside cross draped in plastic flowers and Mardi Gras beads. It was hard to think of a greater contrast than between the Rez and the green, fetid swamps of Louisiana.

"Does the Jewish faith deal in Original Sin?" asked Weismaker.

K wracked his brain and could come up with nothing. To be agnostic in a heartland of born-again Gentiles and missionarized Natives at times could be a challenge. "I don't think so," he said eventually. "I think the deal's a belief in fresh starts."

It sounded plausible enough.

"That seems a good thing to believe in," said Weismaker. "Well, they got enough people on the Ridgeback case. All we got to deal with is John Doe at Chimney Rock. Anything there catch your particular attention?"

K thought back to the prone body at the foot of Chimney Rock. His first impression at the scene had been how peaceful it was. There was none of the chaos that usually lingered where an unnatural death had occurred.

He had felt then that whoever had placed the body in the shadows of Chimney Rock had done it with consideration; had not so much hidden as laid out John Doe under the sagebrush canopy with care, even tenderness.

"Why was John Doe laid out facedown?"

"You are saying he was laid out?" asked the sheriff with interest.

"It looked like that to me," K said, "it looked as if someone really cared. Though who would place a body facedown in the dirt? Who would take such care positioning a body, and then lay it face toward the earth? Isn't it up the dead are supposed to be looking?"

"It is unusual," the sheriff agreed.

"Do you think Chimney Rock and Ridgeback could be linked somehow?" K asked.

"What makes you think that?"

"Just that . . . they all looked so peaceful." K said

"It's not for nothing they call death the Big Sleep," the sheriff said. "We'll know more once we get Durango forensics' results. By the way, I almost forgot: you are on Twilight tonight. Dilger called in—shot himself in the foot."

It was the start of hunting season. K figured Dilger had gotten over-excited polishing his double-barrel. The thought almost compensated for being made to pull a Twilight.

"There is poetic justice after all," K said.

"Why? What have you done?" asked the sheriff.

CHAPTER TWO

When K pulled into Milagro PD's parking lot for his Twilight shift, he saw Young's chrome-infested Chevrolet driving up. The sheriff naturally had omitted to mention that it was Young with whom he was to pull Dilger's Twilight.

So K began the shift as he meant to go on, holing up in his office and playing Spider Solitaire. After seven losses he switched to Mah-jong, where things did not work out either. Some days were like that.

He went into the kitchen to brew himself a coffee. The kitchen was as expected: sink brim full of dirty crockery, worktop filthy with condiments, crumbs, cold cut debris, greasy paper and sticky hand-prints everywhere.

Young was standing at the counter with a foot-high sandwich packed with fluorescent meat and phosphorous cheese.

"You vegetarians don't know what you're missing," Young said by way of welcome, chewing on his Noah's Ark in sandwich-guise. A wodge of saliva-clumped matter flew out of his mouth and landed on K's collar.

"Thank you for sharing," K said.

"I hear some good Christians got made today over there at Ridge-back," Young said.

K measured instant coffee into the last clean mug, filled it with boiling water, stirred.

"Can you smell something?" he said to his coffee.

"Smell? What smell?" asked Young, still chewing.

"Something rotten."

Subtle it wasn't, but still wasted on Young: "There ain't no smell. Lorinda cleaned out the fridge just yesterday. "

• • •

Back in his office K sipped tepid coffee and stared at the wall clock. The clock's ticking sounded like a dripping tap. It was one of those ironies that those who had time—or thought they had it—did not value it. On the contrary. They couldn't wait for it to pass. He couldn't wait for it to pass. Despite everything he had seen today. What did that say about him?

The intercom crackled. Dispatch calling through.

"Trouble at Barbie's. Magnusson just called in."

"Did Magnusson specify what trouble?"

"Just said he could use some support," Gutierrez said.

"I'm on it," said K.

A late shift wasn't a late shift without a callout from Magnusson.

• • •

When K's patrol car pulled up at Barbie's Bar Magnusson was standing outside, looking, as usual, disheveled in his lumberjack combo of check shirt and baggy jeans.

Before he took over Barbie's as his retirement project, Magnusson had been a professor of economics and business management at a Southern state university. The perpetual sorry state of his business gave substance to the old saying "those who can, do; those who can't, teach."

K and Magnusson met up once in a while to play Backgammon. They had first bonded through a shared dilemma as naturalized US citizens and conflicted European-Expats-of-Leftist-Persuasion. They had agreed they were self-serving opportunists, Coca Cola Socialists, neutered lapdogs that nipped—perfunctorily—at the neoliberal claw that fed them.

Magnusson had changed his first name, Gunnar, to Brendan, citing as reason that folks tended to pronounce Gunnar "Gunner," and he was a pacifist. K, full name Franz Kafka, on the other hand had gradually come to realize that by settling in Milagro, San Matteo County, he had chosen one of the few places left in the Western hemisphere—and possibly the Eastern too—where his name rang no bells, provoked no curiosity and drew no comments.

It had taken years of God's own citizenship, of enduring "Cathcarts" and "Cuffcares" and "Caffers," even "Cuthberts," to persuade K to finally let go of the conceit of identity and to begin introducing himself as "K, like M in James Bond." One of many steps on a slippery slope.

"You weren't busy, were you?" Magnusson said.

"What's up?" asked K.

"Is it OK to call you out on a hunch?" Magnusson made it sound as if it was the first time this had ever happened. "If that's what you cops call it—'hunch?'"

"The brothers in the movies may call it 'hunch.' We call it 'wasting police time.'"

Magnusson frowned. When he frowned Magnusson looked like a lost Labrador.

K felt like pulling his ears: "So. What's up?"

"I had a hunch."

"Others have dreams." K said.

"I had a hunch," Magnusson said undeterred, "that something was going to kick off."

"And did it?"

Magnusson shook his head. "I'm overreacting. Getting old," he said sadly. "Sometimes I don't know anymore what's in my head and what's real."

"Don't we all," K said.

"Sometimes one's head's the best place to be in," said Magnusson. "I'm talking about your head, not mine. Sorry about wasting police time."

"Police time's not to be wasted," said K officiously. "We must be mindful of our taxpaying citizens."

"A dwindling minority—now it's official that only the dumb pay tax."

"Might as well do ID checks while I'm here," K announced.

"ID checks?" Magnusson echoed incredulously.

"Open warrants. Fake IDs. Don't look at me like that. Community liaison," K added lamely.

"You can't be serious." Magnusson narrowed his eyes. "Hey, wait a minute. Let me guess—there's something keeping you out on the mean streets, eh?"

"I don't know what you're talking about," K said sanctimoniously.

"So, which one of your redneck friends are you pulling the shift with?"

"Young."

"All's forgiven. Be my guest."

"Thank you," said K, "you go ahead and I'll cloak myself in authority and join you in a minute."

Magnusson chortled, "Cloak in authority? You are a loss to sociology," and ambled into the bar.

K retrieved from the patrol car the paraphernalia of his trade, went into the saloon and swaggered toward Magnusson, who was now standing behind the bar, distributing smears on glasses by means of a dishcloth. K assumed a broad-legged stance and snarled through clenched teeth, "Routine check. Everyone! IDs ready for inspection."

"Oh, my," Magnusson said sotto voce, "I didn't appreciate just what I was getting myself in for."

"Might as well have fun," K murmured sunnily.

He hoped he would be spared cop's luck to happen on somebody on an open warrant, or, as a matter of fact, any other situation that required more than ham-acting the tough-cop routine.

In the first booth was a Navajo couple, long married, K assessed from the way they were disinterestedly sharing the narrow booth. The man was drinking a bottle of Coors, the woman was nursing a glass of soda pop. The woman sat awkwardly. K guessed that she had thought it wiser to accompany her husband when he went drinking than to wait for him at home, worrying about his whereabouts and safety. And here she was, sitting by her old man, though she knew that bars were very bad places for a Navajo. She was middle-aged and heavy set with proud features and deep lines running down the sides of her mouth, wearing traditional Navajo jewelry of squash-blossom ear-rings and turquoise bracelet.

K saw the woman's anguish as she sat in her traditional outfit in a bar, having to sit by and watch her husband drink alcohol and thereby commit a cultural transgression.

Though—who knew?—maybe she was OK with her old man drinking. Maybe it was just cops that made her uncomfortable. As well they should.

When the husband looked up, K realized that special cop atten-tion was exactly what he was expecting. He greeted wife and husband, recited the standard "Routine-ID-Check" phrase; glanced cursorily at the driving licenses offered and handed the IDs back with courteous thanks. The Navajo couple looked at him in stunned unison, as if they could not believe that their encounter with the police was supposed to be over already. The couple's surprise at being treated courteously confirmed what K already knew about the Land of the Free.

The next booth's hirsute occupant was flexing his shoulders and eyeballing K, fixing to act large for the benefit of his date.

"Ahm mighty glad to see y'all working hard for my taxes," he said expansively as he handed K his ID.

"I'm glad to hear you pay your taxes, Sir," said K.

He mustered the couple's IDs with stony mien and glazed dis-interest; returned the cards with a minute nod and moved on before Taxpayer could think of something else to appreciate.

In the next booth were three kids whose gleeful and expectant ex-pressions spoke of their recent transition to legal drinking status. K obligingly pulled his face into the most officious frown he could muster.

"Routine check!" he barked. He took the first ID offered, deep-ened his frown, squinted at the print, and asked menacingly, "Date of birth, Son?" The young man's voice quavered—despite his being legit. K realized that to be fair he had to go on as he'd started, and so repeated the charade for the benefit of the other two. Keeping up the frown took a lot of energy and K's forehead started to ache. He only hoped that his trouble had served to enhance their experience.

Where the bar widened into the backroom there was another row of booths. Here only one booth was occupied. A man and a woman in the semi-dark sitting opposite each other, hunched over the table.

K approached the booth.

The girl had straight brunette hair and sharp features. She was wearing a black long-sleeved T-shirt that shrouded her emaciated frame. The girl's pallor and thinness made K think she was a meth-user. She did not look much past her mid-twenties but had an air of uncompromising autonomy, the kind of steeliness bred by deprivation. She bared her teeth in a hostile sneer as she handed him her ID. The license identified her as Muriel Kowalski.

The young man opposite leaned back languidly and looked at K with an expression that was hard to define. His hair was dark, the color of his eyes amber, almost yellow—like a jaguar's. The young man retrieved his license from a frayed wallet and placed it in K's hand. The sleeve of his T-shirt rode up his arm.

The young man's arm was covered in evenly spaced horizontal scars, thin white lines, each measuring around two inches.

K had dealt with self-harmers in the course of his work. What bothered K was not so much that the young man cut himself. It was the ordered nature of the scars. These scars did not speak of affect, urgency or impulsiveness.

These scars spoke of detachment, deliberation and discipline.

K became aware that he was holding the license without checking it. The young man's eyes were on him, neutral, K thought, with perhaps a hint of expectation. The name on the license was Jared Beausoleil. There was nothing obviously wrong with Jared Beausoleil's license.

K handed it back, nodded, turned, walked.

Not a word exchanged between the three of them. That was some kind of a record at least.

Magnusson was standing outside. K leaned against the wall beside him.

Magnusson asked, "Everything in order. . . ?"

K shrugged.

"Find anything?" Magnusson asked.

K shrugged again. "You know how it is: sometimes I don't know what's in my head and what's real."

"Ha ha," said Magnusson mirthlessly, "honestly—was there something?"

"There's always something. Though usually you only know there was once it's too late."

"You sure are inspiring confidence."

"Glad to be useful."

"Hey," said Magnusson, "are you OK?"

"As much as is to be expected. It's been a long day. Full of . . . stuff."

"Stuff?"

"Better go," K said. He turned away and felt Magnusson's shovel-sized hand patting his shoulder.

"Take care, friend. And thanks for humoring me."

"Anytime," said K.

•　　•　　•

K cruised along Main, took a right on Elm and made another right on Anasazi, which was a lovely place to patrol at night: dark and silent streets, the outline of mountains black against the sky, deer dining on municipal shrubbery, and at this time of year even the occasional bear tempted into the valley by apples ripening in orchards. All was quiet and K saw two shooting stars.

The SUV came careering out of Cottonwood without reducing speed. The number plate was personalized: "King of the Road."

K switched on the flashers and gave chase. The SUV drove on, apparently oblivious to the police cruiser following. It was likely that the driver was occupied, perhaps with his hand stuck in someone's

panties or having his dick sucked, all of which were pretty much routine occurrences for cops on patrol.

K wished for just one occupant, the driver, and a straightforward
DWI scenario. With drunks trouble tended to multiply by the number
of passengers in a vehicle, particularly if some or all of them had been
engaged in acts of a sexual nature prior to being apprehended.

Eventually the SUV slowed down and pulled over, just before it
hit the intersection.

K took the breathalyzer along. He was grateful that his six-foot-
two height brought him eye level with the King of the Road who had
bloodshot eyes, disheveled hair and a spittle-flecked moustache. His
Majesty was so shit-faced he had trouble letting down the window.

"Sshhhhi shhhhere," the guy slurred. There was a snail's trace of
drool running from the corner of his mouth down to the crease in his
neck. Or maybe he had been sick.

"Shhh . . . shhhnut' shhhwro'. . . ."

K yanked open the driver's door, leaned against the vehicle so that
the King didn't topple out and held the breathalyzer under his nose.

"Blow—hard as you can," he commanded in a tone of unassail-
able authority.

"Looks like we got ourselves a new record," he said, peering
incredulously at the breathalyzer.

He leant over the driver, who was mumbling incoherently, pulled
the key out of the ignition, got him under the arms and lifted him out of
the car. He draped the man's right arm over his shoulders and, support-
ing the man's dead weight, started walking him toward the patrol car.

• • •

In the booking room they had to secure a chair by wedging it between
desk and wall, so that the drunk didn't tumble over. K got the breathalyzer out for another reading. The King blew obediently. His lungs
at least were strong and he seemed to enjoy blowing into the breathalyzer. Maybe he ran a party balloon business.

"Wowzer," said Young when he saw the reading. "You caught

him driving? Yikes. Should be in a coma by rights. Tough cookie, huh?"

If the King had been Native, it was pretty certain there would have been more from Young than a remark that damn near sounded like a grudging mark of respect.

Gutierrez patted down the man's pockets and found a leather wallet holding several platinum-issue bank cards, driver's license, a couple of business cards, a photo of two blonde teenage girls, a $107.69 bar tab, and a twin pack of raspberry-flavored condoms.

According to his business card Lucky Easton was Public Relations Representative for XOX.

XOX, the Texan-based energy corporation with big plans, was busy hydraulically fracturing the length and breadth of Quorum Valley and now anticipated the all clear for their pipeline running all the way to Texas. No risk whatsoever to the environment or groundwater, natch.

K wished he'd let the motherfracker smash into a tree.

With the end of the shift near K left it to Young, who probably would leave it to Gutierrez, to notify Lucky's lucky spouse of unlucky Lucky's whereabouts.

In terms of how society's mills of justice turned, it was unlikely that Lucky Easton, King of the Road and Public Relations Representative for XOX TEXAS Hydraulic Fracturing, would suffer much more punishment than being mandated to attend a couple of Safe Driving classes and—perhaps—a month or two's driving ban. That way the cookie crumbled.

"At least I've got something now to put in my report," K said to Gutierrez.

"What was the deal with Barbie's?" asked Gutierrez.

"No deal."

"Nothing?"

"There was something—but nothing that I could do anything about."

"Just like life," said Gutierrez wistfully. "Go home. Get some sleep."

CHAPTER THREE

When the phone shattered the nocturnal silence K felt as if he'd barely slept at all. He groped for the receiver.

"Howza boy?"

K squinted at the alarm clock's fluorescent hands and hissed through gritted teeth.

"What's that? Can't hear you!"

"It is fucking four in the morning!" K roared into the phone.

"Oops. So it is. I am sorry."

"How come you never learn that there's seven hours between us?"

"In addition to all the other things between us? You always say you are an early riser," said Lili, unrepentant and literal-minded as usual.

"Not that early, you cow. What's up?"

"Just wanted to put my coffee break to good use. Serves my kudos to look busy and all that."

"Well, thank you, sister, for thinking of me. I wouldn't like to think you've got no one else to ring. You are working?"

"A gig up at Harrogate. Some HR outfit hired me to strengthen their team spirit."

"So, how are you strengthening their team spirit?"

"*Helping* them strengthen their team spirit."

"Whatever. Too early to piss around with semantics. Any reason you're ringing me during work?"

"Nothing, really. Just felt briefly suffused with gratitude."

"Suffused, eh? They'd lynch me if I used words like that here. Gratitude toward. . . ?"

"You. Well, strictly speaking, not you. Grandpapa—for insisting on calling you Franz. You've no idea how much your name enhances my clients' learning experience. Every time I confirm that I am related to Franz Kafka I've as good as nailed that five star evaluation, even if I sit through sessions playing Kazoomba!"

"Kazoomba?"

"Never mind."

"Don't you think you are being a bit mendacious?"

"Why?"

"Claiming to be related to Franz Kafka?"

"Mendacious? How much more can you be related to someone than being his twin sister—well, apart from being an identical twin?"

"When they ask you if you are related to Franz Kafka, I imagine they don't mean Franz Kafka, provincial cop?"

"Well, they should ask me if I am related to *the* Franz Kafka then," said Lili, undeterred. Sometimes K asked himself if there wasn't something of the sociopath to his twin.

"Your appreciation of being related to me-not-me—that's what you called me for?"

"Hmmm." She sounded muted now.

"Lili?"

"The anniversary's coming up. . . ." her voice trailed off.

"I know," said K.

"Good of you to remember," Lili said testily.

"How so?"

"What do you mean: how so?" she asked.

"I'm saying," said K patiently, "why is it good to remember when there's nothing to do about it? When there's no place to go? That's the thing with ashes. Nowhere to put flowers."

"You're so conventional, Franz."

"Sometimes I think what they would make of us now. What would they make of us do you think? Would they be proud?"

"Proud? You're having a laugh? Daughter lackey to degenerate capitalism, their son a redneck sellout with Hillbilly Received Twangciation?"

"Ouch. What would have made them proud?"

"Hmmm. Maybe, for you a Cannabis plantation, organic and sustainable, natch—and for me, a Maoist-themed tattoo parlor. "

"Tattoos? I doubt it," K interrupted.

"Why?"

"Historically too sensitive."

"Historically?" Lili snorted. "Did they strike you as the kind of people who ever dwelt on the past?"

"They struck me as the kind of people who always ran from something."

"Don't we all," Lili said briskly. "Break's over—got to go. Test the team spirit to breaking point. By the way, it's true what they say about Yorkshire men. Will call you soon, OK?"

"If it doesn't inconvenience you too much, perhaps at a time that is mutually acceptable—to both of us?"

"You just gotta suck it up, little brother," said Lili.

She hung up while K was saying "fuck you too" to a dead line.

K lay and stared into darkness. Sleep wouldn't come.

What did they say about Yorkshire men?

•　•　•

"Just in time," Becky said when K walked into the station. She was distributing mail and messages in pigeonholes.

"In time for?" asked K.

"You're needed in the interrogation room."

"Interview Suite, you mean."

"Whatever," Becky said without a trace of good humor.

K decided against commenting on or enquiring into Becky's mood.

"Who am I supposed to interview?"

"Just observe. They want you to observe. I hear you had a tough day yesterday." Becky's voice had warmed up somewhat. "Just hang and chill."

"Cool," said K. He quite liked sitting in the dimmed light, looking out from behind the one-way screen. It reminded him of monkey houses at progressive zoos.

In the observation room he found Smithson vigorously scratching an armpit while perusing the sports pages of the Milagro Gazette.

"What's going on?" asked K.

Smithson dipped his chin toward the observation screen, which framed a tableau of a grave-faced Gutierrez sitting primly opposite two smirking jocks.

"Looks like he's getting nowhere fast," said Smithson.

"Where's he supposed to get to?" asked K.

"That Indian that was jumped in the park? The drunk dude? It was them. But so far, no cigar. Looks like they ain't gonna sing any time soon."

Smithson was fond of watching vintage police procedurals and it showed in his diction.

"They did what?"

"Jumped him, beat up on him when he was lying there, passed out. I guess he's lucky he's still alive. They meant business."

"Have they said anything so far?"

"Just asked Gutierrez if he was an Indian. I ain't too sure it's been a good idea to send Gutierrez in. These dudes are prejudiced. If you ask me, they ain't gonna spill to no Mexican."

"So much for the great melting pot," said K.

"Reckon we're about ready for a changeover," said Smithson. He pushed on the intercom and called through to Gutierrez.

Behind Gutierrez' retreating back the young men smirked and sneered.

"Ay Jesús," said Gutierrez, looking relieved rather than offended.

"Now you go in and do your shtick," said Smithson.

"My shtick?"

"Whatever cranks your handle. They ain't gonna talk anyways."

"Neither am I," said K and grabbed the newspaper from Smithson.

He entered the interrogation room, nodded at the two young men, sat down and began leafing through the newspaper. He turned pages until he came to the Readers' Letters section, a motley offering of bigotry, parochialism and blinkered optimism that would keep him entertained for a while. And then there was the crossword and the "spot the difference" pictorial puzzle to look forward to.

He wasn't even into the third letter under the headline "Jesus would slap you," when he picked up signs of restlessness from the two suspects. Sneakers tapped on the floor, one of them began rocking on his chair, the other scraped his nails along the table surface.

K looked up, smiled blandly and continued reading.

One of the boys started drumming on the table, the other let the backrest of his chair thud rhythmically against the wall. K raised his head. They looked at him. K looked back.

The rocking boy pitched his chair forward and spread his elbows on the table. His jaw was clenched, his eyes hot.

"You're looking at us like we are some kind of animals."

K considered; shook his head. "Right now I can't think of any animal that would attack a defenseless being for the hell of it." He nodded benignly and went back to his newspaper.

One of the boys cleared his throat. "Defenseless? You kidding?" he hissed. "Gross, that's what they are. Animals—bare human. Get given everything that we have to work for. Need to be taught a lesson."

"What was he supposed to learn from your lesson?" asked K without raising his head from the newspaper.

"Behave civilized. Not stink up our town. Go away."

"Go away," the other boy said, "stink up some other place. Pull their shit elsewhere. We don't need them here. We don't want them here. You go ask anyone: nobody wants them here."

"So you performed a public service?" asked K.

"I guess you could call it that," said the boy with the clenched jaw.

"Bet you don't have the guts to put that into your statements." K pushed pens and statement forms toward them, gathered the newspaper, got up and left.

• • •

K followed noxious coffee fumes down the corridor to the sheriff's office. Weismaker was sitting behind his desk, absently sucking on a piece of rolled-up cardboard.

"Some folk may get the wrong idea, Sheriff," said K.

"I wish," said Weismaker. "They made me attend the public hearing to represent the voice of the Law. Those medical marijuana folks sure know how to have a good time."

"I hear it got voted down?"

"There's always a next time. And the next vote they hold it's going to get pushed through anyways. Tax Revenue! Sweet Dollar Talk got our Mayor hooked. Also, according to that gal who just opened the Herbal Healing Dispensary and that smooth Irish reprobate that's running the Green Light MM Dispensary—Ciaran McGuiness— makes your mouth water that name, don't it?—the choochoo's left the station a while back."

"The choochoo's left the station?"

"Dope ain't niche no more, it's gone mainstream in a major way. There's now more folk that smoke a toke than have themselves a Bud. Why don't we all mellow out together, dude?" Weismaker began to hum in a grating falsetto. The tune seemed vaguely familiar.

"Age of Aquarius? I didn't know that was your scene, Sheriff."

Weismaker nodded, increasing the volume of his humming. He sounded like a demented bluebottle trapped under a bell-jar. As if spurred on by K's concerned frown, Weismaker underscored his humming by languidly wafting his cardboard cylinder from side to side.

"Did they offer samples, Sir?" asked K.

He started to wonder about the stretch of Weismaker's life between Mennonite upbringing and embarking on a career in the police force. Perhaps they could get together one evening for a toke or two of black Afghan, chewing the fat about Haight Ashbury and Jimi and Janis and Joe, while listening to Jefferson Airplane—or whatever complemented Black Afghan.

"Any news from Delgado, Sheriff?"

The humming stopped abruptly. The sheriff put down his psychedelic cardboard roll.

"Post-mortem's scheduled for early tomorrow. One thing's for sure: he had no ID—matter of fact they found nothing on him: no wallet, no watch, no change, no receipts in his pockets, nothing at all."

"Someone didn't want him identified?"

"Or he just liked to travel light."

"What about Ridgeback?" asked K. "Any leads yet?"

"Haven't heard anything," Weismaker said.

"You won't if Ernie Tso's got anything to say about it."

"He'll live, learn and mellow," the sheriff said mildly, "I have a mind to call in some favors though. Input from Redwater might speed the whole thing up. How about Robbie Begay? I bet he'd see things that we don't."

"I was just thinking about him," said K.

"You worked a case together, didn't you?"

"The Anglo and the eagle feathers."

"Sounds like it should be on the library's mystery book club list."

"It was fun."

"Fun? Not sure that's what you get paid for, Son. This here's murder."

"You're sure this is murder?"

"What's for sure is he didn't get to where he was found by himself. Someone put him there."

"It was so . . . serene," K ventured, "not at all like a regular murder scene."

"That still bothering you, huh?" said the sheriff. "We'll know more when we get results from Delgado. In the meantime, go have some quality time with ARGUS. I know how you dig your admin work. You need to make your APC, remember?"

"APC?"

"ARGUS Proficiency Certificate. I ought to set you a deadline."
Weismaker pondered. "I'm sure Becky'll be glad to talk you through
ARGUS—again."

He sighed, reached for his cardboard roll and stuck it into his
mouth with a smoker's urgency.

•   •   •

The ARGUS icon drifted across the desktop in languid loops. It was
having a soporific effect on K. He could barely keep his eyes open.
But then he hadn't slept that much and his dreams had not been restful.

Dispatch crackled into life, an indistinct voice announcing auto
theft on 1741 E Main.

K logged off and saw ARGUS shrink to a toxic green spot.

He strode through reception, mouthed "auto theft" to Becky, and
was out before she could utter "APC."

•   •   •

1741 E Main was a cabin about the length of a single-wide set back
from the road, with a neon sign spelling Main Street Liquors in red
joined-up lettering, on a lot that could have used some resurfacing.

Main Street Liquors stood next to the Aspengrove Trailer park,
from where it drew its main customer base. This Main Street Liquors
had in common with Milagro PD.

In Milagro town Aspengrove Trailer park was known as a
shithole festering with a random assortment of troublemakers, psy-
chos and losers in variable proportion in whom the Good Creature of
God seldom evoked a state of graciousness. So it was all the more re-
markable how rarely Main Street Liquors availed itself of assistance
from the Law—the surfeit that Brendan Gunnar Magnusson required
in the way of municipal resources was, some would argue, balanced
out by the circumspect reticence of Main Street Liquor's owner, Camilla Archibeque.

When K pulled into Main Street Liquors Camilla was outside

leaning against the wall. She was dragging on a cigarette, exhaling slowly, eyes on the distant mountain range.

"Hey," Camilla said and ground out the cigarette with the heel of her boot. "How are you?"

"Mustn't grumble," said K.

"I hear you been busy over there?"

"I guess. Quiet times, busy times—like any business."

"It's a business?"

"It is. Except we prefer it the other way round to most businesses."

"Wouldn't you get bored if there was no crime to solve?" Camilla asked.

"Sometimes even solving a crime isn't that great," K said.

Camilla narrowed her eyes. "How so?"

"Because mostly you wish it had never happened. Because sometimes things turn out so everyone's made unhappy."

"A solved crime makes people unhappy?"

"Sometimes it does."

Camilla frowned.

"It's like Jenga," K tried to explain, "you pull out one piece and everything collapses. A crime's not an isolated thing. It's a landslide. So—what about this auto theft?"

"Auto theft?" asked Camilla.

"The auto theft you called the station for."

Camilla shrugged.

"It's nothing," she said.

"You mean there was no auto theft, or it doesn't matter if there was?"

Camilla looked at him. Platinum hair framed high cheekbones, Aztec nose and dark, dark eyes. Camilla's eyes were so dark they were almost black.

"This is more complicated than I thought it would be." K did not know what made him say that.

Camilla circled the tip of her boot around the cigarette butt on the ground.

"Camilla, are you OK?"

Camilla drew her shoulders together.

"It's not police business," she said.

"I'm planning to retrain as a counselor," said K. "How about you offer me a coffee?"

"I was about to have a coffee myself," Camilla said. "Come on in."

The inside of Main Street Liquors was dimly lit, allowing furtive patrons to purchase their liquor without feeling too exposed. K followed Camilla into the back room at the end of the store and sat down at the small Formica table.

Camilla filled two mugs with coffee and put the black mug that bore the gold-scripted legend "What Happens in Vegas, Stays in Vegas" in front of K.

She sat down opposite K and pushed a sketchbook out of the way.

"Do you sketch?" asked K.

Camilla shook her head. "Not mine." It didn't sound as if she was going to elaborate.

"I always wondered what that means." K frowned at the logo on the steaming mug. "You go to Vegas often?"

"You don't make me for a Vegas girl?" Camilla's eyes held K's, as if expecting a pronouncement.

K began to feel as if he was being invested with rather more than he had bargained for.

"I take you for . . . complex and conflicted."

Camilla looked at him. "You don't give much away," she said.

"Neither do you. But it's not poker we are playing, is it? What I can see is that there's something on your mind pressing on you."

She shrugged. "Look, truth is: it's not easy running this store and breaking even. Hell, in this trade it's not even easy when you're making good money, because it's not clean money. Don't get me wrong, I keep my business strictly legit, but to some people liquor's worse than the devil, and what am I supposed to do, stop them? But you see them walking off with bags full of hooch and you just know someone is going to have to pay for that. Might be the wife. Worse, it could be the kids. Or the grandma. That's where a lot of them get the dough for their liquor from, you know. The old folks that don't know how to say no—or how to protect themselves. I guess I'm responsible for a lot of misery in this town—indirectly."

It occurred to K that Milagro Municipality might want to introduce a special tax from contrite business people for damage inflicted on society. How about "DIRT"—Damage-Inflicted Reparation Tax?

Camilla was looking at him. K looked back. Camilla got a cigarette out of the pack on the table, lit it, inhaled deeply, exhaled slowly, watched smoke curl toward the ceiling.

"You don't mind. . . ?" she gestured with the cigarette.

K shook his head. He guessed that the usually taciturn Camilla was only talking to take her mind off something she did not want to talk about.

If Camilla didn't pretty soon get to what was really bothering her, he'd have to go. If Camilla stuck to her decision not to report an auto theft, he'd have some explaining to do, not to mention having to account for the time spent with her while not pursuing police business. Maybe he could use ARGUS to practice writing a non-report on a non-theft, a damn impressive addition to yesterday's Barbie non-incident. Altogether he was making a pretty good case for his job to be cut. Then maybe he could look into the medical or otherwise marijuana trade. Or clairvoyance.

Camilla looked at K, dragged on her cigarette, looked away. Exhaled smoke through her nostrils. It came slowly and in delicate wisps.

"Have you ever felt out of your depth?"

"Who hasn't? Though I guess there are levels of feeling out of depth."

"There sure are," said Camilla.

K felt a twinge of impatience: "You're feeling out of your depth?"

"I guess that's what you could call it—could be when you're feeling out of your depth you get frightened of being out of control. You start thinking about, how did you put it, everything crashing down?"

"I'm hearing anxiety, but also excitement," K said, bull by the horns and all that.

Camilla bent forward, looked hard at K. "Maybe you should be a counselor."

Ground out her cigarette, reached for another one.

"Life . . . you get older, you start to reckon you're in control. You reckon you are in control of your feelings—and of your experiences. I don't mean disasters or accidents or a bad sickness. Those are just God's will, I guess. There's things in life you can do nothing about. No sense messing with the Higher Power."

Camilla exhaled and watched the smoke drifting toward an unseen current.

"You don't smoke?"

K shook his head.

"Good for you. What was it you just said?"

"Jenga?"

Camilla shook her head.

"That you are anxious and excited?"

"I guess. Sometimes something happens. You start seeing things different, or—maybe things are different."

K listened carefully. He tried hard to understand what Camilla was saying. What Camilla was trying to say.

Camilla had stopped talking. She was chewing her upper lip. It made her seem young and oddly vulnerable.

K saw Camilla as the young girl she once had been. And then things began to make sense. It was strange that it hadn't occurred to him before.

"Camilla—are you in love?"

Camilla flinched as if she'd been slapped. The young girl had gone. Now she looked. . . .

He'd gone too far, carried away by his counselor persona. He could not think of anything to do or say. His mind was blank.

It took Camilla no more than a drag on her cigarette to erase whatever expression there had been from her face, to erase whatever feeling had possessed her. She pushed back her chair, got up, said in a smooth, even voice: "I bet you got important things to do." Stretched her mouth into a smile, and walked out of the room.

K remained sitting, listened to Camilla's footfall moving away from the store room.

He drew the sketchbook toward him and opened it. There was a sketch of Camilla. A sketch in which Camilla looked so much as he'd just seen her, a thwarted, haunted Hera, that K thought for a moment his impression had psychically transferred itself onto a piece of paper.

He turned the pages. There were landscapes: Milagro Mesa, the San Matteo Range, Luna Badlands, Shark's tooth. All intricately done. All carrying an aura of menace, a sense of desolation. Here was Lone Cone. Not looking so much like a mountain as a gateway to a netherworld. K felt that chill spread through his bones. How thin was the Earth's crust separating life above from the molten inferno below.

The store bell rang.

K closed the sketchbook, got up and went out of the back room into the store. Two rugged-looking men were hauling packs of beer out of the walk-in refrigerator.

Camilla was standing behind the counter.

"See you later," said K.

Camilla did not respond.

CHAPTER FOUR

At the station everything was quiet. Becky was reading a magazine titled *Accessorize!* On the magazine's cover was a white girl whose butter-colored locks were threaded with pink and white beads. It occurred to K that a snap taken of Becky Tsosie reading Accessorize! would make a great cover for a book on the wiles of cultural hegemony.

"What's that?" asked K.

"What's what?"

"'Accessorize!' The older I get the less I understand. What does it mean?"

"You wouldn't know an accessory if it hit you in the face," said Becky.

"That's what I'm talking about. Though if an accessory did hit me in the face, I would arrest him," K said grimly.

"What happened about the auto theft, by the way? Go practice your report on ARGUS."

"No report."

"No report? Who was it? "

"Camilla Archibeque from Main Street Liquors."

"Oh. Camilla Archibeque."

"Do you know her?"

"Why are you asking?"

"It was how you said 'Camilla Archibeque.'"

"Hmm. Anyways, Sheriff's got word the post-mortem will be

with us in a couple of hours. Briefing's scheduled for 4. Before that I got a real treat for you."

"Please, God," groaned K.

"Info session at the Elks', 2.30!" beamed Becky. "How's that?"

K wasn't going to give her the satisfaction of arguing. "My cup floweth over," he said fulsomely.

Becky raised her eyebrows. She looked disappointed.

"Who dropped out?" asked K.

"McCabe. That DUI thing at the Library did not float his boat that much I guess."

"Too many gosh-darn liberals over there. Well, I suppose you could give the Elk gig to Young," K offered.

"And leave the tree-huggers to you?" Becky interrupted briskly. "Remember what the sheriff says about not staying in your comfort zone?"

"I don't recall the sheriff recommending taking long-haul trips out of your comfort zone. Can I at least pick what to talk about to those Elks?"

"Let me guess: 'Going Vegetarian Heals Your Karma'; 'Give Up Your Guns and Take Up Knitting'?"

"Origami, I was thinking," K said. "It's all the rage, I hear. A rage for the raging."

"Funny!" Becky curled her lip. "Go ahead. Knock yourself out. Those folks aren't so hot on listening anyways. Besides they'll be too busy figuring out just how much your hair's over regulation length. The talk's supposed to be on 'home safety,' burglary—that kind of stuff. They'll let you know where they want you to go, don't worry. I put everything you need in your pigeonhole. You done this before, right?"

"Yeah, I'll run the DVD and then do FAQ on PowerPoint."

"PowerPoint, eh? Remind me to make sure the sheriff puts that in your next appraisal. And be back at 4 pm for the sheriff's briefing."

● ● ●

The Elks Club was an outsize stone-clad building of a style that hovered between Santa Fe ranch and 1970s suburban shopping mall. The building was surrounded by immaculate lawns—thanks to the continuous deployment of a battalion of sprinklers that dispersed roughly as much water per day as the Hopi tribe used for a year's crop cultivation.

K drove through the gate, past a wooden life-size bear holding a rustic sign with "Elks Lodge" on it in lopsided letters. K saluted the bear, parked, made a futile attempt to smooth his hair with his fingers, gathered the materials that Becky had put together and went into the building.

The Elks consisted of an expansive hall with walls of oak-effect laminate—or maybe it was real oak, who knew. Regardless of how much money the Elks had spent—or hadn't spent, it looked like laminate. K hoped that it was real top-quality, solid oak that the Elks had invested in. He hoped that it had cost the Elks a lot of money to look this cheap.

From the grand hall, doors led to smaller function rooms and administrative offices. Signs pointed to the catering kitchen at the back of the building.

The furniture in the hall resembled something procured from the Addams Family Studio sale. A gallery of God's miraculous creations rendered eternal by the marvels of taxidermy and mounted on walls looked down on visitors: heads of bighorn sheep, deer, elk-bulls, elk-cows, bears, mountain lions, raccoons, beavers, a bobcat crouching on a log, a rattlesnake rearing on a boulder, a humongous stuffed pike in a case, a golden eagle perched on a beam.

"There seems to be no skunk," K said in a mildly inquisitive tone to the floridly complexioned Elk who approached him.

"Beg your pardon?" said the Elk.

K treated the Elk to his WASP smile: a thin-lipped stretching of the mouth, accompanied by narrowed eyes and the briefest of nods. For the WASP to look authentic it was crucial to achieve just the right balance of blandness and repressed menace.

"I'm here for the Home-safety and Burglary Information talk."

"Uh. They said it would be Officer McCabe? He sure did a great job last time he visited with us. We are happy to have you of course, Officer. . . ?" the Elk added as an afterthought.

"Kafka."

"Officer Cathcart, sure am pleased. We scheduled you for the Mesa Vista room. I'll just get Hay-souss to check the equipment. You go right ahead and make yourself at home." he gestured toward the room.

Hay-souss would be Jesús. Though probably of a darker hue than the Elks liked to imagine their Lord. It stood to reason that at the Elks' Club all the Elks would be white men and the staff serving them would be Native or Hispanic.

K squared his shoulders and walked toward the Mesa Vista room.

• • •

"You sure look as if it rained on your parade," said Becky as K walked into the station. "What's up?"

"McCabe, that—"

K choked back the expletive that was the only appropriate way to show how he felt. Becky's tolerance, although otherwise considerable, had its limits at cussing.

Becky's parents, as so many Navajo of a certain generation, had both been fostered by Mormons in the Native Adoption Program, and some things—not cussing, not consuming caffeine and a pervasive sense of loss—had stuck.

"What's he done now?"

"The PowerPoint—I thought it'd be FAQs and safety tips."

"Wasn't it?"

"Well, if you call an NRA propaganda piece campaigning for homeowners' rights to shoot first and ask later, then yes. You keep safe by keeping your gun loaded by your bedside. Better still, have a loaded gun handy in every room of your house.

Have a mastiff that's trained to kill. Don't bother locking your door or your car, because we are a free society. If an intruder dies on your property there shouldn't have to be an inquiry. And so on."

"Oh. What did you do?"

"What was I supposed to do?"

"I bet you did what you weren't supposed to do, huh? Let me guess?"

"No need, I'll tell you. After the damn thing finished I told them it was a spoof to show how *not* to do things. And then I said that I knew that some folk moved here from other places because they reckoned we still had old Wild West justice. Then I advised anyone looking for that kind of fun to move to Alaska and wave to the Russians from there."

"You are kidding?"

"No."

"What did you do then?"

"I distributed brochures and left."

"Well, I'm sure we're going to get some follow-up calls. And guess who's gonna have to field them?"

"I'm sorry, Becky."

"You really are upset, huh?" said Becky. "That bad?"

"It's everything, the people, the place, all those critters they kill and nail to the walls. There's hardly space left. All ears and antlers and eyes. . . ."

"The eyes are glass," said Becky. "Are you trying to tell me you picked a fight with those Elks about their trophies?"

"I didn't. But I wish I had. If they introduce Open Season and make it legal to take out some of those good ol' boys. Don't look at me like that. I won't take them out, OK? I'll just scare them, graze their fat asses maybe. They need to feel some pain, don't you think?"

K was working up to one of his rants.

"For an older guy you are kind of cute, especially when you get angry," said Becky.

Speaking of having the wind taken out of your sails.

"If I didn't need you to CMA, I'd file a complaint about your ageism," K said.

"CMA?"

"Surely that's the first thing they teach you? CMA: Cover My Ass."

"Oh, I know it as CYA: Cover Your. . . ."

"Most important principle of any public service."

"Well, why not make it a double? There was a bit of sexual harassment in there too," Becky suggested.

K wondered if, when Becky's age, he would have dared to speak to a woman nearly twenty years older than him in the way that Becky spoke to him. Should he feel flattered or perturbed? Then he wondered if this was the way she spoke to every cop—Young and McCabe included.

"Just so you cool down: us Diné don't rate trophies either," Becky called after him.

• • •

In the meeting room tables and chairs had been placed in a horseshoe shape around the whiteboard that covered most of the wall. A few seats had already been claimed by the placing of random objects—a notebook, a copy of the National Enquirer, a pack of Reese's Peanut butter Cups, a Walmart shopping bag.

Basically everyone had their preferred seat. The golden rule was to keep that preference hidden from the team, because as soon as someone's favorite place was known, everyone else would do their damnedest to prevent them from ever getting to sit there again. It was one of those games that brought zing to teamwork.

K strolled into the Incident Room and made straight for a seat at the center of the table. Then, as if noticing only now the notebook that had been placed on it, he shook his head mournfully and went to the chair by the window.

K leant back in his favorite seat and took in the view—cottonwood groves now turning into the golden colors of fall bordering the city limits; distant peaks of the San Matteo mountain range, pale blue sky and drifting gossamer clouds.

'Yet again I triumph, me; Rumpelstiltskin my name be,' murmured K. It was quite a few years now since the move to the new building and they had yet to find out that K always got to sit in the seat he actually preferred.

K nodded a cautious, sober greeting at Juanita Córdoba. Juanita Córdoba nodded back and took the seat next to K. Naturally the eyes of the squad, pack of sex-crazed hyenas, were on Officer Córdoba and therefore by association on K. In a way they were a trinity of squad outsiders, Córdoba, Gutierrez and K, non-Americans, according to the ruling belief of what was a real American: born in the USA, white, Christian, preferably Born Again, with rudimentary command of just one language: English. "If English was good enough for Jesus, it sure is good enough for me," as the state Senator said when voting down bi-lingual education.

Córdoba looked at her watch. "When's this starting? The sheriff was outside just now."

"They're waiting for the folks from Merced and all."

"Oh," said Córdoba, "I got a rape crisis training at the Community College in an hour."

"You know those Tullulah cops," K said.

"Sure—they're real attached to their mountain."

"More like attached to their coffee."

Weismaker entered, ushering in Officers Wertenbraker, Uhlig, Mills and Eckhart out of Tullulah, Merced, Ciego and Gopher PDs. How they would be able to help with John Doe was anyone's guess. Maybe Weismaker had just wanted to treat them to an opportunity to leave their backwater lairs where they likely spent most of their working hours picking their teeth and counting sprinkles on donuts.

Córdoba leant toward K and whispered, "Looks like the sheriff's invited them all?"

K inhaled the scent rising from Córdoba's warm, coppery skin, a delicious mélange of soap, peach and just the slightest whiff of fresh, healthy perspiration.

"The more the merrier," he said sagely.

"There's nothing merry about a murder case," Córdoba admonished.

"We don't know for sure if it's murder yet," said K.

"Yes, we do," said Córdoba just as the sheriff summed up the results of Delgado's forensic pathology report: "Fracture to base of skull. Signs of a forceful impact on chest. Bruising indicates that John Doe was alive at the time. Fracture was not the cause of death though: the cause of death was suffocation. Skin discoloration due to oxygen deprivation. Traces of synthetic fibers in lungs. No signs of struggle. Could be he was unconscious prior to being suffocated."

"So someone hit him and then—suffocated him?" Córdoba whispered, "That's weird, isn't it?"

"Was he hit?" K whispered back

"He has that bruise and the fracture," Juanita Córdoba said.

"Hardly a frenzied attack."

"That's what makes it weird," said Córdoba. "It is such a detached . . . it's not messy, like most murders are, you see?"

K remembered the order, the calmness of the crime scene. The dead man's body stretched out in that sheltered space. The birds circling high above.

"A better place," he said.

"What?" asked Cordóba.

"Nothing," said K.

"We'll be glad for y'all's input as soon as we've got through this." Weismaker's face was stern. "Couple of tattoos. One: small, left inner biceps, probably DIY: skull in sphere with letters SW. Within the inner margin of sphere shapes that could refer to four sacred mountains of the Navajo Nation seal. Anyone know what SW's supposed to stand for?"

"Gang?" suggested Uhlig, whose Gopher outpost surely had never dealt with anything more severe than a TFIF DUI and public littering.

"Possible," said the sheriff, "Next: tattoo on right inner wrist, setting sun with DAD, letters RIP below."

In the bright light of day the projections of John Doe's tattoos were hard to make out. One definitely looked like a DIY job and it was doubtful that the other one would have won any prizes at tattoo conventions either.

K was still considering Córdoba's comment. The more he thought about it the harder it was to see how Doe's injuries—skull fracture and bruises—fit in with the cause of his death—suffocation. K's main association with death by suffocation was mercy killings: relatives dispatching a terminally ill loved ones by placing a pillow over their face. Compassionate, speedy, efficient: a brief struggle and good-bye to a world that held nothing anymore but pain and suffering. In peace now and forever, Amen. In the eyes of the law it was still homicide though, never mind how altruistic the objective.

"Why don't you say something?" he whispered to Córdoba.

"Say what?"

"What you just said about things not fitting together?"

Córdoba shrugged. A frown had edged two small vertical lines on her forehead. Her face was stony. K looked around the room and realized that in Juanita Córdoba's place he would not say anything either. Even as a male who could pass as member of the dominant majority he preferred to keep quiet unless the situation obviously demanded that he speak.

"Body tested positive for alcohol, BAC of 0.04%, so under the limit," said Weismaker. "Traces of recent marijuana and crystal meth consumption, preceding death by six hours or so. Now for the composite reconstruction."

Becky pressed keys on the computer. She looked strained. "It would be better to see if someone lets down the shades and switches off the lights."

Gutierrez got up, went over to the windows and pulled down the shades, and in the darkened room the reconstructed image of the dead man became visible.

High bridged nose, wide forehead, broad cheek-bones. Full-lipped, sensual mouth contrasting strong, fierce features. An expression of anger or pain. There was something disconcerting about the eyes—maybe that they lacked focus or that they reflected no light. The face was bloated and contourless. Maybe John Doe had begun to decompose when he lay there under Chimney Rock, when he lay there dead with his face in the dirt.

In the wilderness were plenty of scavengers, bugs that would have not have passed by the chance of a meal—all those creatures inhabiting the earth, feasting on that great gift that had been bestowed on them, carrying away, ingesting and digesting particles of John Doe who now was, in a sense, part of the ecosystem around Chimney Rock. And therefore immortal.

Weismaker asked, "Does this kid seem familiar to anyone?"

There was no answer from the darkened room.

"Lights, please," said Weismaker

Gutierrez got up and began pulling up the shades. Gutierrez, being relatively recent to the squad, had taken to volunteering for the chores that kept his colleagues sitting it out on their asses, waiting for the weakest link to break. Gutierrez hadn't been here long enough to comprehend that he was screwing with one of the squad's favorite diversions—playing "Who's the Sucker."

"Initial reactions? Anyone recall him? Recall anything at all?"

"He seemed kind of familiar to me. Could be he was a troublemaker."

Becky said, "I don't know. When I first saw the photo-fit I felt somehow. . . . But it was gone in a second."

Córdoba asked, "Delgado say anything about the likeness of the composite? Sometimes the deterioration is so bad they have trouble making a 'fit look real."

"They didn't specifically comment on the reliability of the image," said the sheriff. "So there's nobody here that knows the guy, recalls seeing him around? No? So our priority has to be to ID John Doe."

"Put up posters, like in Walmart, City Hall, the college," Gutierrez suggested.

McCabe snorted.

"Get the Milagro Gazette, and the Navajo Times and the Appleton

Daily to publish the photo-fit," Gutierrez said, bravely soldiering on.

"That's a possibility. But we'd have to take the risk that this is how his relatives learn that he's dead."

"Send out the photo-fit and dental chart to every dental service in the area, public and private," said Gutierrez. You did not get to be a Latino cop in a town like Milagro without perseverance and a tough hide, even if you had to hide your hide.

"That seems like the best course of action," said Weismaker.

Another snort.

Amazing how much a snort could say.

This one said that McCabe deemed any praise or encouragement of "ethnics" as affirmative action of the most heinous liberal tendency. It was only a matter of time until Gutierrez would be forced into acquiring the finer points of how to swim with sharks without having chunks torn out of his skinny ass.

"We'll send dental charts and photo-fit out today to every area dental service and then follow up the public ones with a personal visit," said the sheriff. "There's a good chance he was treated in the IHS. If he's from around here, Redwater's the most likely. We'll start visits tomorrow. That's it, folks."

The squad began to file out of the Incident Room.

"I'm going to make it on time for my training session." Juanita Cordóba looked at her watch and gathered her papers. "I just remembered: That's what my grandmother called it: A Better Place."

"Called what?" said K.

"Death." Cordóba said.

McCabe cocked a fat thumb, directing Gutierrez toward the last lowered shade.

"That one always stays down to prevent light damage," said K.

"Huh?" said McCabe.

"You probably missed the implementation of Statute 14: 'Rules for Natural Light Source Management,'" said K helpfully, "Something about City Hall Health and Safety regulations."

McCabe stopped chewing his gum.

Gutierrez' eyes roamed from K to McCabe and back to K.

"Lousy bastards," spat McCabe, "I'll be darned."

"There's Big Government for you," K said encouragingly. "Looks like the People didn't get the White House back after all."

"Yep," said McCabe, "but first I'm going to talk to the sheriff. This crap's gone too far."

"Next they'll tell us how to make our beds," said K.

"Damn right," said McCabe and stomped off, chewing furiously.

"Thank you," said Gutierrez, "for refreshing my memory pertaining to Statute 14."

"You are very welcome," said K.

• • •

"Is it Ornery Day today?" Weismaker growled. The mug in his hand emitted evil fumes.

"Pardon me?" said K, startled. Had Weismaker already heard about his encounter with McCabe?

"We got some calls from the Elks about the Home-Safety and Burglary information session."

"Hmm," said K, cautiously. His memories of the event were sketchy. For some reason he could now only remember laminate paneling and the mounted heads of massacred animals . . . their glass eyes. . . .

Weismaker was regarding him pensively.

"Anyhow. Tomorrow you drive down to Redwater and do the hospital. If they don't come up with anything, try the Beautiful Smiles Dental Clinic. He's most likely to have been treated at one of those places. Then go see Benally and his family. Whoever did it must've used a vehicle to get John Doe to that place. So they'd have driven past Benally's outfit. Ask if anyone has heard anything, seen anything—dogs barking, lights in the night. Ask the kids. Teenagers are always up at night, asleep in the morning."

"Dom's kind of old school that way. He probably makes sure his kids get up and do the Dawn Blessing."

Weismaker looked skeptical. "Why do you think traditionals are dying out? Another thing: Go over any tracks you can find over there. We are still real short of details. See if Redwater'll let you borrow Begay, he's the King of Tracks."

CHAPTER FIVE

K loved the drive to Redwater, loved the effect of seasons and the changing light on the land. In springtime a carpet of Desert Paintbrush lapped at Needlerock's base. Its reflection tinted the sky crimson, the plain shimmered green with desert flora that briefly asserted itself. In winter a day could start with a blanket of snow, melted to nothing and every drop drunk up by the thirsty earth come noontime. Summer was the season of sandstorms, of whirling dust devils and many shades of colored sand. Fall brought rain and mud and air washed crystal clear of pollution and dust.

Today was one of those breezy days when gauze-like clouds drove delicate shadows across the land and pale blue light blurred the landscape and made you feel serene and that all was well with the world.

K passed the weathered "Welcome to the Navajo Nation" sign; the 55 mph speed limit sign; and his favorite, the "Speed monitored by aircraft" sign; drove past the abandoned hogan on the hill crest west of the highway where not so long ago had lived an old man and his sheep; and was approaching Redwater. Now he had to decide where to start his search: Redwater Indian Health Service hospital or the Beautiful Smiles Dental Practice.

He detoured to the gas station, where he was captivated by the various kinds of Tcheezos on display: Tcheezo Puffs, Tcheezo Giant Puffs, Crunchy Tcheezos, Hot Tcheezos, Hot and Crunchy Tcheezos, Extra-hot and Crunchy Tcheezos, Extra-cheesy Tcheezos. He bought a copy of the Navajo Times. In view of the likely epidemiologic impact of Tcheezos it seemed fitting to make the hospital the first point of call.

Redwater Hospital consisted of a central building, from which departments fanned out in individual wings, with a stairway leading to the basement. The hospital's hexagonal central hall evoked a large-scale ceremonial hogan, a tribute to Navajo traditional healing offered up by an institution drawing foremost on the tenets of Western biomedicine.

K descended the flight of steps along a wall adorned with murals of sand paintings. He wondered if the hospital had solicited any feedback from the community—in particular what the few remaining traditional Medicine Men had to say about having their sacred sand paintings, an integral part of Navajo healing ceremonies, de-contextualized and employed for decorative purposes only. But they probably hadn't asked any traditional Medicine Men, because those tended to live way out in the boondocks and did not speak English that well.

The Dental Clinic's entry door had a glass panel through which the empty waiting room was visible. The receptionist was a woman in her thirties with long hair that she wore open. The woman smiled at K.

In Anglos, seeing a cop in uniform immediately registered in their behavior. To most Navajo whether K wore a uniform or not did not seem to make much difference. Maybe this was because bílagáana socially represented the dominant majority and therefore, even as civilians, were, relatively speaking, close to police status. Or maybe it was because bílagáana pigs had no jurisdiction on the Rez anyways.

"Are you here for an appointment?" the friendly receptionist asked.

"An inquiry," said K. "I'm from Milagro PD, following up on the photo-fit and dental chart we sent you to identify a body."

"Did you email it with an attachment?" asked the receptionist.

"Yes."

"I forwarded it to the doctors. They're all out for a meeting—over in the Main Building. They ought to be back soon. You want to wait?"

"Sure," said K. "Did you have time to look at the email?"

"I read it."

"Did you look at the photo-fit?"

"Is it the photo of a dead person?" the receptionist asked unhappily.

"It is a composite reconstruction, it's an impression of how this person that was found dead, looked alive," explained K.

"I am expecting a baby," the woman said.

K nodded. "You don't have to look at the photo. We just need somebody here to look at it. Is there someone else who works in reception that sees most folks that come through?"

"Elsie Nez. She won't mind. She's Christian."

Christians had no problems with the dead. They worshipped them in fact. Their own god was most frequently displayed during his final earthly moments writhing on the cross, and to get into their churches one had to walk through burial sites.

Still, Christian missionaries had managed to be extremely successful with a people with whom death was such a taboo.

One of the first things Dom Benally had said was that he wished he could move away. Dom had not been neurotic. He had been following his ancestors' beliefs about the polluting power of death.

This was why the elders had not trusted hospitals. Even when tuberculosis ravaged the Tribe they did not want to be treated at the hospitals. Hospitals were not healing places. Hospitals were death houses. In the early days the hospitals had been obliged to hold a purification ceremony every time someone died—though the elders would have probably preferred the hospital be burnt down.

Now ceremonies were no longer necessary. People visited hospitals when they needed to, visited their dying relatives and recently a Navajo-operated funeral parlor had opened just opposite the hospital. Mourners sat in the same room as casket and corpse and did not mind. In the olden days that would have been a definite no-no. The old ways had relied on everyone minding a multitude of taboos and prohibitions. Those who transgressed promptly fell ill, went crazy, suffered endless bad fortune. Elders warned of lost ways and inevitable catastrophes. Just look around: drug use, gang activity, drinking, violent deaths, cancer, mental illness—all the price of forgetting the traditional teachings.

K sympathized with the pregnant woman's fears.

"Is Elsie Nez around now?"

"She's just on her break. She should be back any time now. She's always straight on time," the woman added as an afterthought.

She looked at the clock and gathered the files littering her desk into a tidy stack.

"Oh, there she is!"

K had not heard the door open behind him. The woman walked past him, opened the door that led to the reception office and put her purse in a locker.

"Elsie, this officer is from Milagro. He—uh—wants to show you something. I'm going on my lunch now."

Elsie Nez said, "You got twenty minutes," and looked at the clock.

"Sure," said the pregnant woman and hurried out the door.

K suspected she was avoiding seeing him produce the photo-fit, but then twenty minutes for a lunch-break were not much, even if she went no further than the hospital canteen.

Elsie Nez was a short, wizened woman, who probably ate lunch in her car with the air-con running. She did not look leisurely enough to stand in line in the canteen, or sociable enough to meet up with others to eat in one of the fast-food outlets or moderately priced restaurants that catered to Redwater's hospital workers, school teachers and BIA officials. Elsie Nez' hair was drawn back in a bun in a style often seen on the female members of religious communities who would have preferred the veil, but for some reason were prevented from wearing it. She was dressed as she wore her hair, austerely. No jewelry; hospital ID suspended from a black cotton strap.

"When are the first patients due?" K asked.

Elsie Nez glared through a pair of steel-rimmed spectacles.

"In twenty-two minutes," she said, without consulting the clock. "She said you wanted to show me something."

It didn't sound like a question, more like a criticism of her colleague.

"Can I come in?" asked K, and entered the reception office without waiting for an answer.

"I guess," Elsie Nez said. She looked around her workstation as if deliberating on a near unsolvable dilemma, then dipped her head toward a chair.

The waiting room when seen from the reception office area looked very different. K felt sheltered, as if barricaded in a fortress. Maybe this was why receptionists so often were dragons: being "on the other side" really did impart a feeling of control and power.

Elsie Nez sat down warily next to him, looking as if she'd rather keep K at a distance—preferably over on the other side. K explained the purpose of his visit. On the wall the digital clock showed the relentless march of time, the scroll of digital seconds advancing digital minutes, a display that in its own way was quite as effective as those mechanical clocks found on medieval churches where Death chased skeletons round and round with his scythe.

Elsie Nez sat and glared.

"I'm here to see if someone can identify a person who died," K said.

"Uhuh," said Elsie Nez blandly.

"Do you have a good memory for faces?" asked K.

"Uhuh," said Elsie Nez.

"If this person has been treated here, could you identify him?"

Elsie Nez shrugged her shoulders. "I guess."

"How long have you worked here, Ms. Nez?"

"Mrs." said Mrs. Nez.

"How long have you worked here Mrs. Nez?" repeated K in the robotic tone of detached officialdom.

"Since they built the hospital."

God help them, thought K.

Mrs. Nez looked at the clock.

K opened the folder. He found in himself a reluctance to show

Elsie Nez the photo. He put the folder before her. He looked away, at the clock, at the gum tree withering in the corner of the waiting room, at the bluebottle ramming its body against the window, again and again. Why did flies do that? Was it because they did not understand the concept of invisible though solid matter? Was it determination? Bloody-mindedness? Optimism? Did bluebottles get concussions?

K looked at Elsie Nez looking at the photo-fit. He tried not to read her expression, then realized that even if he tried, there was little to read.

"Is it a likeness?" Elsie Nez asked.

"We don't know," said K. "Don't worry if you don't recognize him. I'll show it to the dentists too, and there are plenty of other dental practices we can try who might know him."

"I do know him," said Elsie Nez.

"You do?"

Elsie Nez looked at the clock.

"I need to open up now. Come back at 4:30."

There was no arguing.

"I'll leave these with you for now," said K.

"Uhuh," said Nez, shuffling files without looking at him. She started to prepare her workstation for the afternoon surgery with the unyielding focus of an android.

At the doorway K turned around.

"Could you open the window?"

"Huh?"

"To set the bluebottle free. We are all God's creatures."

• • •

In the hospital's parking lot K called Redwater Navajo Nation PD and asked a voice whose tedium was so palpable that it damn-near froze the line to speak to Officer Begay. The line went dead. K waited. He was not sure if he was being put through or had been cut off. This was one of the few occasions when he would have actually welcomed muzak. He pressed the mute phone to his ear until he felt like an idiot, then ended the call and redialed. The voice answering sounded, if anything, even more bored.

"Officer Begay," said K tersely.

"I put you through," said the voice, positively clinking with frostiness.

The line went dead.

Was she using the past or future tense? Did she mean that she had put him through already and would not do so again, or had she announced her intention of connecting his call?

"Fuck this," he said and was about to end the call when a voice barked, "Hello?"

"Robbie?" said K.

"Yeah?" said Begay.

"It's K. I didn't mean you."

"Potty mouth."

"Sorry."

"No need to be sorry," said Begay, "I can guess."

"You'd be right," said K. "Any chance you can help us out?"

"Sure. I know how generous Milagro PD is with freelancers," said Begay when K had filled him in. "Ha ha. Just kidding. How about you pick me up when I'm done here? There'll be still enough light to look things over. See you later."

• • •

With time to kill, K drove over to the flea market in search of lunch.

The flea market was pretty deserted. There were no more than a handful of sellers scattered around the vast, dusty lot. K drove past a pickup selling hay camped out at the entrance. The Chinese family selling household items was there; the old man who always got dropped off by his family to sell beadwork was snoozing under a lopsided parasol; and today there was just one of those stalls that sold counterfeit DVDs, CDs and games.

K parked and strolled toward the food shacks. He stopped at the Chinese family's stall because he could not bring himself to ignore the kids' hopeful faces. Once he stopped he realized that he could not move on without buying something. He decided on a bottle of detergent, $1 at the Dollar Tree, $2.82 here. He rummaged for his wallet. One of the daughters held up a red travel alarm clock. He shook his head and gave her two dollar bills and four quarters. The girl put back the clock and counted out 18 cents change.

K quickly walked past the stall where the old man dozed over the beadwork he was supposed to sell for his family. Even if he'd been awake, the old man's prices did not lend themselves to mercy-buys. K stopped at the stall of the woman selling the DVDs. There were all sorts of genres, romance, bromance, action, war, horror, weight loss. K obligingly shuffled through the DVDs even though he didn't own a DVD player. He felt the woman watching him. He looked up and smiled.

"Most of my business is boxing and adult," the matronly Navajo lady told him. She pointed to a couple of cardboard boxes sitting under the trestle table. She seemed not to care that he was in uniform. But she'd know that he had no jurisdiction here. Maybe loads of cops crossed the state line to stock up on counterfeit porn on the Rez.

"Do customers who like boxing also go for adult?" asked K.

"Hmm, good question. Let me see." He could see that she was really thinking about it. A good businesswoman needed to consider her enterprise from any angle that folks threw at her.

"Not so much, I don't think," she said pensively. "They are different customer bases, you know? It's the young kids that go in for boxing, and the . . . uh. . . ." she faltered. "Let me know if there's something you want. I got a real big range."

K dug neither boxing nor boxers—excepting maybe Mohammed Ali—nor did he dig porn, toward which he had a bigot's attitude. The few individuals employed in the porn industry whom he had met had the downtrodden, resigned aura of people who had the kind of life that had given them plenty of opportunity to get used to being treated like shit. There was nothing liberated about them. K was of the opinion that the disrespect of any social group or member of society compromised society at large. He said as much to the woman, whose eyes glazed over as soon as she realized that K was not a prospective customer. She probably had him for a Christian. Still, she wasn't going to let him get away without making a sale.

"Here," she said, and momentarily brightened as she held out a DVD to him, "I reckon you'll like this."

K took the DVD reluctantly. He was relieved to see that she hadn't chosen a Born Again rally for him but rather a wildlife program presented by an elderly gent who was shown squatting amongst indulgent-looking gorillas.

K handed back the DVD. "I have no DVD player."

Still he admired the woman's psychological astuteness. Of all her stock, the gorilla program probably did come closest to his interests.

"No DVD player?" echoed the woman.

"Not even a TV."

The woman was not deterred. "You can watch it on your computer too, you know," she said.

"I don't have a computer either."

The woman widened her eyes:

"How do you pass your time?" She sounded appalled.

"I keep a small colony of prairie dogs that I try to teach circus skills," K said.

"Yeah, right," snorted the woman.

He had overlooked that jokes told by weirdoes had no amusement value; people simply found them disturbing. And as quirkiness went, training prairie dogs was probably not very high up the scale of amusing pastimes anyway. In fact maybe training prairie dogs was a plausible hobby for a bílagáana. After all many bílagáana came to the Southwest to commune with the Vortex, looking for extraterrestrials and indulging in all manner of activities they claimed were spiritual. K just hoped that the woman didn't think "training prairie dogs" was code for being into bestiality. He waited a beat to see if she would start rummaging in her below-the-counter box, but she turned back toward the National Enquirer, whose title page promised revelations about a tycoon's nanny being cryogenically frozen for the benefit of his future grandchildren; the president's wife, who was having the face of a beautiful Brazilian pauper transplanted onto her ageing visage in an exclusive Swiss clinic; and the ex-president's extended family living as illegal aliens on a Chicago housing project dealing in classified substances. A lot of news for so little money.

K thanked the canny purveyor of porn and walked toward the food stalls. He decided on the one that had a seating area covered with a tarpaulin roof. Tables and chairs were metal and foldable, of a style that had furnished canteens in 1950s residential schools. It was probable that the furniture had been sourced from a school that had wreaked misery on generations of Native children. That it was now used by Natives enjoying traditional meals of steamed corn, squash, muttonstew and fry bread seemed like a small historical victory.

K walked up to the counter, a wooden plank laid across two oil drums, and ordered a tortilla and grilled chili pepper. In K's opinion this was the best meal that $3 could buy.

In the cooking area an old woman began to pat and stretch a ball of dough.

Ten minutes later the meal was ready. K lifted the paper plate and inhaled the bittersweet scent of the pepper and the doughy smell of the tortilla. He took a sip of coffee and bit into his chili burrito. That you never could tell how hot a chili was part of the treat. This one was perfect: first the taste of caramelized sweetness, then the hot kick that lingered on the palate and then the earthy taste of charred pepper. The coffee was hot, fresh and strong. K ate slowly, savoring every bite. It was tempting to stay on, sit in the afternoon sun, have another chili—on fry bread this time—maybe take a drive toward Needlerock. But duty called and he had fifteen minutes before he had to return to the hospital and Elsie Nez. He got himself a coffee refill and flicked through the Navajo Times.

Readers' Letters, being full of complaints, aspersions and disclosures about the corrupt, self-serving machinations of officials, dignitaries and politicians, was his favorite section.

K gulped down his coffee and rolled up the newspaper. He walked past the stalls. The DVD seller was still busy reading the National Enquirer; the old beadwork seller was still snoozing and the Chinese family was sitting on upturned boxes, holding steaming bowls at chin-level and pushing noodles into their mouths with chopsticks. They ate quickly, with focused concentration, in silence. By the time K got into his car, they had finished eating, stowed away their bowls and were tidying their stall in anticipation of customers.

CHAPTER SIX

The Dental Department's waiting room was empty except for one man pressing a dripping bag of ice cubes against his cheek. The pregnant receptionist was sitting beside a pile of files. She nodded at K, got up and went to the back of the office. When she returned she held open the reception door for him.

"Elsie's over there."

Elsie Nez glanced at the wall clock. It was 4:33.

K decided not to apologize, but to relish on this occasion the privileges that being a police officer afforded. As far as Misuse of Office went it was pretty tame, though maybe this was just the beginning of a steep descent that would eventually lead him to accept backhanders, trade deferred parking tickets for sexual favors, solicit confessions by vigorous application of socks stuffed with soap bars...

"What about patient confidentiality?" asked Elsie Nez abruptly.

"You are helping with a police enquiry."

"Uh-huh."

Elsie Nez opened the second drawer of a large, battered-looking filing cabinet. She flicked through the files, which were, assumed K, sorted alphabetically. K looked toward the window. On the windowsill lay a dead bluebottle.

Elsie Nez removed one file from the drawer. It occurred to K that this was the second time she had taken the file out: the first time would have been when she was looking to match the photo-fit to the file. Elsie Nez opened the file, pushed it toward K.

"Noah George. Twenty-eight years old. I'm pretty sure it is him."

Elsie Nez had put the dead man's dental chart that K had given her next to the chart in the file.

She drew a finger over the two charts: "They exactly correspond."

"Can I take a copy of the file and dental chart?" asked K.

"I guess," she said, gathered the file and went to the photocopier.

K took the photocopies from her. "We may contact you if anything else comes up."

"He did not look much like that," said Elsie Nez, pointing to the photo-fit.

"Alive he was a handsome boy," she added as an afterthought.

K wished she had not said this.

It would have been easier to leave with his view of Elsie Nez as a joyless, robotic bureaucrat intact.

•   •   •

In the hospital lobby K made his call to Weismaker. "I think we made an ID. Noah George. Twenty-eight years old. The dental records match in any case."

"Well done," said Weismaker without much enthusiasm. "What now? Would you like to come home?"

"No. I'm going over to the admin department now to see if I can get the medical file released," said K. "Then Robbie Begay and I are going to Chimney Rock for the tracks. I'll take him back to Redwater and then I'll call on the Benally family."

"Remind me to write up your overtime," said Weismaker, sounding weary. "Later."

The hospital's lobby was filled with patients waiting in front of the pharmaceutical dispensary. Medication was dispensed through a hatch beneath a window, similar to a bank teller's counter. Above the window was a sign with instructions in English and Navajo:

1) Go to the machine and take a number
2) Wait until your number is called*

64

3) Go to the window and show your ID
4) Receive your medication

*Listen out for your number! If you fail to respond when your number is called, you have to get a new number.

At intervals a voice barked numbers through the loudspeaker. Most of those waiting were elderly. K watched an old man struggle to his feet and shuffle toward the dispensary hatch when a stern voice rasped: "Forty-two." Numbers were announced in English.

K looked at signs pointing in every direction, trying to make out the one for the Administration Department.

"Are you lost, Officer?" asked someone behind him.

K turned. The question had come from a young Navajo in a paramedic uniform. K looked at the man's expression and wondered if the question had been asked in a spirit of helpfulness or provocation, as in "Damn pig can't find his way out of a paper bag."

"In more ways than one," said K.

"Glad to help," said the young man. His eyes glinted.

"I am looking for Administration."

"I'm going that way," said the paramedic.

His voice was nearly drowned out by the speaker system barking "Forty-three."

In the waiting area nobody was moving.

"Forty-three!" The voice came on again, this time sounding even sterner.

The young man followed K's glance. "The old folks don't always get the numbers. If their hearing's bad . . . and their English not that strong. . . ."

"Why aren't numbers called in Navajo?" asked K.

The young man snorted. He jerked his head toward the dispensary. "Coz they don't know the numbers in Navajo."

The young man walked at a brisk pace.

"Those bilingual signs?" he said abruptly. "Who's gonna benefit from those? The old folks that speak Diné never learnt to write it. The young folks don't speak it. They don't need them. They hardly employ anyone who can speak Diné anyways."

"Why the signs?" asked K.

"I guess for the bílagáana passing through: 'Wow, how multicultural is this! Real Indian writing on the wall!'"

"Indian writing on the wall," K repeated.

"Admin Department," said the paramedic. "Have a good one."

"You too," said K, and watched the young man stride away.

The paramedic had left him standing under a large sign that said Administration Department. Actually the sign was unnecessary. At the end of the working day medical files were returned to Central Administration, where accounts, invoices, insurance claims and third-party reimbursement were processed. The corridor was full of hospital workers pushing trolleys loaded with green medical files. K was reminded of Fritz Lang's "Metropolis."

He followed the procession to the end of the corridor. One by one the trolley-pushers punched a code into a keyboard. The door lock clicked open; the trolley-pushers walked through the glass door and disappeared down the long corridor behind it.

A majority failed to get the code right at first attempt. They punched in numbers, pushed against the door; shook their heads; tried the numbers again; rummaged for slips of paper with the code—some were prepared and had stowed the code in the plastic wallet holding their ID, and others tried again and again, muttering under their breath, until someone in command of the code came along and let them in.

Considering the workplace efficiency that everyone was so hot on these days the security code sure swallowed a lot of time. If time was indeed money, K estimated that it would be more economical to employ a human doorkeeper.

K positioned himself in front of the code-locked door. It was not long before a trolley-pushing drone materialized, dressed in scrubs and wearing a preoccupied frown. K stepped out of her way and held up his badge. "Mind letting me in?" he asked.

"Sure," answered the scrub-clad employee.

K was surprised how easily she'd agreed to his demand. The woman punched in the code, pushed her hip against the door to prop it open and wheeled the trolley through.

"Make sure you arrest all of them," she said with an encouraging nod. "They are guilty beyond reasonable doubt."

"Would you be willing to be called as witness?" asked K.

"I'm looking forward to it. You know where to find me," said the woman and walked on.

• • •

The Administration Department was an open plan without a reception area. Now it was a question of finding somebody who'd admit to being in a position to respond to his inquiry. As K damn well knew, "pass the buck" was a favorite organizational pastime. After all, he'd played it often enough himself.

So far he'd been lucky anyways: he'd obtained the identification of John Doe, now Noah George, without being made to produce release papers or engage in laborious confidentiality agreements (though someone's head could still be made to roll for that); he'd been let into the Administration Department's hallowed halls without further to-do, though the manner in which he had been let in suggested employee subversion as prime motive, rather than a desire to smooth the path of the Law. By law of probability it was time now to trip over some stumbling stones.

Staff hurried between tall filing cabinets, carrying piles of green files. As some files went in, others came out. To K it looked as if people shoved in files wherever they would fit and dragged out whatever came to hand. He guessed that this could not be the case, unless the Administration Department's purpose was to create work for itself to ensure that it continued existing. In that case the work now being done by twenty-five could probably be handled by two moderately efficient-at-being-inefficient administrators.

K resisted the impulse to call out "you are all arrested!" though it was conceivable that some workers would prefer being hauled away by the Law to doing whatever it was that they were being made to do and call productive work.

He looked around the open-plan office in search of a friendly face. His eyes settled on an amply proportioned woman of middle age with purple-rimmed glasses, wine-red velvet top and tightly permed hair. If her appetite for colors indicated appetite for life, she was the one. K walked across the office, conscious of the eyes of under-employed bureaucrats following his trek. He sat down without waiting to be asked and flashed his badge at the lady in red. She did not look particularly impressed. K looked at the woman's ID. It was suspended from an intricate beadwork strap that showed scenes of rural Reservation life.

"I've never seen beadwork like that," he said.

"My granddaughter made it," said the woman proudly. "I taught her, but now she's way better than me."

"How old is your granddaughter?"

"Nearly seventeen," said the woman. "I started teaching her when she was real little, couldn't hardly hold a needle."

"The old skills live on," said K.

"Sure hope so. We need to keep on teaching them," said the woman. "Since she's started liking boys she's not been so hot on the beadwork though," she added in a confessional tone.

"She'll come back to it," promised K.

Pleasantries out of the way, he cut to the chase: "Who can I speak to about authorizing access to a medical file for an identification enquiry?" He hoped the red lady would nominate herself. Before his hopes could fly they were dashed. From the way the red lady pursed her lips it was clear to K that she wasn't including herself in his quest.

"Uh, let me see. Access to files, hmm, Delma . . . Delma John, she's the liaison manager. You need to ask Delma. Her office is back over there, third door. Her name's on it."

K thanked her and she said, "You bet!" a turn of phrase that K associated with Texan Anglos. In his experience Navajo were not much given to clichéd verbiage.

He walked as instructed and found the door with Delma John on it. He knocked on the door, badge at the ready. There was no answer. He counted to twenty. It was surprising how long it took to count to twenty. He knocked again. This time he thought he heard something and opened the door.

The room was small, more cubicle than office. It was windowless and all available walls were covered with shelves stuffed with blue, red and black folders. A woman sat behind a desk facing the door. Her skin was waxy, her hair lank, her eyes sunken. She looked as if she had not had left the office in decades. K held up his badge, introduced himself, stated the purpose of visit.

"Who sent you here?" asked the woman in a tone that was somewhere between anxious and threatening.

K decided to play it safe.

"I was directed to you," he said weightily, as if a higher power had guided him.

Mistake.

"You have to come back with an official request for data disclosure from your superior that states the purpose of the enquiry. You have to sign a Confidentiality Form."

For the dedicated bureaucrat there was but one higher power: the Superior. The woman opened a drawer and pulled out a sheet of paper, which she pushed across the desk toward K. "Confidentiality Form. Fill it in and return it with your official request."

"Will we be able to take along a copy of the medical file?"

"When we have the official request," said Delma John with finality.

CHAPTER SEVEN

Redwater Navajo Tribal Police Station was an older drab-looking brick building with large windows, its entrance sporting a large sign with the seal of the Navajo Nation. Inside the impression of drabness was changed by the panoramic view of Redwater and Needlerock offered by the station's vantage point.

Evidently the majestic view was doing little for the receptionist who was sitting at the front desk. To describe her as bored would have been a cosmic understatement. To adequately convey the degree of ennui she emanated one would need to create an entirely new vocabulary. Bored to tears; bored shitless; bored out of her skull; homicidally bored; bored into zombiedom; walking on a razor's edge of sociopathic boredom did not cut it.

Layers of makeup caked her face and gave it a mask-like quality. It was a small miracle that she managed to chomp on a wad of gum— or maybe it was bile—without chunks of makeup dropping off her face like stucco off a facade. K watched, mesmerized. He let his eyes wander to her desk, expecting to see hillocks of foundation debris.

K approached the Navajo Kali's desk cautiously. She blinked twice—perhaps it wasn't blinking but that her lids were drawn down by the mascara's weight—and said, "Yes."

"Thank you," said K expansively, and walked past the reception desk.

"Hey! Wait!" rasped the girl. "Where you going?"

"You said 'yes,'" said K.

"No. I didn't."

"Yes, you did."

"I meant 'what do you want.'"

"You should try to make a complete sentence—sometime," said K in the most avuncular tone he could muster.

The girl stopped chewing. Now K understood what people meant by "if looks could kill." The girl flexed crimson talons.

"I would like to speak to Officer Robbie Begay. Is he in, Ma'am?" K asked in the tone of exaggerated clarity that some people used when they addressed someone with certified learning difficulties. Though he hoped that he would not talk to someone with learning difficulties like this. He was talking to the receptionist in the way that he guessed the receptionist talked to people, old people, country people, Jhons— anyone ignorant of the ways of the metropolis Redwater.

"Hold on," said the girl.

She extended her arm toward the phone and stabbed at numbers with a long acrylic nail. "Someone for you. Huh? Don't know."

"Who are you?" she called to K.

K stifled the impulse to embark on an existentialist exploration of the question and recited name, rank and station. The girl repeated the information in a droning monotone that was a mascara-coated eyelash's breadth away from outright insolence. She hung up the receiver and made what K took to be a pointing motion with her artful claw. K remembered the way to Robbie Begay's office quite well. To give the girl the benefit of exercising her makeup layers, he asked, "Where do I go?"

• • •

Robbie Begay was a broad-shouldered man with a happy eater's rounded belly, thick black hair in a crew cut and rimless spectacles that belied his phenomenal track-reading skills.

"Long time no see! How are things in the Land of the Enemy?"

When revenue from the oil and gas industry dried up, Milagro had made a bid for the tourist dollar and reinvented itself as "Gateway to the Mysterious Land of the Ancient Anasazi."

Anasazi was the term an early archaeologist exploring the cliff palaces up on the mesa had picked up from some passing Navajo. The archaeologist dutifully recorded Anasazi as the proper name of the people who had built spectacular cliff palaces that could only be reached by ladders bridging vertiginous heights and who for reasons unknown had only briefly inhabited the settlements they had risked so much to build. And so it came to pass that the great cliff-dwelling pueblo people were now universally known by the name given to them by their old Navajo adversaries: "Our Enemies' Ancestors." Sic transit gloria mundi.

"Shoot," Robbie Begay said. "It's your John Doe case over at Chimney Rock, huh?"

"Uhuh," said K. "Looks like we got an ID. Delgado forensics came out when the body was found, but that was before we knew anything. It'd help us to have a pro take another look."

"You calling me a pro, bro? I got no Certificate!"

"What? No Level Three Vocational Certificate in track-reading?!" asked K.

"Nope. Nor a Level Two, or even One. That's what all those academy rookies that they are going to get to replace me have. But what the heck, I'll come out with you anyway. It'll be good to get out of here."

They walked out past the girl who sat immobile, except for her jaws working the chewing gum.

"I'll give you a ride and bring you back," said K, "unless you prefer to use your own ride. Then you can submit a Fuel Reimbursement Form for your gas."

"It'd probably get processed in time for the Second Coming. I'll ride with you."

Begay inhaled the crisp afternoon air. "Sorry about the girl. She's some relative of the boss. K'é and all that. You know how it is."

"Oh boy," K said.

"She got some muscle. Any time one of us tries to get her written up, they get written up instead. Anyone else with that attitude and no friends in high places would have been made gone a long way back, that's for sure."

K nodded. He knew about k'é. Some Anglos called it nepotism, but the age-old network of kin mutual obligations was what had helped the Diné overcome the worst of times and grow to become the United States' largest tribe. It was just that k'é and modern-day bureaucracy at times made uneasy bedfellows.

"I wonder what her grandma thinks of her," he said.

Begay snorted.

"Do you mind looking at the photo-fit of our John Doe, Robbie," asked K, "to see if you ever had any dealings with him?"

Begay was known for his track-reading abilities as well as for his phenomenal visual memory.

"Sure," said Begay. He still sounded pissed.

"Sorry to put this on you," K said.

"What? No—it's got nothing to do with this. I guess I chew on things too much."

"You still chewing on your boss' relative?" asked K.

"She's only the tip of the iceberg," said Begay. "Look at THAT—and then maybe you can imagine what else he gets away with. Oh brother."

"Uhuh," said K sympathetically.

"Let's get on to happier things," said Begay, and stretched out his hand for the dead man's photo-fit. He studied the image carefully.

"I don't think we've ever booked him," he said. "Leastways I can't recall having had dealings with him. But now you got an ID, right?"

"It's just that he was found nearer to Redwater than Milagro. He could have died—been killed anywhere."

"I don't remember this kid. I've not met him, I'm pretty sure. What's his name?"

"Noah George, if the ID we have on him is correct."

"Noah George . . . George. . . . There're no Redwater Georges far as I know. Would he be of the Goatrock Georges maybe? There's a whole outfit over there. There's been a bunch of them up in Milagro too. Used to work the mines in Tullulah. They moved down when the mines closed. I recall a Norbert George; they all have names beginning with N—their Anglo names. Don't know if they even have Diné names anymore."

"Have you?"

"Bet your sweet ass I have. My cheí did it the proper way—first smile, all that."

"What is it?"

"I thought you know some about the Diné way?"

"OK, sorry, none of my business."

"Maybe one day, when you've proved your worth."

"Ch'íidii."

"Not bad, you still got the accent wrong though. Anyways, where were we? Norbert George: Old Bertie used to be a big man in the community, ran all types of gatherings up there on his camp: Powwows, NAC meetings, sweats. . . . He picked up all that stuff someplace on the plains. One day he's this complete Apple, wannabe-bílagáana: Born Again, Sunday school, bible studies, all that. Then he comes back from visiting over there, Oklahoma: Wowee! Must've run into some Brothers. And now he's into Indian Identity in a big way. Doesn't do anything by half, our Bertie. So he gives up the Christian thing and being an Apple and becomes, uh. . . . What's red through and through?"

"Strawberry?"

"Strawberry doesn't sound . . .uh . . . also it's not Native."

"Neither are apples."

"That's the point. An apple is NOT Native. It is not Native and it is red on the outside and white inside. Geddit? Hmmm, cactus fruit? Bit prickly. . . . Watermelon? Nope, green outside . . . doesn't work. Hey, we've got ourselves a real gap here."

"A conceptual niche."

"Yep, whatever. Fact is there's no word for someone who's red through and through."

"You mean Indian."

"I seem to recall you talking me to sleep with symbolism and metaphor, and signifiers—signifiers was it? Remember? When we were working on that bílagáana and her dog-blessing ceremonies?"

"How could I forget?"

"Anyways." Begay furrowed his brow. "Where were we? Norbert George comes back, no Apple anymore, works at being a real Indian and gets busy, goes to NAC meetings, powwows, drumming circles, sweats. . . . Then he becomes this kind of cultural activist, starts to initiate all these meetings, has NAC gatherings in his camp, organizes powwows. Stuff really takes off for a while. Until someone burns down his hogan. Bertie takes it real hard. Gives up everything, shuts down his outfit and moves away. Can't remember where, I think somewhere way over Page, out in the boonies. He died a broken man, they say. And they never found out who it was that burnt down that hogan. Though some think it was his wife. She didn't like the old man's powwows one bit. He expected her to make all that fry bread and stew for every meeting. Also she was a proper old dragon, Norbert George's old lady. And real Christian 'til the end. Thought everything that floated Norbert's boat was a bunch of heathens' devil work. Have you noticed how mean those Christians can be? Anyways, my nalí was involved when they investigated the arson attack on Norbert George's ceremonial hogan. My nalí was a real famous track-reader. 'Course could've been almost anyone that did the burning. Loads of folks were pissed at old Bertie."

"Really?" asked K. "Why's that? Doesn't sound as if he did anyone any harm with his, uh, cultural revival?"

"Bertie got loads of folks real pissed, believe me. For a start, the Anglos did not want all those wild Injuns around taking hallucinogenics and forgetting to be grateful for being second-class citizens; the Traditionals thought it was a corruption of the old ways; the old folk were not so much into the carnival aspect of Indian identity . . . hey, did you catch that? I almost sounded like you there. Anyways, old Bertie's followers were basically a bunch of New Age fringe Indians. Nowadays, of course. . . . Anyways, those Georges, if I'm thinking of the right ones, they've never been lucky, you know. Always something bad going on for someone in that family."

K signaled a right turn at Chimney Rock.

Begay said, "This where the real bad crash happened."

"Yes," said K. "Did you catch the callout too?"

"I was off duty. They said it was real bad. The guys who went out there said it was the worst they'd seen for a long time."

"Noah George was found a couple of miles from here, on the east side," said K. "Dom Benally found him on his morning run."

"Maybe I should start running, huh?" Robbie Begay patted his belly. "All that fry bread really sticks to the ribs. Anyways . . . business."

"It's likely that a lot of the tracks got messed up, there'll be our tire tracks and prints, all kinds of stuff," K said. "Delgado forensics were pretty sure he didn't die at the scene—they say that he was taken there when he'd already been dead for a while."

"Quite a lot of fresh tracks here," Begay said.

"Fresh?"

"Well, traffic that came here after the rain last week. Ah, I see."

They were passing Benally's camp. "I guess a couple of his kids have rides too? Stop here for a minute, OK?"

"Hey," K said, "take the kit. State of the art and never used."

"Hope my nalí does not see me, wherever he is," Begay muttered. "Got a camera too, huh? Fancy, fancy."

"Here's what I got so far," Begay said once he'd hoisted himself back into the patrol car. "Understand that I'm an auxiliary, OK? No guarantees, no liability, got that?"

"You want me to sign Terms & Conditions?" asked K.

"Why yes, dude. You know how I like to do everything by the book, right? Better drive on, else there won't be enough light left."

K drove on slowly.

"Here we go: I got the tracks of six cars I guess belong here or were visitors. This was the patrol car you were in when you came here?"

"Yes," said K.

"Great. That makes it easier to eliminate your vehicle's tracks from this search."

"Where would you like me to stop?"

"I'd say not to get too close. Where did you stop last time?"

"Well, we didn't know, so we got really close. Dom Benally was over there waving at us."

"Can you remember where exactly Benally was standing?"

"Over there at about three o'clock, where the boulder is."

"Let's stop here," said Begay.

They got out of the car.

"Your right rear tire is getting bald," Begay said.

"I'll get it seen to, promise," K said obediently.

"That's not why I said it. It just makes it easier to tell your vehicle from any other tracks that might be there."

Begay walked to the other side of the gravel track.

"Ah," he said after examining the ground, "that's a good start, real good in fact."

"Glad to hear it, Robbie. But why?"

"Because you've hit it real lucky, leastways in one aspect: apart from yours there's only the tracks of two other vehicles that've passed here after the rain. And the body was left here when the ground had dried out, after the rains, huh?"

"Just two other cars?" said K. "Then one of those tracks belongs to whoever left the body here?"

"Not 100% cert, but pretty likely, I'd say. Unless the perps walked all the way from the roadside, or got dropped off by helicopter . . . there's a lot of footprints. To move our guy they would have needed two people for carrying the body. His weight would make their prints deep. These prints here are pretty average: look at the depressions in the dirt. Some look like kids' prints."

"Benally said his kids and their friends like coming out here to target-shoot."

"That'll be their prints then. And here are Benally's. See those prints here, that deep indent is his heel, then here further on—toe, here again heel, looks like he's a fast runner—got a really long stride. And these tire tracks here would be forensics I'd say, nice straight trail and then they stopped over there. See—they knew where they were going. With these other tire tracks, see here? They keep zigzagging. Like somebody casing the area to look for a good place. Looks as if they hadn't made up their mind where to drop the body when they were driving along. So I guess that these tracks right here are what's real important."

Begay circumnavigated the tire tracks.

"OK," he said, "let's take a walk. You keep your eyes to the ground too."

They inched toward the boulder.

"Coyote tracks crossing," said Begay.

"Benally said that's the reason why he changed his route—he heard a coyote and felt somehow that something wasn't right. How old are those tracks?"

"They aren't fresh. See here? How the edges of the imprint have dried and are starting to kind of crumble into the depression? See?"

"Uh-huh."

"Couple of days at least."

"So that could've been the coyote that Benally heard?"

"That I don't know. This area is pretty well stocked with coyotes. And they like traveling in packs sometimes. So you stopped here and reversed and turned there, and here is where Benally was waiting for you?"

"Yeah, over there by the boulder."

"OK, so that's your vehicle here. That there is forensics. Here's Benally. Here are the forensics' prints—two individuals, shoe sizes between ten and twelve, so it's likely men walking on over here. . . ."

Muttering to himself, Begay methodically inventoried the area around the boulder. Watching Begay at work K began to understand why they called it "reading" tracks. The tracks were the text and the landscape the book bearing the text. Nothing existed in isolation.

Everything was connected to something else. To understand the tracks you had to understand what went on around them. You had to understand the natural order of things to notice when they were out of order. And then there was what modern-day forensic investigators would call expertise in behavioral psychology that was necessary for higher-order track reading. To discover the tracks and imprints that were relevant in this vast, unyielding expanse you had to establish a working hypothesis first of how the source of the tracks—person or animal—would have been most likely to act.

K looked at Begay scrutinizing the area, considering and discarding possibilities, building hypotheses, walking in the footsteps of his ancestors, drawing on knowledge that had been accumulated for hundreds, maybe thousands of years, using skills honed since the great migration across the Bering Strait—probably.

Begay reappeared on the other side of the boulder, stooped and peered at the ground. He put on gloves and carefully scraped soil into a bag that he handed to K. He walked around again, examined the ground on the other side.

"OK," he said when he had circled back to the car. "You ready? See, what I think happened is this: the perps take this road, maybe because they see Chimney Rock or maybe because they see all the debris on the roadside left by the big crash last week. So could be they are thinking that they can dump the body there or maybe even start another fire and burn it there and maybe no one will notice that there is an additional body. So they take the turn-off and decide against leaving the body at the crash. They probably see Chimney Rock and hope that they'll find an easier way to get rid of the body. So they drive that way and they kind of zigzag because they're scouting the area for a good place. Then they drive along there in the direction of the canyon over there and they pass Chimney Rock and that boulder and they stop over there, by that piñon, and turn round and drive back. And they stop right here. And one of them gets out . . . now that is funny: that one here's got real small feet . . . sneakers, size six. Could be a kid. So the kid's the scout. Walks around here and then goes that way and a bit further down here, and then has another look over there—see? OK: goes back to the vehicle here, and tells the other guy: 'this is the place, dude.'"

Begay was getting into his reconstruction now; he was acting out the hypothetical scene like a man possessed: "So buddy gets out here. He's a cowboy, or at least his boots are: size thirteen, soles well-worn and I'd say authentic Mexican, not some Walmart piece of crap from China. See the shape of the sole here? That's the real deal. They walk round the vehicle—by the way, have I told you it's a pickup? Near-new tires—nice profile here: Michelin, no cheapie. So they unhook the ramp, as they've got the dead guy on the back of the pickup, and Tall Guy starts pulling the body off the pickup—see here his prints get deeper, and the kid takes some weight too: I'd say it almost floored him: prints here are real deep."

"You sure it's a kid?"

"There ain't too many size six guys around," said Begay,

"Size six'd be about small average for a female though?" K persisted.

"Why are you so hung up about the perp's gender?"

"Because of your assumptions," K said primly. "It's as if you don't believe that females can commit heinous acts."

"That makes it positive discrimination, right?" said Begay, undeterred. "Besides, I am one that knows females can commit heinous acts. I'm a survivor, remember?"

"Gloria whacking you with a frying pan a heinous act? More like divine retribution. Was it the bottom?"

"Was it—what?"

"The bottom, like the base of the frying pan? Or cooking side down?"

"Does it matter?"

"Just that it would help me to picture it," K said.

"Can't recall. Besides, I ducked, so she caught me on the shoulder. Else I'd be in a wheelchair, maybe, and she'd have to push me around, wipe the drool off my face," mused Begay.

"Sound lady, Gloria. What's she doing now?"

Begay snorted. "Moved to Taos. I hear she got a job running a store for this Anglo lady. One of those Taos stores, you know—crystals, dream-catchers, those cards with the hanging man, whatchamacallit?"

"Tarot."

"I guess. And they run Spirit Safaris."

"Spirit Safaris?"

"Yeah. Too bad."

"Too bad? You think running Spirit Safaris out of Taos is worse than hanging out with you?"

"Boy, you sure are a friend. And you're wrong. If Gloria was still sweet on me I could carve a niche for myself maybe."

"As a Spirit Safari guide?"

"Got it! It's a growing industry. You are your own boss. You got all those Anglos following you, instead of just one dumb—"

"Watch it," K said.

"How did we get there?"

"Your sexism," said K.

Begay shrugged. "Anyways. Tall Guy starts walking backward carrying the torso and your gal's carrying the body by his feet. And they walk in here: Tall Guy first and Lil' Buddy second. And they put Dead Guy down here, facedown—there's an imprint of his face, there's his hip-bones and over there his knees. My guess is they carried him facedown coz' they didn't want to look at him, or him looking at them. It's hard carrying a body face-side down; real hard, matter of fact. So anyway, they put the body down and your gal leaves a nice print for us here, with some clay with interesting stuff in it stuck to it."

"Why interesting?"

"Because this dirt's not local, and looks kind of special, so if you ever come across someone you suspect is the perp, then you've got some little thing in your evidence drawer that may help you nail them. No guarantees, though."

"What about the truck?"

"Medium size pickup, not pimped or anything, I guess something more up-market—no Nissan or Ford, I'd guess—maybe a Chevy or a Toyota, but I'm saying that on account of the Michelin tires—cheapos buy non-branded at Big-O's. But it's hard to say. Kind of new, coz' there ain't no oil, coolant or other fluid leaks at all where the truck's been parked. And they'd have to stop here for a while to dump the body. But I saved the best for last. This right here's your winning ticket."

Begay took the camera, crouched down and took photos from several angles.

"Here." He held the screen to K's face. "Can you see what I'm talking about?"

"It's the tire track."

"Sure is. Notice anything special?"

"You're giving me a clue there. Anything special?"

K stared at the photo. He saw dirt, crumbled soil, furrows that cut across it and that he assumed were part of the tire tracks.

"Uh. . . ."

"There." Begay pointed his finger at something. "See what I mean now?"

The honest answer was no, not a damn thing.

"Yeah, I think there's something," K said.

"I read faces like I read tracks," said Begay. "Hey, did you ever see that movie where Gary Farmer says 'Stupid fucking white man' to this Anglo?"

"You saw that?"

"Nope. Just a clip on YouTube. Coz. that's what we Indians often feel like saying to dumbass white people."

"Thank you. I got your point. Shall we keep on playing guessing games or do you want to tell me what it is that you want me to see?"

"No need to be pissed. I'm sure you have your strong points—somewhere. OK, so this is what I want you to see. And as you are not seeing it, I'm going to explain it to you: that's a close-up of the tire mark. The right-hand rear tire to be precise. And here is what I'm talking about: it's an imprint about two inches across—you see that V-shape against the grain of the profile? That's some damage to the profile that gives you a unique identification point. You see this and you know you've got the truck that was used by the perps to ditch the body. Don't worry. I'm going to make it real clear in my report—I kind of like using jargon: 'unique identification point' sounds so much better than 'damaged profile.' And now brother, take me home, they'll be missing me at the station."

"Listen: when you send over the photos and your findings, can you write a full report on what you've seen and your conclusions? Just write down what you told me over there—the unique identification point, the shoe sizes, all that. I'll upload the photos as soon as I'm back at the station and email them to you and the voice-notes too. You can bill us separately for the report. Weismaker'll take the fee out of our Expert Consultation Fund."

"And the track reading?"

"Uh, 'Cultural Consultation'? How would I know? I don't do the accounts."

"Are you sure they'll cough up?"

"That's a cert. We're dealing with Weismaker, remember?"

"Yeah, but who's Weismaker dealing with?"

"Don't go cynical on me."

"Don't forget I did this on Redwater time, remember?"

"How about you write the report in your own time and bill us for 'Private Consultation Services'?"

"I'll remember that 'Private Consultation' shit. Might come in handy when I get fired."

"Look, how you bill it doesn't matter from our end. Weismaker'll make sure you get paid whatever."

"OK. I'll write the report, just because at least you got me to spend some time outta the station."

"That bad, huh?" asked K sympathetically.

"Don't get me started. It's worse than bad. You had a good look at that Sheryleah? The whole team's getting to be that way, like they're about to audition for some freak show. And the politics are real bad. We're all getting to hate each other's guts. Any chance of a transfer to your outfit?"

"We'd love to have you, I'm sure. But we are not spared our tribulations either, you know."

"Yep, I do. I've had a couple of run-ins with those redneck crazoids over there. Regular hillbilly terrors. And to think they have the gall to poke fun at us Jhons. You got Weismaker though. He's pretty cool—like, he's all you want a sheriff to be, don'tcha think?"

"I do, mostly."

"Mostly?"

"He keeps bugging me about my IT skills," said K unhappily.

"Well, you probably deserve it. Is it really that bad?"

"Computers don't agree with me."

"You mean like alcohol with Indians?"

"Worse."

"You are genetically indisposed to PCs?"

"It is a myth that Indians are genetically predisposed to alcoholism."

"That's a relief. Let's meet for a brew sometime when no one's looking. Anyway, where were we?"

"You were singing the praises of my work environment."

"Yep, sure was. Since Johnny Nakai and Alf Nataani left, things just haven't been the same. Now what we've got is twenty-four-seven professional brown-nosers and busybodies. They're real good with computers, though—really dig their paperwork." Begay shuddered.

"What about Lewis? Lewis King? He's a good man," protested K.

"Don't think he's gonna last much longer either."

"I saw him over there at Ridgeback."

"Called you out for backup, huh? I hear he got Window Rock to come up too. Guess what happened?"

"I guess what happened is what Lewis said was going to happen."

"If what Lewis said was going to happen was that nothing was happening—that's what happened."

"Maybe go after that transfer so we can work on our double act. Meanwhile you can do some cultural mediation."

"Damn. You really have no Native cop on the squad?"

"Nope. There's just two in the whole team—Becky and Lorinda."

"Lorinda?"

"The lady who cleans."

"Figures," said Begay.

"Well, we could use some Apples."

"Strawberries. Or make it Cactus-pears. At least that's got a sting to it. If things don't get any better this son of Dinetáh may well be forced to move away to the territories of the Ancient Enemies."

"The land of opportunities."

"True. Who says I've got to stay a cop anyways? There's always the Spirit Safari option."

"Unless Gloria's Anglo lady has trademarked it."

"Who cares? Spirit Safari. Spirit Stampede. Spirit Bonanza. Spirit Anything's sure to wow those Anglos. I feel more cheerful already, don't you know."

"Sometimes a little perspective's all you need," K said.

CHAPTER EIGHT

Dusk had fallen and traffic was heavy. Pickups returning from oil-fields loaded with metal drums, winches, ropes and brooms drove northward at speeds unsuitable to the winding road. Pickups tailgated compacts; compacts overtook trucks at blind summits; heavy goods vehicles accelerated around bends. Damn the Rez speed limit of 55 mph, and the 65 mph allowed this side of the State Line. Woe to those who drove responsibly and adhered to the speed limit. Those pussies were tailgated within an inch of their bumpers; mercilessly chased up blind summits; forced onto soft shoulders or into ditches.

But right now K was King of the Road, commanding a mobile speed-enforcement device. What joy to behold the patrol car's instant impact on drivers. Now all those hard-ass dudes were crawling along behind him like a bunch of debutantes afraid to crease their ball gowns.

In the rearview mirror, K saw a metallic blue pickup charging onto the oncoming traffic lane. The truck was approaching at great speed, the driver aiming to overtake as many vehicles as he could, clearly not giving a damn about traffic on the oncoming lane. The road was approaching another blind summit. The pickup's maneuver was reckless, if not homicidally aggressive. When he had almost drawn up level with the squad car, the pickup driver finally noticed the reason for the traffic's snail-paced progress. Spotting the patrol car, he braked frantically and tried to insert his truck back into the lane. Not one of the drivers he had overtaken let him back in: "Die, motherfucker, die!"

K left the decision to mete out capital punishment to the righteous and turned right toward Chimney Rock. Immediately the turbo-charged choir of howling engines and shrill acceleration filled the desert air as drivers made up for lost time and the enforced postponement of the thrill of risking their lives and those of others on the United States Deadliest Highway, a highway so deadly that not even renumbering it some years ago from Highway 666 to Highway 288 had succeeded in making it any less lethal.

K drove through the Benally compound's open gate and parked next to the assortment of pickups, compacts and souped-up lowriders—most likely the older Benally kids' rides.

Dom Benally came out of the trailer and was immediately surrounded by a pack of dogs that yipped and clambered and formed a roving fur ball with multiple protruding wagging tails and legs like a canine god Shiva. As soon as K got out of the car the dogs were upon him. He felt paws on chest and hips, wet nozzles on arms and groin, the rhythmic beating of muscular tails against his legs. He patted a head, scratched an ear, petted a shaggy fur, pulled a matted tail, trying to distribute his attention evenly.

"You really dig dogs, huh?"

"They dig me," K said modestly.

K was relieved to see that Dom seemed to have picked up somewhat since his ordeal.

"How are you?" he asked.

Dom shrugged. "You're just in time for coffee. You've missed out on Wanda's stew. And we're all out of hay. Come on in."

The trailer was filled with the smell of coffee, simmering stew and the warm yeasty aroma of baking. Wanda was busy stacking dishes.

"Franz!" said Wanda, walking over and reaching up to envelope K in one of her generous hugs. She had to stand on tiptoe. "It's good to see you! It's been a while."

"Hi! Hi! Hi!" piped the Benally children, who were sitting round the large table.

"Wow," said K, "I know this is what old people always say, but you really all have grown something shocking. Last time I saw you, you were all midgets that high," he held his hand two feet from the floor, "and I had to run after you and wipe your noses."

"Yeah, I remember," said Geena, the oldest daughter. "That was when you were just starting to go bald. Your implants look good though. Almost natural. By the way, have you gotten used to wearing your dentures? Remember you got to brush 'em regularly, just like real teeth."

Wanda and Dom shook their heads.

Wanda said, "Multiply that by five and you know what we are going through."

Dulcie, Trevor and Warren, who were doing homework at the kitchen table, giggled. Dom put a percolator of coffee on the table and Wanda retrieved a tray of cinnamon rolls from the oven.

"Help yourselves!" Wanda said, pointing at the tray. "They're not glazed, I was kinda short of time."

"In that case I'll have to have two, to make up for the missing calories," said K greedily.

"You just go ahead, there's plenty. You need to put some meat on your ribs anyway." She squeezed his arm affectionately.

The cinnamon rolls were fluffy, oozing caramelized cinnamon-spiked sugar.

"Hmmm," sighed K, "do you know what you should do with your baking and your green fingers, Wanda? Open a plant nursery with a café. You could put out tables and folks would have coffee and cake outside and that would put them in a mood to buy some plants. There's your business plan."

"I'd love to do something like that, for sure. But running a nursery-café is a very bílagáana thing to do, don't you think?"

"Being a social worker is a very bílagáana thing to do. At least running a nursery-café is a fun bílagáana thing to do."

"Before that vegetarian eats all the cinnamon rolls and goes into hyperglycemic shock, we should start on the statements," Dom said.

The smile vanished from Wanda's face. The children fell quiet. "It's better to get it over with," Dom said apologetically.

"Sure." K looked around the table. "I would like you to brainstorm together what you remember. Anything can be important, even if you don't think it is. Let's just see what comes up. And then each of you gets to write a short statement about what you have seen. Does everyone know what the inquiry is about?"

The children nodded.

"Dad said not to go and play over there, 'coz it's a crime scene," Warren said, savoring the grown-up word.

"That's right," said K.

"What is a crime scene?" asked Warren.

K looked at Wanda and Dom. Wanda gave a tiny, almost imperceptible shake of the head.

"What is a crime scene?" repeated Warren.

"It's a place where a crime has happened," said Geena.

K waited for Warren to come back with a response that he considered logical: "What's a crime?" but Warren nodded seriously as if he now understood everything. "Can I have another cake?"

"You had two already!"

"It's not cake, dummy, it's a roll," said Trevor. "What's a crime?"

"A bad thing that should not happen," said Wanda.

Trevor frowned. Before he could come up with another question, K said, "The questions I have are pretty straightforward, really. I just need to know if anyone saw or heard anything unusual during Monday evening or Monday night."

"I saw a tiger," said Warren.

"You saw a tiger?"

"Yes, it was that big," he spread out his arms, "and it had a real mean face, and it wanted to eat a . . . buffalo. But then it went asleep."

"A buffalo?"

"We watched one of those nature programs," said Wanda.

"The tiger wanted to eat a buffalo?" asked K.

"Yes," said Wanda. "A water buffalo."

"Oh, I see," said K.

"We were all gone during the day. The school bus brings them back around 4:15. Dulcie, Trevor and Warren come back on the bus. Dulcie has a key. She looks after the boys until we get back. I'm usually back by 5 . . . depends. Dom by 5:30. With Geena it depends what she's got going on at college. And Jimmy works late so he's usually the last to get home. On Monday we had dinner at the usual time, cleared up, looked at the homework, Trevor's spelling book. . . . Dulcie wanted to practice Spanish."

"Como está usted, señor?" asked Dulcie.

"Muy bien, gracias. Y tú?" said K.

"Then there was the Broncos versus Raiders game, and everyone watched that and we made some popcorn," Wanda continued. "And then Warren brushed his teeth all by himself, because he's a big boy now, and then we had a bedtime story and he went to sleep."

"I have a singing toothbrush," said Warren.

"Wow! What does it sing?"

"Just, like. . . ."

"It's a musical toothbrush. It plays melodies," Wanda explained

"A musical toothbrush. I wish they'd had those when I was a kid."

"Your teeth look great."

"I never got any candy, that's why," said K.

"Really?"

"Pretty much."

"Poor you. I'll pack you some cinnamon rolls to take home," said Wanda.

"Remind me to play the pity card more often," said K. "So you were all watching the game?"

"Yeah. Then Trevor went to bed pretty much straight after the game, that would have been 8:00, 8:15, maybe. We hit the sack pretty early too—Dom gets up real early because of his running and I like some time in the morning to straighten myself out and get my head clear for work. I can't think of anything, least I didn't notice anything out of the usual. Of course we were all still jumpy on account of the crash last week. That really shook us up. So any traffic noise kind of makes us jump."

"Was there traffic noise?"

"Sometimes the wind carries the sounds from the road. Traffic noise travels pretty far."

"Did anyone drive past the house?"

"I wasn't looking out that much. Mostly we were doing chores, watching TV. I didn't pay attention."

"It's not a throughway. Do you get many cars driving past?"

"Depends. Not now so much, but in summer it can get pretty busy. Kids going to their boonie-parties, we get hikers and rock climbers too, for the canyon. On Monday, I did not notice anyone. But then I was real busy."

"I've been trying to think back too and I can't recall anything," said Dom, "except the coyotes I heard that morning. I guess in my mind they were linked to the accident. Maybe that's why I felt like a premonition of something bad about to happen. That's what I remember: in my bones I felt something bad was going to happen."

"How do you feel something in your bones?" asked Warren.

"Something bad?" asked Trevor.

K could see that Dom's remark worried the children.

"So what about y'all?" he said briskly. "Anyone see or hear anything? A noise, a light, a car driving along here?"

All the children shook their heads, except Dulcie.

"What about you, Dulcie?"

"I saw a truck," Dulcie said.

"You saw a truck?" asked Wanda, "When did you see a truck?"

"It was kinda late."

"When?" asked K.

"Late."

"How late?"

"Well, kinda really late. . . ."

"What time?"

"... about 2."

"2 am? What are you doing up at that time?" asked Wanda.

"Texting Janelle," Dulcie said.

"At 2 am? Now I know why you look so pale and always have shadows under your eyes."

"I don't always text her at 2 am, just . . . this was something important, alright?"

"I bet about some stupid boy," said Trevor—probably astutely, K thought.

"What exactly did you see, Dulcie?" he asked.

"Well, I got up, because there was something important I wanted to tell Janelle and I did not want to forget it in the morning, so I got up to text her. I didn't mean her to answer me or anything, I just didn't want to forget. I went in the kitchen not to wake up anybody, and I didn't even turn on the light, and I was texting and then this pickup comes in from the highway. Sometimes there's guys who like to look at crash scenes, you know? The truck was going that way, toward Chimney Rock, it was going real slow, and mostly it had its lights dimmed, but it turned them up a couple of times. It didn't go straight. It kind of changed sides. I figured it was some drunk dudes going off to drink some more."

"Did you see the truck? "

"Well, kind of. Not really clear. I mean it was dark, so I didn't see everything. Not who was driving, or anything. But it was a white pickup. I'm pretty sure it was white, or else maybe kind of cream-colored maybe or silver. But I know it was real light. "

"Make?" asked K, half jokingly.

Dulcie took the question seriously. "No, I couldn't tell. I'm not real good on car makes anyways."

"Anything else you can think of?"

"No, I texted Janelle and went to bed. I'm sorry. I didn't pay any attention. I didn't know it was important," Dulcie said regretfully.

"Of course not, you couldn't have known. Can you write this up in a statement for me? Just write it down exactly as you've told me."

He handed out statement forms.

"I want one too," protested Warren.

"You can't write," said Dulcie.

"I can draw real well."

"Here you go," said K and gave Warren a form.

"I'll do you a real nice . . . what's it called?"

"Statement."

"I'll do it in my room."

The others stayed at the table. Trevor squinted at the ceiling.

"If you haven't seen anything, you don't have to do a statement. Your mom can write it down for you."

"I want to. I want to," said Trevor, "My spelling's real good."

Geena was the first to hand back her signed statement. It was short and to the point, confirming that she had neither noticed nor seen anything out of the ordinary. Jimmy wrote a similar statement, followed by Wanda and Dom. As far as K had determined the only statement of relevance was Dulcie's. By the way Dulcie concentrated as she wrote her statement it was evident that she was a good student.

"Remember, no detail is unimportant. Everything counts," He said.

Dulcie nodded and continued writing. When K scanned the completed statement he saw that it was clear and concise, written in a hand that looked more mature than he would have expected of a thirteen-year-old girl.

"We need a guardian's signature as well," said K.

Wanda nodded. She read her daughter's statement. "Pretty good," she said. "I wish you'd act like that when I tell you to do something." She poked her daughter in the ribs with her elbow and signed the statement.

"Is there anything anyone would like to add?"

They shook their heads.

Trevor was still writing. "Wait, wait!" he said.

He scribbled furiously.

"I'm done! I'm done! Wait. I gotta sign it. Here!"

"Well done," said K. Trevor's letters looked like a bunch of drunks trying to go on a party in a gale-strength wind. He had watched some tigers, and the Raiders had won, but he liked the Broncos and they had made popcorn and he did not like the salty one.

"So you don't like salty popcorn," said K.

"I do! I do! It's Warren doesn't like salty coz he's a baby."

"Oh I see now. Indeed. The witness states clearly that he prefers salty popcorn."

"Witless! I'm a witless!" said Trevor happily.

"How true," said Dulcie.

K leafed through the statements. "We are almost done here. Just one more."

Warren was at his desk, bent over the form. The desk was covered in crayons and Warren was covered in crayon. There were yellow, red, green and blue splotches on his hands, arms, ears, on his nose and eyebrows.

"I see you've been working real hard," said K.

Warren nodded, busy applying colors to self and paper.

"I got to get back now and give these to the sheriff."

"A real sheriff?"

"You bet!"

"I haven't finished."

"I think the sheriff will be real happy."

K took Warren's index finger, rubbed red crayon over it and pressed it down on the form. "A special witness signature."

Warren had produced a splendidly grumpy tiger face sticking out of what K assumed was grass. No buffalo.

"Got 'em all," he said, and held Warren's statement up for Dom and Wanda to see. They grinned and K could see the pride in their eyes.

"Here." Wanda held out a paper bag. "I packed you this. It's not an intervention, OK? Just didn't want you starving."

"I had worse interventions." He smelt the parcel. "Cinnamon and sugar are antidepressants, did you know?"

"I'm an old hand at self-medication," said Wanda. "How else would I end up like this? "She pulled at her love handles.

"It's always good to visit with you guys, even though I wish the circumstances were different."

"It's always good to see you, Franz," said Wanda. "It seems like a real long time."

"It was, judging from how the kids have grown since I last saw them."

"They really dig you, you know?" Wanda said. "You're good with them. You'd make a good dad, I reckon."

"I still feel I could do with a dad myself."

"There are not many of those around, huh?" Wanda asked.

"I feel I'm getting a taste of you in social worker mode," K said, and turned away from whatever it was that he saw in Wanda's eyes.

"Take care, shik'is," Wanda said. "Dom promised when all this is over he'll run a sweat."

"That would be good," K said, "when all this is over."

K drove home, fed Wittgenstein a tin of sardines and spent what remained of the evening on the porch steps with a bottle of beer, looking up at the stars.

Wittgenstein, crouched on the banister, looked down on him, and together they listened to the melancholy two-note call of the blackcapped chickadee.

CHAPTER NINE

The morning started well enough with a rosy dawn sky, strong coffee and one of Wanda's cinnamon rolls. It stood to reason that all would be going downhill from here.

In the mirror, K's reflection was grim to behold, eyes a thunderous grey and hair an unholy mess, as if the devil was fixing to build a nest in it. In preparation for the day's trials, K shaved with more care than usual and even ran the brush through his hair a couple of times. The brush looked as if it had been used on Wittgenstein, though K had no memory of ever grooming the cat—he'd be missing an arm if he had. Wittgenstein, in any case, was acting aloof.

"What's up, friend?"

K scratched the cat's head.

Uncharacteristically, Wittgenstein licked his hand. Perhaps the cat held some affection for him after all. That, or his hands smelled of sardines.

• • •

At the station K made straight for Weismaker's office. The corridor smelt as if pest control had paid a visit and fumigated the building. There was an acrid, burnt stench in the air that constricted the lungs and irritated the throat. Maybe Smithson had fed Meyers the green tuna and antique mayo sandwich that had been festering at the back of the fridge and they'd had to clean up after Meyers.

K realized with a sinking heart that the smell came from Weismaker's office. He knocked on the sheriff's door. Weismaker was seated behind his desk, sipping from a mug. Maybe the sheriff really voluntarily drank this stuff with its robust bouquet of burnt tires with assertive undertones of skunk.

"Just in time," Weismaker said. "Take a seat." He looked round his office. "Uh . . . wherever."

All available surface was taken up with files, folders, papers, newspapers. Some were stacked, some stacks had collapsed, some had slid to the floor.

"Are these to be sat on in any kind of priority?" K asked.

"That one might be glad for your butt in its face," Weismaker said crudely.

K sat on the file as instructed. He did not find it a comfortable position.

"ID's been confirmed by Delgado forensics. I pulled the file on the dead kid, Noah George. Made some reading." Weismaker pointed at a blue Manila folder.

"Where did you get that?" K said.

"Right here. The kid had quite a jacket. Didn't the name sound familiar to you?"

"Not me. But I mentioned him to Smithson and he thought he knew him from somewhere."

"Here, look at the files." Weismaker pushed a couple of folders toward K.

"You got hold of the Redwater medical file?" K was impressed.

"Got it released and had it couriered over first thing."

"Couriered?"

"Young," said Weismaker. "He needed some cultural liaison experience to put on his resume."

"Why not arrange a secondment at Redwater PD? They'd be happy to instruct him."

"Uhuh," said Weismaker noncommittally.

The police file was a hefty tome. Noah George had had more than a couple of run-ins with the law.

"Actually he was on probation when he died," Weismaker said. "He's got a whole bunch of DWI and DUI jackets. He was close to getting sent down to Federal. For the last ten years, since he turned eighteen, he barely managed a year without collecting a couple of convictions."

K opened the file. There he was. Noah George. Alive. Looking into the camera as someone had told him to when he was being booked. Under Noah George's photo was a bar with his name, DoB, and date and time of arrest.

Maybe Elsie Nez had been right about Noah George being a handsome boy alive. In this photo his jaw was clenched and his scowl fierce. He looked as if he knew that nothing would ever go right for him. He looked like somebody who was busy plotting his life around his grievances.

"Is it all DUIs?" asked K.

"Couple of assaults and possession charges. And one complainant decided against filing a report."

"What were the circumstances?"

"A relative. His mother I guess. That's where he's registered at— her home—his mother's home. She made a 911 call, about six months ago. Córdoba took the call. According to Córdoba's report the woman had bruising on her face and on her arms. He had destroyed some of her stuff—vandalized the kitchen. What I got from Córdoba's report is that she tried real hard to get the lady to file a complaint. You know how she works with the Women's Shelter on Domestic Violence Awareness. Usually she's real good at getting the vics to file a report and following up cases, but no luck here. This is why this file's for information only. My guess is if Córdoba had reported on the incident, Noah George would've been shipped to Federal—might have saved his life. Too bad. Hindsight's always twenty-twenty."

"Was there a Missing Person's on him?"

"No. Kind of strange that. Probation as a rule mandates that people stay at their registered address. If they don't, it's a violation. Let's you and me deal with next of kin. The social worker I leave to you."

THE QUALITY *of* MERCY

NNoKs—Notifying Next of Kin—were dreaded by everyone in the squad. Informing a family of a relative's death was difficult enough in any case. But murder was the worst. With any other death the bereaved had an option of reassuring themselves that the deceased wouldn't have suffered; they had lived a good life; passed serenely to higher pastures; death had come as a release courtesy of a merciful God. There were as many variations, as many versions of comforting stories, as there were families.

With murder it was different. What was there to say? What could the relatives of a murder victim tell themselves that gave comfort? K had witnessed many different reactions. Almost all had been hard to bear, heartbreaking even. A few had been of the type "Motherfucker had it coming"; "Good riddance"; "Knew it had to end like this."

These reactions made it easier for the bearers of bad news. "Go, Tell, Beat It," to most officers was preferable to having to sit through breakdowns, tantrums, tears and self-recrimination. Though often enough those harsh responses were in themselves a defense against grief. Sooner or later the irremediable fact of death would sink in—if luck would have it, long after the cops had split.

NNoK visits were always made in pairs, never alone. Being two, however, made it necessary to coordinate responsibilities, which in turn tended to complicate things. It always depended who you worked with. Sometimes there was a shared reluctance to be the bearer of bad news and you had to draw straws or something. Sometimes you were partnered with someone whose social skills or sensitivity were somewhat underdeveloped, which meant you better prepared to administer the Heimlich should they happen to choke on their feet in their mouths. Equally perturbing were those who took a ghoulish pleasure in a "hard job, well done." Fond of instructing fellow officers to make cups of tea and fetch boxes of Kleenex, while perched on the edge of the seat with a Beagle-puppy frown and lachrymose expression that screamed "your pain is my pain" at 160 decibels; these folks were a monumental pain in the ass.

Then there were characters like old-timer Tom, whom K had

been partnered with in his early days at the squad. Old Tom had been due to retire shortly and preferred to conclude NNoKs with a hearty: "When you gotta go, you gotta go."

The first time this happened K thought Tom was asking to use the bathroom. In fact, "when you gotta go, you gotta go" could be taken in any way: a pithy statement of acceptance of the universally shared inevitability of death, an announcement of the intention to leave, or a request to use the bathroom; a crafty three-in-one. This having been an era before Evidence Based Practice and Customer Satisfaction Feedback, they'd never found out how Old Tom's approach had gone down with the bereaved.

In time K had started to positively appreciate Tom's style—after he had been paired with Young on a couple of occasions.

NNoKs were amongst those onerous duties no cop of sane mind and sound disposition particularly relished doing. But if the job had to be done, then Weismaker was the man to do it with.

"Coffee before we go?" asked Weismaker.

"Yes, please," K heard himself answer. Maybe it was not just Catholics who believed that mortification of the flesh was a virtue.

Weismaker said: "We better take my truck. She lives at Cottonwood Trailer park, down by Walmart. It's bad enough we're wearing the uniform. The neighbors don't need to be seeing a patrol car camped out in front of her trailer."

Weismaker's private car was a rust-infested Ford pickup with, as far as K could see, as few features to recommend it as Weismaker's coffee. K, who himself was frugal in the choice of vehicles, had found his sixth-hand Datsun pickup on the Walmart parking lot with an optimistic "Buy Me" sign on its windscreen. He had bought the Datsun because it had reminded him of a stray mutt waiting to be rehomed. And like the mongrels at the animal rescue shelter, the little pickup had proved a reliable, resilient ride that needed minimal repairs and generally ran as if it was made to last an eternity. Weismaker's Ford, on the other hand, was more like a geriatric patient being kept alive by medical interventions. When Weismaker turned the key in the ignition, the engine made noises that could at best be described as reluctant. When the engine finally caught, after Weismaker had gone through a series of mysterious maneuvers which either were based on technical knowledge or more likely on Weismaker's magical thinking, the spluttering was so painful that K considered begging for clemency: "Do not resuscitate. Just put it out of its misery."

The number and standard of trailer parks in a town were, as a rule of thumb, an indication of the state of a community's fiscal affairs. Where there was scarce employment, low wages and high mobility, trailer parks were often the most practical solution to people's housing needs.

The standard of trailer parks could vary considerably: some made residents commit to the meticulous upkeep of trailers and plots, and had a catalogue of draconically enforced rules and regulations. High-end trailer parks levied hefty monthly fees that were only marginally lower than the rental price of a mid-range condo. They were big on white picket fences, manicured lawns, designer flowerbeds and ornamental birdbaths.

In Milagro, the residents of high-end trailer parks were in the majority Anglo. They were the kinds of folks who took a stand against non-Anglo residents moving in—because it just wasn't fair to encourage these people to live there, it being too big of an ask for them to have to keep up with the general standard. And they were generally much happier among their own kind anyways. And they made the value of realty plummet.

Then there were the mid-range trailer parks that were preferred by families with children, where rules were mainly geared toward minimizing occasion for conflict between residents. Though trailers could be pretty much kept in whatever state residents wished them to be or could afford them to be, the majority of residents in these trailer parks strove to maintain the best standard they could afford, or even higher if their credit rating allowed it, thanks to the fuel of sociometric rivalry.

And finally, there were the down and out, last stop before destitution, English-as-a second-language trailer parks, compounds that contravened all Anglo ideals of domesticity and decorum. Here the dominant society's mantra of appearance over reality was inverted. People had little money to spare and were damn sure that they wouldn't spend what little they had on paintjobs that they wouldn't be able to enjoy anyway. Why spend all that green to make your neighbors happy? Much better to take care of the trailer's interior. The exterior of a trailer was therefore not always an indication of how it looked inside. Sometimes a tattered, lopsided, patched-up trailer would cocoon a spotless interior that was as homely as any home could be.

The Cottonwood Trailer Park was in the last category, one of Milagro's least august trailer parks. It was variously described as a "dump," an "eyesore" and a "public disgrace." K had his suspicions that this was because of Cottonwood's high contingent of "minority" residents: the trailer park was a multicultural mix of Navajo, Ute, Hispanic and Latino residents with a minority of people who were artlessly referred to as "White trash."

In the bygone days of Political Correctness, White trash had been the one social group that had an all-round exemption from being protected by it. Almost everyone, whether liberal or conservative, whether brown, white or black, had seemed to think it was OK to make jokes or prejudicial comments at the expense of White trash. Society had ignored poor Whites at its own peril. Their discontent had been like a pressure-cooker with a shut valve that slowly but surely gathered steam, until an explosion was inevitable.

But even now when the political tide had supposedly turned, when aspiring to a more tolerant society was no longer virtue fueled by decency, but failure inspired by spinelessness, White trash remained the losers in life's lottery they had always been. According to the core mantra of the limitless potential of individual achievement that was the American Dream, they had failed, pure and simple. They, or their forebears, had been too dumb, too feckless, too damn lazy to make it. They were squatters in God's Own Country with a thwarted sense of entitlement, which was the most dangerous sense of entitlement. Still they were surrounded by dusky faces whom they felt they should rule over rather than having to live side by side with—folks who should surely have been deported and repatriated by now.

The only thing that had changed was that their rivals for society's bottom rung were no longer owed sympathy for hardships endured via colonial atrocity, political oppression and social prejudice perpetuated by the dominant order.

Cottonwood Trailer Park, like a Hindu Dalit colony, was situated south of Walmart, where it occupied a depression at the foot of town, next to a gulch beneath which the city's wastewater flowed. The Cottonwood was separated from surrounding wasteland only by a cattle grid that was perhaps the legacy of a long abandoned farm. There was no cottonwood as far as the eye could see.

It looked more like a squatters' camp than an official trailer park. It was a motley assembly of trailers and shacks that ranged from single-wides to makeshift shelters that would not have looked out of place in a shantytown. Tarpaulins and plywood were the preferred patching materials. Here and there a halfhearted attempt had been made to separate one trailer from the next by means of improvised boundaries that looked more symbolic than effective: A couple of chairs placed apart and tied with red ribbon; posts hammered into the ground with a length of wash line between them; a couple of traffic cones positioned at either end of a yard. There were a lot of vehicles around that looked as if they were being kept for parts and that contributed to Cottonwood's general impression of being a junkyard.

"What's the address?" asked K.

"25 Cottonwood. Doesn't look like they're numbered through though. I'd rather we didn't have to ask anyone."

Sometimes Weismaker's truck came in handy. When they drove through the trailer park at a slow crawl scanning the trailers for numbers, the old Ford looked right at home. Weismaker and K had nearly completed an entire circle of the trailer park when they finally hit on No. 25.

It was a single-wide trailer that had once been white, with a faded blue door and peeling blue window frames. The flaking paint revealed black tar underneath. No attempt had been made to separate No. 25 from its neighbors, and no effort to prettify the property. Rickety stairs that looked as if they had been nailed together from broken-up wooden crates led to the front door. The trailer's one advantage was that it stood at the edge of the trailer park and had great views across the plain to the Mesa.

Weismaker parked the truck where it would not block anyone's way. As if by agreement they sat in silence for a moment, before Weismaker reached for the file. K followed him up the steps. The sheriff paused, then knocked. There was no response.

Weismaker knocked again, this time more forcefully. They heard a scraping noise, and then shuffling steps.

A voice called, "Háísh?"

"Police," said Weismaker.

A key creaked in the lock, a pulling at the handle, and the door opened slowly.

A loose nail wobbled on the hinge. On the door frame the paintwork had peeled away almost completely. A few strips of weather-beaten blue and bleached-out green, remainders of previous paintwork, clung to the brittle wood. A small, elderly woman stood in the doorway.

"Mrs. Ella King?" asked Weismaker.

The old woman nodded.

"May we come in?"

She nodded again and stepped aside.

Weismaker motioned for Ella King to lead the way.

The living room was spacious. It had wood-clad walls and was sparsely furnished. There was a Formica kitchen table that looked like it had come out of the 1950s; four folding chairs around it; a sofa of about the same period as the table, covered in faded chenille; and in the corner, a high-backed rocking chair. There was an old TV sitting on a crate covered with a woven rug. On the sewing table before the window was an old black Singer with a length of vividly colored fabric protruding from it. Over the TV was a large framed black-and-white photograph of a young man in uniform, his earnest face in half-profile, his eyes looking into the distance.

Ella King motioned toward the sofa. She waited until they had sat down, then turned the chair at the sewing table around and sat facing them.

Ella King was dressed in the style favored by older Navajo women: a pleated, flower-patterned skirt reaching almost to her ankles; high-collared, long-sleeved velvet blouse; white socks; and red striped sneakers. She wore turquoise and silver squash-blossom earrings and a silver bracelet with turquoise inlay. Ella King's black hair was threaded with grey, pulled back in a bun and fastened with a silver and turquoise beret. She had the broad forehead, high cheekbones and delicate features characteristic of Athabascans.

Ella King, her hands folded in her lap, looked at the two policemen before her.

"You got news for me?"

They nodded.

"Has he done something else bad?" asked Ella King.

The men shook their heads. Weismaker cleared his throat. It was this noise that seemed to have an effect on Ella King. Suddenly her composure left her and she looked frightened. The fear rendered her mute. She sat, looking at them, wide-eyed and unblinking, reminding K of a trapped bird.

"Shíma," said K, "we are not completely sure yet, but a body was found and we have reason to believe it is your relative, Noah George. We are so sorry," he added, helplessly. Then he added with the small reservoir of hope that he always kept until the end: "When did you last see him?"

With all his might he was willing her to say "Tuesday" or "yesterday."

Ella King seemed to share his hopes.

"On Friday," she said "He was home most of Friday."

Their deflated hope must have been visible on their faces. Ella King became very still. She had stopped looking at them, as if she was trying to withdraw. She said nothing, did not ask them anything.

Weismaker said, "Is there anything that would help us tell if it is your son? Scars, tattoos, anything that you can think of?"

"Shídeezhi biyáázh," the old woman said. "He had a couple of tattoos. One little one, here."

She pointed at the inside of her upper left arm.

"Can you describe the tattoos?"

"This one—I haven't seen it much. It was on the inside of his arm. He probably didn't want his relatives to find out. We would've got real mad at him. I think it was . . . like a skull or something. It had some letters. SW. I remember because I asked him what it stood for. I thought it could be for South West maybe. But he said no, it was not that."

"Anything else?"

"The one here," Ella King tapped on her right wrist. "He had it done for his dad. To remember his dad."

She looked at them and found there the news she did not want to know. Slowly tears started rolling down her face. They ran into the deep grooves alongside her mouth, they dripped down on her blouse leaving dark splotches. Weismaker and K looked at the floor.

It was Navajo custom to look away when a person was crying or upset. Strangers to the culture often found this callous—"The poor woman is crying and they all look away and no one thinks to comfort her"—but whenever K had been around and observed this he had felt it a peculiarly comforting custom. People could cry with others around them, but they were not pried on; they simultaneously had a containing group around them and the dignity of privacy. It was very different from how most Anglos reacted. Anglos always wanted to feel useful and had a tendency to be proactive. As soon as the first tear rolled, somebody'd jump up and run off for a box of Kleenex, someone else would hug or shoulder-pat or keep asking "are you alright?"

When K had first experienced how Navajo reacted to a grieving person he too had found it unsettling, as if he was being made to ignore a person's grief. Gradually he'd come to appreciate the ability of people to stay silent.

They could hear the old woman trying to suppress her sobs, and they sat looking at the floor. A part of K started to wish that they had not been familiar with Navajo custom. Then they could've proceeded in the Anglo way: Kleenex; cup of tea; thank you, Ma'am and farewell. Instead they had to sit it out. But as they sat together in silence the small unintentional community they had formed began to work its magic.

Ella King shifted on her chair and they were called back from the journey into her grief. They blinked, blinded by the here and now.

She asked, "Ahwee nohsinish?"

"Aoo," answered K for both of them.

The old woman rose slowly, as if she had to remind herself how to move.

She walked over to the sink, unscrewed the percolator, filled the bottom part with water and the top with ground coffee, reassembled the percolator, set it on the gas stove, lit the flame; slowly and methodically, as if no task in the world was more important than this. She went to the cupboard, opened it, took out three cups. She put the cups on the kitchen counter, opened another cupboard and took out a jelly jar with sugar. The percolator began to bubble and steam. The smell of coffee filled the kitchen. Ella King stood, looking at the percolator as if waiting for it to start talking. The coffee boiled over, hit the stove with a hiss. Ella King spooned sugar into cups, poured out coffee, stirred each cup in turn. She took the first cup and brought it to Weismaker. She returned to the counter, picked up the next cup and brought it to K. Then took the last cup and returned to her hardback chair, sat down, looked into her cup, began to take small sips—and did not move her eyes away from the black steaming liquid in the cup.

K looked at his cup and wondered if she had deliberately chosen a particular design for each of them, because she felt they suited them. From the variety of patterns and motifs on the cups he guessed that she got them at yard sales. The cup Ella King was using had a yellow sun, palm trees and a flamingo on it with the legend "Welcome to Beautiful Florida." Weismaker's was a photo-transfer of prairie grass with the friendly face of a horse looking out as if encouraging a game of hide and seek. The cup Ella King had given K was turquoise-green with a narrow horizontal stripe of aquamarine blue. K favored blues and greens. Turquoise was his favorite color.

They drank their coffee in silence. Ella King, looking into her cup as if she expected it to answer her question, asked, "What happened to shiyáázh?"

"He . . . his body was found near Chimney Rock by a person who was running there. The runner called Milagro Police. We went down there. There was nothing on him . . . on your boy to show us who he was. We had to identify him, that's why it took us so long to come to see you. The doctor in Delgado said that it is likely that he passed away a couple of days before he was found at Chimney Rock. We don't know what the circumstances of . . . why he passed away."

Ella King nodded into her cup.

"Did someone kill him?"

Ella King lifted her head and held their eyes.

K realized that people ageing visibly was not a cliché. Ella King's skin was like yellow parchment, stretched tightly over her skull.

"He had a fracture to his head. They couldn't say for sure what caused it; it could have been some kind of an accident, or there's a possibility that he suffocated." Weismaker's voice sounded hoarse.

The old woman's mouth worked as if she wanted to say something, but had difficulties saying it.

The policemen sat silently.

"Suffocated?"

"There were some signs that before he passed away air had stopped getting into his lungs."

"Why?"

"We do not know for sure. Maybe he was smothered. They say that maybe somebody held something over him to . . . stop him breathing."

"Of all the ways to go . . . no air . . . no breath. . . ."

As if to make up for the lack of oxygen the young man had suffered at the end of his life, the old woman began to fight for breath, her chest rising and falling as she sucked the air in great agonized gulps. Weismaker and K compulsively compensated for her hyperventilating; they breathed slowly, deeply. It took some time for Ella King's breathing to calm and grow slower.

"Was he on drugs?" Ella King asked suddenly, as if she had made up her mind to pre-empt any more terrible news.

"There were some traces of drugs in his body."

"He promised . . . he said everything would change. He was going to get through that probation. He was looking for work." She shook her head. "He was trying to change . . . he promised. No. I'm lying to myself. I am not telling the truth. I know things are not good. I know when he does things that are no good. I just turn my head, I guess. I'm old. I'm tired. I had mostly worries with him. Hopes too, sometimes. When he is good, he is OK. He is a nice kid. But somehow he always gets back to trouble. Or trouble gets to him. Do you know how his dad died? He was on a drunk and he fell asleep in City Park and those bílagáana kids beat up on him. High school kids. They said that is something high school kids like to do, like a dare or something, beat up on a drunk Indian. And they told folks about it later. Told their friends that they got themselves an Indian. Then someone told on them, I guess a teacher or something, and the police came for them. They got just a little time in prison, like a couple of months, no more. They said that Noah's dad did not die from the beating, they said he choked on his own vomit. For us it is murder. They killed a man who didn't do anything to them. They beat up on him and he could not defend himself. Those kids are men now, still running around, and no one minds. That is Noah's excuse when he gets into trouble. It is because of how his dad died. He says he gets into all this trouble, because he has no dad to look out for him. He was ten when his dad died. Just old enough to understand what happened. It hit him hard. He was too little when his mom passed. He didn't understand. But when his dad died, he was old enough. That's when he comes to live with me. Noah is like his dad, he can be real happy one moment, and then he'll turn and you better get out of his way. What he always says is that what happened to his dad showed him that nobody cares about you when you are an Indian. You got everything against you from the beginning. But I think he wants to get caught. He is waiting for bad things to happen to him. He always expects bad things . . . and now. . . ." Her eyes filled with tears. "It would not be so bad if he didn't get into drugs. Sometimes he comes home and talks, talks. He is up all night. Sometimes cleaning the house . . . everything he cleans. I tell myself: what a good boy. He wants to help. I am hoping. . . ."

"Do you know who Noah might have gotten drugs from?"

"I don't know. He kept some bad company, people that was trouble."

"Do you know those people?"

"Don't know them. We had some words about it. I said, 'Why don't you stick with your own people and walk in beauty? These bílagáana don't care about you. It is people like them that hurt your father. And now they are making trouble for you.'

He got real mad at me. I don't know if he maybe liked this one girl, a white girl, he didn't want to hear anything bad against his bílagáana friends. That was his other side. Once he was a friend to someone, he was a good friend."

K thought of the assault report that Juanita Córdoba had written, but that she hadn't processed as an official complaint, because Ella King refused to file a complaint against her son—her nephew, actually. In Navajo terms, Ella King, Noah's maternal aunt, was Noah's bimá yázhi, his little mother.

"Who are these people that live here that he was friends with?"

"There are a couple of them he started to hang out with. There's some around. And some guy who lives somewhere else, but he visits all the time."

"Do you know any of their names?"

Ella King shook her head. "I'm not sure. He mentioned some,

but I forgot. The girl's name . . . Lara . . . or something. Marcia, Monica, maybe. It was more a name that bílagáana have, like a short name. He always found someone that would give trouble, if there was hózhó one way and bahadzid the other, he would choose bahadzid, shíyáázh."

"Have you relatives nearby, Mrs. King?" asked Weismaker. "Anyone that we can call for you?"

"I don't need nobody with me. They were not there for me when Noah's dad was beaten dead by those boys. I don't need them now. They were not there for Noah when his dad died. They were not there when Noah needed a relative to show him how to grow up to be a good man. They don't care for him in life. I don't need them to care for him in death. It's too late. It's all too late now."

"Mrs King," said Weismaker.

"Don't worry," said the old woman. "I can see you are not bad people. I know you will try to find out what happened to my boy."

"We'll come back as soon as we find out what happened. We will be back, when anything new comes up."

Ella King began to gather the empty cups.

"Shimà," said K, "when we saw him over there at Chimney Rock, there was a horny toad right by him."

"Na'ashǫ'ii dich'ízhii?" said the old woman. "For us he is cheí, the protector. Maybe he came to look after shiyáázh?"

At the door she said, "You know, he was born with the umbilical cord around his neck. He was nearly lost. We used to say that's why he was so afraid of being without air. As a kid we couldn't even get him to wear a turtleneck."

And she closed the door.

CHAPTER TEN

K phoned Social Services to make sure that Noah George's social worker, listed in his police file as Dinky Sapps, was available for "an enquiry relating to an open case."

The rising popularity of TV police procedurals and crime fiction had left their mark on police practice. Both the Law's and layman's appreciation of police work had been much enhanced by filmic and literary takes on it. There were cops aplenty who modeled themselves on fictitious counterparts. From time to time K liked to indulge in enigmatic hyperbole, preferably delivered in a languid Southern drawl, his favorite detective being a moody, recovering alcoholic with a poetic take on Louisiana swamp life. His police officer meme usually got a far more positive reception than his natural persona ever did. Renegade cop—tough as nails but with a touch of the blues—yeah, baby.

Whether K's assumed persona or his officious turn of phrase was the cause, or if the San Matteo County social work department was just exceptionally efficient, K hardly had to wait at all before he got a call confirming that Dinky Sapps was available forthwith.

K felt tempted, but did not dare, to ask if the name Dinky Sapps was genuine or if the social worker had adopted an alias maybe for altruistic reasons to brighten up her clients' mood. Who could possibly be pissed at being mandated to go and meet a Dinky Sapps? In fact K had been so perturbed by the quaint eccentricity of this name that he had half anticipated that Social Services would confess to a practical joke when he asked for Dinky Sapps. But judging from the call-back

Dinky Sapps really existed, unless Social Services were exceptionally adept at being devious—which they probably were. The question was whether they'd bother to apply their virtuoso mendacity to inventing silly names for their colleagues—which they probably would not.

•   •   •

San Matteo County Social Services were located west of town, a couple of miles outside Milagro city limits, next to what the municipality liked to refer to as the Industrial Zone. The Industrial Zone was a few acres of wasteland reclaimed from an arroyo that ran muddy waters in spring and fall and that hosted a haulage enterprise, three warehouses and the municipal recycling station.

Whoever had been responsible for town planning had paid but scant consideration to the convenience of Social Service clients. Milagro had no public transport. The Roadrunner Bus Company had recently terminated its intriguingly scheduled regional route that contrived to cross a 12,000-foot summit at 2 am, a time when even in summer there was the chance of snow flurries, not to speak of the kamikaze black ice run that the mountain road turned into during the cold seasons. Maybe the Roadrunner Bus Company had been involved in a national conspiracy to dispense with poor people, a coach-load at a time. Maybe that scheme had now been abandoned in favor of the more efficient Death by Tcheezos and Crystal Meth.

The only other communal transport was the Casino bus that trawled the Rez pimping for trade and that ferried gamblers to the casino free of charge. Thanks to cunning logistics, buses to the casino ran about ten times more frequently than buses from the casino.

Milagro also had a taxi service that consisted of an ill-tempered and ill-suited wife and husband team who used steeply prized journeys to unburden their woes on wary passengers. Every tip not given exasperated the couple's temper further and led to more conjugal strife, which in turn discouraged customers. What Milagro's taxi service did was in fact encourage drunk driving. Most folks preferred to risk a DUI charge than having to endure a trip with Mr. and Mrs. Nagandgripe.

Other than that, only the small municipal airport connected Milagro to the big world—the state capital—but an airport wasn't that much help to folks who needed to get around Milagro Town and San Matteo County and had no access to a ride. Most of the folks who had dealings with Social Services did not own a vehicle.

There was no footpath, no boardwalk, no shade on the way to Milagro Social Services. It was a two-mile hike in dirt and ditch next to the road. In sync with the inclination of greater American society, car owners had little empathy for people who walked. Pickup trucks did not swerve; cars did not slow down; pedestrians were expected to stop, suck in their bellies, jump in the ditch, when a vehicle passed by. K had seen mothers pushing prams along the road while coaxing reluctant toddlers to keep up, forced into dangerous maneuvering because drivers didn't take their foot off the accelerator. K had driven by many such scenes without being able to help. Police regulations strictly prohibited officers giving rides to citizens—unless citizens fiercely resisted being given a ride.

K's drive took him past small clusters of people making their way to the Social Services building. After the schlep through the city's wasteland periphery, Milagro Social Services building came as something of a surprise. It was an Eastern Seaboard city-slicker's fantasy of Southwestern bucolia; it screamed Santa Fe nostalgia, Rancho cum Hacienda cum Rio Grande Pueblo sprawl in burnt sienna enlivened with pan-Indian decorative doo-das. The grounds were landscaped with regional flora with a few cast-iron Kokopellis scattered about.

Newspaper pages, coupon strips, Styrofoam cups and trash bags—transported by the wind and deposited by clients—swayed in sagebrush, piñon and juniper trees; whirled along walkways driven by wind funnels; came to rest on gravel paths and Buffalo grass-planted ledges. The municipality had probably envisaged that the citizen participation and empowerment it so keenly promoted would establish itself differently, but there was no denying that citizens had participated and—damn it!—had added to the landscaping.

At the entrance a revolving door led to an open reception area, displaying murals of historical scenes from Anasazi life: mesa land-scapes; cliff palaces; serene women grinding corn; infants propped in cradleboards; bronze-skinned hunks in loincloths carrying deer on their backs; warriors returning from slaying the enemy; old crones weaving baskets. There was much to see. Who knew how the majority of Navajo clients felt about the prominent display of the ways of the Enemies of their Ancestors? Maybe they did not feel much about it at all. There was after all an ample supply of modern-day adversaries; no need to grind on the past and dwell on historical vexations and the foes of bygone days.

The receptionist—Felicia, as identified by her nametag—was a middle-aged Navajo woman with iridescently rimmed spectacles and bouffant hair that must have required an ozone-depleting amount of hairspray to hold it in place. Hairspray that many of the center's clients would have gladly put to another, mood-altering, use.

Felicia fixated K in a manner that he could not interpret as encouraging. In attitude, if not in appearance, Felicia seemed pretty close to Redwater PD's Sheryleah. Felicia did not chew gum though. She just glared. And eventually she spoke.

"Yes," she said, making it sound like, "No."

K stated whom he had come to see, heard his own voice, terse, clipped.

Felicia took up the phone and dialed.

"Room 113, end of the corridor," she said.

K walked in the direction she indicated, through glass doors separating the reception area from offices. The corridor was long, with gleaming polished floors and office doors leading off to the left. The walls were white, broken by one continuous line in turquoise about a third up the wall's height. The line was the first thing that K liked about the building.

He knocked on the door of Office 113. A moment passed before he heard a voice call: "Come in."

Face-to-face with Dinky Sapps, K congratulated himself on the accuracy of his conjecture. Dinky Sapps was short, plump and in her late fifties. On first glance she exuded bustling joviality. Blonde, of florid complexion, Dinky looked pretty much as most bílagáana in these lands did—out of place.

Crimson burnished hides desiccated by the merciless sun; thin, brittle hair; pale watery eyes; scabbed, scarred skin heralding mela-noma—oh Lord have mercy for they do not comprehend whither they moved. Good news though for the one reliable growth industry: med-ical skin care. Skin cancers proliferated amongst the displaced pallid sons and daughters of the northern hemisphere. And with global warm-ing and the diminishing ozone layer they were certain to increase.

Dinky Sapp's freckled skin showed signs of precancerous chang-es here and there. The woman seemed to like colors. She was dressed in what looked to the untutored eye like a loosely layered outfit of skirt and tunic, in turquoise, pink and orange of vaguely Native pat-tern. Dinky Sapps was of the species "Sedona Woman," someone who dug "Native Spirituality" the way you dig around in a pick 'n' mix candy display; resorted to crystal healing to supplement her pri-vate healthcare plan; and believed that the Vortex worked just swell for her. Her office was decorated with baskets, rugs, sand-paintings, cradle-boards and Kachina dolls. Crystals dangled from the window.

"Hi there," said Dinky Sapps with grating cheer, "how can I help you, Officer?"

"This is regarding one of your clients."

"Oh my! I like your accent!" trilled Dinky Sapps.

Her expression was appreciative, not to say roguish, and her eyes roamed rather freely over the length of K's body before settling on his face.

"Anything I can do to help you, Officer! Which of my clients are you concerned with?"

"Noah George."

"Noah? Oh my! What has he done now?"

Not very good with boundaries or confidentiality then. A minute in and she had already managed to implicate her client. Her ex-client.

"He is dead, I'm afraid," said K, in the officious monotone that

116

seemed to have invaded him since he had entered the Social Services building.

"Dead? Oh my! I don't know what to say," said Dinky Sapps.

"We are conducting an investigation into Noah George's death, Ma'am. Any information that you can give us is helpful."

"Certainly Officer," Dinky Sapps responded in a similarly officious tone.

At least it hadn't taken her long to pick up on his antipathy and discard him as quaintly accented romance-fodder. She went to a filing cabinet, retrieved a file and said in a tremulous drawl, "I'm afraid Noah was not one of my hopeful ones."

K found Dinky Sapps' phrasing interesting in its ambiguity.

Did she mean that she had not felt hopeful about Noah George; or that Noah George didn't feel hopeful about himself; or that he did not feel hopeful about Dinky Sapps; or that the Criminal Justice system had little reason to feel optimistic about Noah's prospects for rehabilitation?

"He was always in some kind of trouble, that boy. In and out of jail. DUIs mostly. Common assault. Drunk and disorderlies. Not sticking to probation terms. Nothing big mostly, but if you ask me, he was working up to something. It would have been federal prison at the next count, I reckon."

"What makes you think that?"

"He was real angry. Not just young-man angry; growing-out-of-trouble angry. He was boiling inside. Like a ticking time bomb. Nothing could reach him."

"What was he so angry about?"

Dinky Sapps shrugged. "Just angry. I think with him it had become a habit. It was in his blood. Maybe his Daddy dying. Thought his Daddy had been murdered by white boys and the system was on their side, because they were white and his Daddy was an Indian. He said this country doesn't care if Indians are murdered. If he had been born a bit earlier in time, I guess joining AIM and becoming a militant would have been a way for him. He was too late for all that. All that was left was drink and drugs and getting rowdy. That's about it."

"Did you like him, Ms. Sapps?"

"Like him?" No trace of bonhomie left now. "I got 121 clients on my books. A lot of them are what we call Revolving Door. Mostly what we do is firefighting. Small crises; big crises; an intervention here; an intervention there. One fire extinguished. And the next sure to come. And you never know how much that next one is going to destroy. You ask me if I liked Noah George: I guess the answer is no, Officer, not so much. I like the ones I can feel some hope for. We all need something to keep us going, don't we, Officer?"

"No hope at all for Noah George?"

"None that I could see. I have been in this job thirty years. There's some you can't get through to. Noah George was one of them. Don't get me wrong. He was a charmer. A smooth talker. He knew what to say, what to promise, when to be contrite. I bet he was a wow with the ladies too. But after a while you learn that it's just words, and nothing, absolutely nothing behind them."

"You sound angry."

"How do you want me to sound? So many resources; so many policies; so much time—and where does it end? A young man dead. And before you ask: yes, I do feel guilty. We always feel guilty when something goes bad. We always think there's something we could have done better. Something we missed."

Something about Sapps' use of "we" was pissing K off. Was she using the royal 'We'? Or was she distancing herself from her personal responsibility by distributing hypothetical blame amongst those of her profession?

"And what do you think you may have missed in this case, Ms. Sapps?"

K knew he was being provocative, but decided to take the risk of pushing Dinky Sapps.

The woman looked at him, momentarily silenced. But it only took a beat for her to collect herself: "Nothing that anyone else would not have missed as well," she said smoothly.

"There seems to be a lot of cohesion in your profession," said K.

The social worker looked at him blankly. If there was nothing more to say here was at least an opportunity to pull some stereotypical cop genre moves. Had he been a smoker and had smoking in public places been permitted, now would have been the time to tuck a cigarette into the corner of his mouth, to casually strike a match on the wall or his thumbnail or the sole of his shoe. Not being a cigarette smoker and not carrying matches and smoking in public places not being permitted, K smiled his thin-lipped American Alpha Male-Clint Eastwood crossed with crocodile anticipating a feed-smile, and nodded emptily.

"I'd like to look through Noah George's file," he said.

"You will have to do that outside, Officer. My next appointment is due."

"Yes Ma'am. Is there some place for me to read the file?"

"Room 117 is unoccupied. A colleague on extended sick leave," said Dinky Sapps pointedly, as if this proved the vicissitudes of her profession. She pushed Noah George's file toward K.

"Where would you like me to leave this when I'm done?"

"Leave it with Felicia in Reception. Just let her know it's mine."

"Thank you, Ma'am," K said to the woman.

Neither attempted to shake hands or exchange reassuring platitudes.

K made his way as instructed to Room 117. If Dinky Sapps' office had been a display case of Native arts and crafts, Office 117 was devoted to a sickly evocation of childhood. There was an extraordinary amount of pink. Pink cushions, pink wall-hangings, pink curtains draped over the windows, pink fluffy toys. Either this social worker worked exclusively with children or was a specialist on counseling hebephrenic clients, or the pink hyper-saturation heralded a psychotic breakdown. For a moment K was tempted to return to Dinky Sapps and ask her if she could find him another office. He assessed the office for the area least assailed by pink and sat behind the desk, swiveling the chair toward the window, so that, should he happen to look up, his glance would fall out rather than in.

Noah George's file was old-time. Dinky Sapps reports were hand-written, her handwriting round and school-girlish. Noah George's contact with Social Services and Dinky Sapps went back almost ten years. As Dinky Sapps had said, Noah George had been in some or other kind of trouble ever since adolescence. Most incidents were trivial enough; affray, drunk-and-disorderlies, vandalism. Then came the DUIs, and there was an escalation. Not only was Noah George a repeat offender, his DUIs got more extreme; his alcohol blood level climbed with each conviction. Referrals to rehabilitation programs alternated with jail terms. Each intervention was followed by a con-viction. It seemed that Noah George had dedicated his energies to becoming a problem drinker. At his most recent conviction his alco-hol-blood level had been so high it was a wonder he had been able to maneuver a car at all, never mind drive it.

Dinky Sapps' entries on her meetings with Noah George were procedural rather than reflective. Mainly she had recorded dates of appointments and made brief notes on issues "raised," "addressed" or "flagged." These seemed to be the social worker's operative terms: raising, addressing and flagging.

Noah George's life, Noah George himself, remained opaque, a fretwork of incidents and misdemeanors, held together by "pro-fessional interventions," if that was the right term to use. Nothing here of a young man whose anger could not be appeased, the kid whose daddy had been murdered, whose relatives had hoped that their yáázh would learn to walk in the way the Diné's ancestors had prescribed—the Beauty Way—a young man now dead of causes un-known, murdered.

But there had been something that could be of use, maybe. K leafed back through the file until he found what he was looking for. The references were ominous though oblique. Whether they pointed to mere association or direct involvement, here at last was something worth following up. K got out his notebook and copied down names, dates and details, meticulously. Avoiding mistakes meant not having to come back. That made paying attention to detail well worth it.

K closed the file, raised his head, and surfaced into a froth of pink that brought on something like hyperglycemia. He left the room and walked along the cool white corridor, following the single turquoise stripe to reception, feeling lightheaded and spaced out. Maybe it was the contrast between Noah George's life history and the message the office's resident was presumably trying to convey through pinkness. But then the office's usual occupant was off sick. K handed in the file, turned crisply on his heel and left the building without further word or glance.

It was now too late to do anything other than return to the station and follow Dinky Sapps' example: process paperwork; log issues; raise queries; address points of attention; flag necessary courses of action.

• • •

"That Felix John was jess asking 'bout you in Reception." Young made it sound like an accusation.

"Felix John?" asked K.

"Ain't he your buddy?" said Young.

K inclined his head expectantly and smiled winningly.

"The Indian guy that always whines about discrimination and racism," snorted Young, "the Human Relations wotsit."

"Wotsit," said K.

"Better get him in and have a liberal heart to heart about social injustice and stuff," said Young and stabbed his thumb toward reception.

"Better do," K said to Young's back.

He went into his office. In his office the phone was ringing.

"Felix John's out here," said Becky. "He wants to see you about the Noah George case."

Not Noah George. The Noah George Case. That was the trouble. A person became a case in no time at all.

• • •

Felix John was standing by the reception desk studying the notice board. He was a broad-set man with wide cheekbones and a smile that did not quite reach his narrow eyes. He extended his hand. His grip was powerful, not the Navajo customary brief repose of hand on hand, but a firm handshake bílagáana style.

"Would you like a coffee?" asked K.

John shook his head. "I'm good."

Either he had experienced Weismaker's joe or he meant business and did not want to dilute his message by accepting the Law's acrid hospitality.

K showed Felix John into his office and motioned toward a chair. The chair creaked as John cautiously lowered his body on it. He really was a very broad man, though his body's mass did not make him look obese, but forceful and somehow compelling, like a well-fed bear whose mood it was difficult to gauge.

John looked at K, nodded and briefly bared his teeth. His smile exposed pointed incisors that dazzled white against his brown skin. Maybe not a bear but a mountain lion, thought K.

"Go ahead," said K.

Behind steel-rimmed spectacles Felix John's eyes narrowed. "Go ahead?"

"Well, if you start that minimizes the risk of me getting things wrong."

"Right here for this minute maybe," said John, unimpressed. "That strategy don't take you far enough though."

"Sure doesn't," agreed K and saw Felix John's lips twitch.

"The dead man at Chimney Rock—they identified him as Noah George? It is Noah George? No mistake?"

"As far as they can be sure it is Noah George, yes. Was."

"It seems that they—you—are not sure about cause of death? At least that's what Bachman says."

"You've been to see Bachman?"

"Newspaper folks are usually more forthcoming than cops, I find," said John.

"That's because they can afford to be," K said, unwisely.

"Are you trying to tell me something?" asked John, not missing a beat.

Building rapport word by word, thought K with a sinking heart, and tearing it down syllable by syllable.

"Don't want to take too much of your time—Sir," Felix John said. "What I want to know is: are there indications that it was racial?"

"It is early in the enquiries," said K.

"Early?" John raised his eyebrows. "It's been . . . how many days?" He counted on his fingers. "Would you've taken that long if the victim was white?"

K lifted his shoulders. Felix John had a point. Of course. It was unlikely that the discovery of a white John Doe would have met with quite as low-key a reaction from the wider community. A dead white man spoke of the coming social apocalypse. The suspicious death of a white person signified that soon NO ONE CAN SLEEP SAFE IN THEIR OWN BED ANYMORE.

"We are too early in our enquiries to make definitive statements."

"So was it an accident? Or murder?"

"I don't think it is helpful to speculate at this stage."

"For you—or for us, the citizens?" asked Felix John.

"That's all I can say at this time," said K.

"Thank you for your time," said Felix John, and rose, unsmiling. He nodded and left the office without offering K his hand.

"Oh fuck," said K.

CHAPTER ELEVEN

By the time K drove home darkness had fallen. A metallic green SUV was parked in his driveway.

It was too late to turn back.

K drove up and parked alongside the SUV, though it would have been easier to park behind it. As soon as he opened his car-door, the SUV's door opened.

Juliette lowered herself out of the SUV and came toward him.

"Hi," K said warily.

"Hey."

Juliette was wearing fashionably faded jeans, a denim shirt over a white tank top that accentuated her tanned skin, sun-bleached hair falling over her shoulders.

"I had a long day, Juliette," said K, as if using her name would stop her.

Juliette came closer, slowly, until she was so close he could feel the heat her body radiated.

"Look," said K.

Juliette kept coming closer, inching toward him until her toes touched his. She stood silent and still. He could hear her breathing. Felt her shirt brush against him in rhythm with her breath. Felt her breath quicken.

"Juliette," said K, helplessly, "I don't think this is a good idea, for either of us."

"I know," she said and tilted toward him so that he felt the entire length of her body against him.

He unlocked the door and held it open. Already he hated himself.

• • •

Juliette was asleep. She had thrown off the sheet and lay on her back, an arm over her eyes.

K looked at her breasts, smooth belly, diamond stud in belly-button, long legs, pubic area waxed and what remained of her pubic hair styled into what he thought they called a Brazilian. Juliette's Brazilian pubes were new and cinched it for him. The lost bush was the straw that broke the camel's back. As a matter of honor and principle he could never be compatible with someone who spent time and money on pubic coiffure.

How many things divided them, him from Juliette, Juliette from him. The only time they got along was while they were getting it on. Out of, let's say, seven hours, or 420 minutes, sex including all preliminaries and post-coital etiquette took up about seventy minutes, at the outside. that meant they got along around 19% of the time, which was actually not too bad, except that most of the remaining time, 350 minutes, they were asleep. He couldn't begin to imagine what a whole twenty-four hours in Juliette's company would be like.

Out of 1440 minutes with . . . OK seventy minutes of sex, just to make the calculation easier, that still made almost 5% of time when they got along. More than he'd thought. Intuitively he'd have put it at about 2%. If they had to live together then the frequency of sex would decrease, its duration shorten, and with it the percentage of time that they were OK with each other's company.

There was a self-help book in there somewhere; maybe he could patent this as the "Definitive 'Calculate the Value of your Relationship' Algorithm." The formula would have to be adjusted according to age though. When you were young, even three minutes of sex, around 0.02% of your time, were worth any amount of aggro and tedium otherwise endured; the older you got the less you were prepared to sacrifice your personal comfort zone for the sake of making the beast with two backs.

K gathered his clothes, took them to the bathroom, locked the door, stood under a scorching hot shower, toweled off and dressed. He prepared coffee and went into the bedroom. Juliette was awake, sheet drawn up between her legs, limbs golden against white bedding.

"Coffee's ready," said K.

Juliette raised her arms, stretched and ran her fingers through her hair.

"Have a shower, I'll get you a towel," said K and bolted out of the bedroom.

In the kitchen, dressed and sipping coffee, Juliette looked less sure of herself, more vulnerable. K could think of nothing to say, nothing that was friendly, respectful and simultaneously discouraging of yet another repeat. Juliette finished her coffee, K took her cup and put it in the sink. Wittgenstein was sitting on the windowsill regarding Juliette with a cold, disapproving eye.

K held open the door for Juliette. He locked the door, raised his hand to a half wave, mumbled "Running late," and walked to his truck quickly. He drove off without looking back, feeling enduring shame mitigated by a smidgen of relief.

• • •

Behind the reception desk Becky was elbow-deep in schedules, forms and message slips.

"Hey, Becky. Is there anything you can tell me about the Sam Wellies?"

"No," said Becky.

"Really? Nothing?"

"You don't even say good morning and then you ask me something like that?"

"Good morning," K said sheepishly.

"Too late now."

"Really, I am sorry. Guess my head was someplace else. So what about the Sam Wellies?"

"Don't you get it?" Becky said, "we're not supposed to talk

about them. OK?" She shoved a fist-full of message slips toward him. K struggled to find something conciliatory to say, could think of nothing, mumbled, "sorry," again, gathered the message slips and made toward his office, chastened and confused.

Juanita Córdoba appeared at the far end of the corridor, silhouette bathed in light, long legs, curvaceous hips, slim waist and perfectly molded breasts. Down boy, down.

K ducked into the men's room where he stood over the sink, mechanically rinsing his hands and staring glassily at his reflection. He bent toward the tap, wet his face, then neck, then hair before realizing what he was doing. Water dripped from hair to shirt.

K was patting his neck and shoulders dry with a wad of paper towels when McCabe entered the restroom.

McCabe, narrow-eyed, mouth cutting a compressed line through bolsters of florid flesh, dipped his chin and waddled over to the urinal while tearing at his fly. He pissed as if he was trying to hose down a wildfire about to spread out of control. Then, abruptly, the flow stopped. McCabe flexed his knees, grunted and zipped up. He walked over to the basin, regarded himself in the mirror and smoothed back his hair with both hands.

"What did you say?" asked McCabe.

"I was just wondering when they took away the "Now please wash your hands" sign."

"Sign?" said McCabe, "There ain't never been one."

"Maybe they should put one up," said K to McCabe's retreating back, mentally tracing the trail of microbes on McCabe's pissed-stained hands through the station: hair, door-handle, refrigerator, drawers, cupboards, coffee-machine—every damn surface in the kitchen, which was McCabe's favorite place to spend time in during working hours—when he wasn't called upon to lend his expertise to the NRA.

K rinsed a paper towel in water and wiped the door handle, opened the door and wiped the other side as well. Huzzah for displacement activity.

Lorinda, walking by with her cleaning trolley, stopped. "I don't clean good enough for you?"

"People don't wash their hands," K said grimly.

"Uhu, you telling me."

Lorinda watched McCabe disappear into the kitchen. "I bet it is those self-same folks that always say bad things about other people—that they are dumb, and lazy, and dirty, huh?"

"You got it. Weird, huh?" asked K.

"I don't think it's weird at all," said Lorinda. "It's just folks that don't like themselves push their bad feeling about themselves on others."

"You see this often?" K asked.

"You're Native, that's what comes your way, more than for white folks, I guess."

"If those folks understood themselves, would things get better?"

"Might, might not. Don't matter anyway. I walk with the Lord. I just pray and forgive. Mostly I don't get mad anymore."

"I do. All the time," said K.

"You want to go to church. I know a bunch of people that it has helped become better. Myself too. I was in a heap of trouble when I was younger. Try it."

Lorinda nodded her grey head at him, and pushed her cart onward.

What a shame. The conversation had started so well. Just once it would be great to hear something insightful without a Jesus-appendix. And this from a People whom history should have taught what there was to expect from Christianity.

• • •

K piled up the notes he'd made on Noah George's Social Services file and dialed Redwater PD.

"Yes," said a voice that sounded as if it was cushioned by a fist-sized wad of chewing gum.

"Officer Begay," K barked into the receiver.

"Which one?" droned Sheryleah.

"Robbie."

"Officer Robert Begay. Who are you?"

"Officer Kafka, Milagro PD."

Silence. Maybe Sheryleah had choked on her chewing-gum.

"Begay here."

"Hi Robbie. It's K."

"How ya doin'? Getting on OK with your inquiry?"

"I had a look through Noah George's social work file. Looks like he was in trouble for a long time—ever since he was a teenager."

"That's not so unusual."

"Probably not. Anyway, his social worker kept things kind of minimal, but—Noah used to run with a gang."

"That's not so unusual either. Bored young men trying to connect with their warrior past and all that. What's the name of the gang?

"The Sam Wellies."

"The Sam Wellies?" asked Begay.

"Ever heard of Sam Wellies?"

"The Sam Wellies or what 'Sam Wellies' stands for?"

"I just asked Becky and she chewed my ass. She wouldn't tell me anything."

"Some folk are sensitive that way."

"What about you, Robbie?"

"You know me," said Begay complacently.

"OK then, shoot," said K.

"You know what Sam Wellies stands for?"

"Yes, and I'm not going to say it out loud," K assured Begay.

"I don't mind. You can't be a cop these days and avoid saying certain words just because you happen to have traditional . . . uh . . . sensibilities. It's a long time since they offered to hold a ceremony when we face a dead body. Why ask Becky about stuff you know already anyways?"

"Multiple source data collection," K said weightily.

"Argh," said Begay, "So yeah, Sam Wellies stands for Skinwalkers. Hold on, let me knock on wood or something. Only kidding."

"They're still around?"

"They've been around for a long time. Folks back then were terrified. There was a lot of bad things happening, livestock dying, and people getting sick through witchcraft. So when the gang bangers ignored all these old taboos and called themselves Sam Wellies it was an end of the world kind of deal, you know? It was like they wanted to go beyond just being badasses. In our tradition Skinwalkers are like your demons or witches with their special way of doing evil. Do you know how Skinwalkers came to be?"

"Go on," said K.

"Are we having a little cultural instruction session?"

"Sure. If there's time left I'll tell you about Yom Kippur."

"Can't wait," said Begay.

"You are not interested in the traditions of my ancestors?" asked K.

"You'll not file a grievance 'cause I been politically incorrect?"

"These days there'd be nobody on my side. Otherwise I just might. To help me focus on positive things."

"Maybe I should try it too. So anyways—I'll give you my nalí's take on Skinwalkers: he kind of explained them as historical trauma, you know? After the Long Walk everything went bad. Like folk had been through all that hardship. They'd seen their family and k'é starving, dying. They couldn't help each other. Then they return to Diné Bikéyah. Only the government's given them the badlands and has kept all the good land. So the Diné start getting at each other's throats, envy and all that. The Skinwalkers came out of that, hurting and killing people because they wanted their stuff—basically."

"What about their supernatural powers?"

"Who says they have any? How about you go and read up some of those anthropology books?"

"Don't you believe they have supernatural powers?"

"I keep an open mind."

"Walking in Harmony between Conflicting Beliefs," said K.

"Ain't that just beautiful?" said Begay "I'm gonna use that next time I'm trying to impress a bílagáana."

"The copyright's mine," K said.

"Good old bílagáana tradition; put it down on paper. Anyway, how did we get here?"

"The Sam Wellies."

"You shouldn't even say the name because it can bring evil on you. So most folk would avoid saying the word and just call them Sam Wellies, which I guess also makes them a little bit less scary, because it's like a funny name, right?"

"Becky didn't even want to use that name."

"Yeah. But I hear she has this relative that's been in a heap of trouble, so maybe she's extra sensitive."

"A relative that's a Sam Wellie? I didn't know that."

"There's a lot of things you don't know, bro. So, anyways, when this gang starts up that calls itself the Sam Wellies, the elderlies get real worried. Young people only taking on the evil, destructive part of the culture, and that's almost worse than not taking on any traditions at all. You get it?"

"I think so."

"Guess they thought SW stuff was less evil when a traditional did it than when a young gang banger did it."

"So what's up with the Sam Wellies now?"

"They keep going. Some bros grow up and get out of the life—find a job or Jesus or the love of a good woman. Some don't change, they get killed, kill themselves, disappear, get kicked out. Gangs don't dig running around with grandpas. Your average gang-banger finds some different kind of trouble to get busy with by the time he's twenty-five—if he makes it that long. There's a whole bunch of possibilities for a body to get into trouble on our sweet Rez. You just takes your picks. These gangs have peaks and troughs. Sometimes they get real active and dangerous, other times they keep quiet and not much happens. Always depends on politics, and—dig this—the kind of music they listen to and films and stuff. Years back we had us a real spike during 'Natural Born Killers'. It wasn't just bílagáana kids who fancied themselves as serial killer outlaw heroes."

"There's mention of stuff in Noah George's social work file that's pretty bad. I mean it goes way beyond juvie delinquency."

"What are you saying?"

"I'm not sure. The social worker put it in a way that there's something there and not there."

"I'm getting a headache."

"There are some names in the file. Maybe you have something on them? If you do, I was thinking—"

"—we organize ourselves a little field trip?"

"Yes, Sir," said K.

"Don't see why not. Seeing that gang activity on the Rez has been declared a particular concern of the PD in this year's fiscal budget—or is it this fiscal year's budget?"

"Why this year? There's been plenty gang trouble for about half a century."

"Longer. We Diné were the marauders of the Southwest, remember? That's why they sent us to Hwéeldi; that's why our Pueblo bros ratted us out to Kit Carson. We were Trouble."

"Not still bitter, are you?" asked K.

"More like all this talk about gangs has made me nostalgic."

"I'll pretend I haven't heard that. So why the sudden concern about gangs?"

"Who knows? Probably they need to spend to get next year's budget approved by Window Rock or the BIA or whoever hands out the green. I lose track. Don't know who pays us and who we are supposed to butter up. They need to waste time and money on something. They've had Elderly Abuse; Drunk Driving; Domestic Abuse; Auto-theft; Littering. . . . Anyway, I'm glad to confirm, Officer Kafka, that I will be available to participate in a joint gang initiative."

"I wouldn't mind a little trip."

"You and me both, bro. Why don't you come on down and we go through the database together. I'm here, waiting."

• • •

K was about to knock on Weismaker's door when it opened. Bach-man, in crisp white shirt and pressed khaki chinos, smiled a greeting and hurried out. Being the editor of a local paper kept you pretty busy.

K entered the sheriff's office. The stink of McCabe's piss still clung to his olfactory nerves like a demonic invasion, which had the possible advantage that it modified the smell of Weismaker's coffee. Next to the coffee-machine stood a cup, full to the brim. As editor of the Milagro Gazette Bachman was a brave as well as tactful man, but he was not *that* brave and tactful.

"Help yourself," said Weismaker, gesturing toward the coffee-machine.

K nodded noncommittally and sat down.

"Bachman's running the story. The Navajo Times already got ahold of it. I've not given Bachman much besides the boy's ID and that it is an open investigation. We are asking people to contact us with any information. That's about it. No forensic details, no cause of death. Best to keep an open blotter and see what comes up. Told Becky to put relevant calls through to either of us."

"Felix John came to see me. He'd already been to see Bachman. Said he got more from Bachman than from us."

Weismaker shrugged.

K reported on his visit to Dinky Sapps and Noah George's file. The sheriff, with his bat's ear that perceived the slightest pipsqueak of ambivalence, said pensively, "Those kids need someone to hold out hope for them, huh? Even if they dash it time and again."

"Well, maybe some are more trouble than others. With some it helps to believe in a higher power, I guess—gotta have faith to keep the faith, maybe."

"You are not yourself into faith so much, are you?" said the sher-iff astutely. "Personally, I reckon you don't have to believe in a higher power to believe that there's a little bit of good in everyone."

"I don't know," said K.

"I think I know," said Weismaker. "Now either have some coffee, or find something to do to restore your faith in humanity, Son."

"Quite a lot would have to happen to do that," K. said. He felt like a temperamental teenager.

"Keep me posted. So long." said the sheriff.

CHAPTER TWELVE

Inside the station it had been easy to forget the Indian summer sunshine outside, soft breeze ruffling golden leaves, cotton-puff clouds drifting across the deep blue sky. At the roadside a prairie dog stood sentry, guarding the entrance to the colony's burrow. In the distance a gaggle of prairie dogs chased each other around a tree. Beneath another tree a portly prairie dog stretched himself tall and leapt upward, trying to grab a low-hanging branch loaded with bright orange berries.

K pulled the patrol car over. He watched the prairie dog leaping, missing, toppling, getting back on his hind legs, stretching, leaping, toppling over again. Until, at last, he got purchase on the branch. He pulled the branch down, hunkered on his haunches, fastened his incisors on the branch and began stripping it of berries.

The prairie dog's Buddha-pose; his soft-furred potbelly resting between his legs; his contented, contemplative munching; his fat cherubic face as appealing as a baby's dimpled cheeks, filled K with a surge of pure delight.

Around these parts people who looked kindly upon prairie dogs were usually tourists and a dwindling number of Navajo elderly who nostalgically remembered eating BBQ prairie dog way back. For the majority, rural folks and ranchers, fauna fell neatly and unequivocally into four categories:

Category One: For raising and eating.

Category Two: For hunting and eating.

Category Three: For guarding and petting.

Category Four: For exterminating.

Categories One to Three had been put on this here earth by the Good Lord for people to enjoy. Regarding Category Four K was not quite clear what had been the Good Lord's intention for putting moderate pests on this here earth. Apart from the dramatic ones like plagues of locusts and venomous snakes, what was the deal with field mice and prairie dogs and pigeons? Varmints all of them, said the ranchers. Shoot 'em, smoke 'em, poison 'em, gas 'em—whatever floats your boat.

The powers that be seemed less united on the terms and conditions of the Good Lord's anthropocentric master plan. And so it was that up on Milagro Mesa prairie dogs were a protected species, watched over by the BLM, who dutifully rehomed colonies, rebuild burrows and provided veterinary care when needed; while down in Milagro city limits prairie dogs were vermin with municipal environmental services expending substantial funds on "managing colonies" by gassing them.

K remembered that it was that time of year again. In the municipal calendar the prairie dogs had no more than a couple of weeks left. There they were, foraging and playing and guarding their burrows, raising their young, teaching them what prairie dogs needed to know to survive, thrive and procreate—all in vain. Not one of them would live to know another season.

• • •

At Redwater PD reception was deserted. Maybe Sheryleah was on nail-filing break. K gathered speed and marched through to the corridor leading to the offices. The building was quiet, apart from the swishing sound made by the revolving blades of the ceiling fan. He walked along the corridor to Robbie's door and knocked. There was no answer. K waited and knocked again. There was no answer. K retreated to reception, took out his cell and dialed Robbie's extension. The phone went to voicemail.

"Where are you? I'm out in reception. I hope you come back quick, wherever you are, before your ogre comes and gets me."

K ended the call and had just put the cell back in his shirt-pocket when he heard a door open and shut. Sheryleah appeared at the far end of the corridor. She looked at K with a basilisk eye; her expression could have turned the whole tribe of Israel into pillars of salt. Sheryleah's makeup needed some repair; a smear of lip-liner streaked across her cheek, an eyelash dangled at a precarious angle, the upper lip Cupid's bow smudged to the shape of a crimson carp's mouth. Sheryleah stalked past K without a word and settled on her perch at the workstation.

K took out his cell and redialed Robbie Begay's number. This time there was an answer.

"Yeah?"

"Yeah," said K flatly.

"Come on up," said Robbie. He sounded wary.

K rapped on Robbie's door, opened it when he heard a mumbled "come in." Begay was rubbing at his face with a Kleenex.

K kept his eyes down, rummaged in his jacket's pockets. He lowered himself on the chair that stood at the desk. He drew a folded piece of paper out of his pocket. He fixed his eyes on the paper and began to smooth out creases. He pushed the paper across the desk toward Begay.

"Here's the names of those Sam Wellies. Got them from the social worker's file," K said to the desk. "Everybody in there was involved in a couple of incidents. Petty delinquency, misdemeanor, that kind of thing. Some indication of involvement in more serious stuff too, though insufficiently substantiated."

"What was the serious stuff?" asked Begay in a voice wavering between crisp and croak.

"Pretty serious. Really serious—if it turns out they were involved. One of those crimes deliberately committed before a body turns eighteen so they'll still be classed as 'juvie.' The stuff that's sometimes dealt as 'coming of age rite.'"

"That 'get one in as a juvie' jive's still going—matter of fact it's pretty endemic."

"We are not talking petty crime like auto theft or vandalism. This was bad—really bad."

"What are they supposed to have done?"

"Boiled a guy's head."

K raised his head and looked at Begay. Begay aimed the crumpled Kleenex at the trash basket, threw and missed.

"Somebody pushed this kid's head in a vat of boiling water. They held him under until he was dead. They must have used metal rods or something. It was on one of those boonie parties."

"But they weren't pulled in?"

"Apparently not."

"This is the stuff you found in his file?"

"It's one of the few things his social worker put in his file. About everything else she was kind of vague."

"Must have thought he did it?"

"Guess so."

"What do you think?"

"I try not to think," K said.

Begay frowned at the list. "Let me just put these names through the database, OK?"

"Any of those names familiar?"

"That one for sure," said Begay. "Troublemaker. No shit he wasn't involved with. Exploding meth-labs; hit and runs; domestics; arson; theft; affray."

"Should we call on him?"

"If you feel like digging six foot down."

"He's dead?"

"Unless there's been a resurrection. Died just a little while back—couple months ago."

"What did he die of?"

"Here it says hypothermia."

"In summer?"

"Well, with a lowlife like that no one's gonna bust their ass to determine cause of death."

"But it was in summer?"

"I think so. Didn't pay too much attention."

"Probably had plenty of other things to keep you busy," said K pointedly.

Begay's eyes darted to K's face and away.

"What about the other names?" K asked.

"Nothing right now, but that doesn't say there's nothing there. Besides I only started here twelve years ago, anything earlier I wouldn't necessarily know. They'd have to be repeat offenders or from a notorious family."

"Notorious family?"

"Trouble runs in families. Let's say one elderly has a criminal inclination, you will see that running down through the generations like a curse. Mostly it's the men. I guess you don't want me to talk about the traditional ways or Walking in Beauty right now?"

"Not right now perhaps," K confirmed.

Begay nodded resignedly. He looked at the paper.

"So there are four here minus one: three left. That can't have been the whole gang though? They usually run in crowds of seven to ten. Eight's ideal for a gang."

"Like group therapy," murmured K.

"Huh?"

"Group therapy," said K, "the ideal number for a therapy group is eight."

"Gangs is group therapy."

"Gangs as alternative group therapy?" K asked. It was an interesting thought. "What about that one?" He pointed at the next name on the list. "Fancy running them all through the database?"

"Sure—you got all the details and everything we need right here. Somebody did their homework, eh?"

"Yeah. Dinky Sapps."

"What?"

"Dinky Sapps. The social worker."

"Is she. . . ."

"Is she what?"

"Dinky?"

"I'd say she is annoying. But that's me."

"Sure. I bet you find most people annoying?"

"Yep. Some days more than others."

"Uh. So. . . ."

"There was only one part of the file that had any meat. The only part where she'd put some work into it. Everything else, record of meetings, casework notes, careplan or whatever they call these things, was bare-bone minimum. Careplan my ass. It was plain she didn't care."

"Maybe she knew she was wasting her time. Didn't think there was any hope for the guy."

"That's what she said—that Noah George was beyond help."

Robbie Begay sighed. "Believe me, I know how she feels."

"OK. But you are a cop. We are cops. We see the worst of humankind, right? We are there to apprehend wrongdoers, not to help them. We are just there to protect citizens."

Begay looked up. "Boy, have you changed your tune. Did they give you some brainwashing serum or something?"

"I'm just saying," said K, "we are not helpers, we are protectors—that's our job description."

"Just when did you start bothering about the job description?"

"I'm trying to make a point," said K. He was starting to feel impatient. "I'm saying that it was Dinky Sapps' specific duty to help Noah George. That was what she got paid for. And I don't think she did a good job with him. You could see in the file that she just did not care one bit. Treated her job like an assembly line: clock in, clock out. Did the bare minimum statutory mandated process: Meet the guy however often he's mandated to. Make the meeting last however long it's supposed to. Mention the issues you are supposed to. Tick the boxes you are supposed to. And then tell folks there's no hope for the guy."

140

"Wow," said Begay. He shook his head. "Are you done?"

"I could go on for hours," said K through gritted teeth.

"Don't," said Begay. "You got a Tylenol?"

"Am I giving you a sore head?"

"Not just you," said Begay.

"Glad to hear it," sneered K.

"Let's get to it." Begay had switched voice to official. "Let's look at those names. You reckon no way that social worker would've bothered to get ahold of all these guys' details if she didn't have some suspicions, right?"

"Something like that. Though beyond their names and DoBs she hardly documented anything at all."

Begay drew the piece of paper closer, squinted and began typing.

"This here's such a common name, I can think of about a dozen people that are called Vince Benally, right off the bat."

"Vince is a common name?"

"Around here it is. Don't know why it is so popular though. Maybe an actor or something?" Begay peered at the screen. "Yep. There's a whole bunch of 'em. Maybe Vince's a good name for troublemakers?"

"Or a name that creates troublemakers?"

"Can't see why," said Begay, giving the issue serious consideration. "Rambo, yeah, that might make you a bit hardass. Or Zorro—sounds kind of pesky too. But Vince? Hey!" Begay stabbed a finger at the screen. "We got lucky! Just one with that DoB. I guess that's our boy."

"And?" asked K.

"Hold on," said Begay. "I'm just pulling up what we got on him. Slow system and all that."

K leant back in his chair and looked out the window toward Needlerock. The rock was swathed in haze and looked more like a mirage than a physical entity. Maybe there was a sandstorm going on. It was close to the season of the first frost, the season of Redwater Fair, which was inevitably a week of heavy rains that turned the fairgrounds into a slick plain of mud and turned people against the fair's management committee who had once again neglected to invest some of the profits into improving the fairgrounds.

The time of the first frost was also the time of the Yeíbicheí—the Nightway—the nine-day healing ceremony that must only be performed during the cold season.

Begay, squinting at the screen, spluttered "hehehe."

"You find something?" asked K.

"Wolf turned sheep—watchamacallit?"

"Wolf turned sheepdog? Or something like that? So. . . ."

"Vince Benally. Quite a dude. Kept himself pretty busy in trouble. Got himself a jacket too. Guess what Vince is doing now?"

"BIA?"

Nope."

"Cop?"

"Close."

"Teacher?"

"Closer."

"I'm all out of ideas," said K.

"Youth worker. How's that? Right over there at the Adolescent Center." Begay pointed his chin in the south-westerly direction of the Community College.

"Ought to be clean then," K ventured.

"The biggest crimes often take place closest to the Law," said Begay darkly.

"The biggest crimes are often committed by the Law, you mean," K posited.

"Speak for yourself."

"What do we do? Go visit?" asked K.

"Better shoot him an email first."

"If he's working with kids he's not going to be sitting at his desk checking his emails."

"You'd be surprised," said Begay.

"Well, we haven't got the time to wait until he's got it. Also with

142

an email he just can pretend that he hasn't got it: 'Email? What email? Must've gone straight to junk.'"

"Made up your mind he's dirty?"

"Not necessarily. Just that he'd do what I'd do, matter of fact."

"Which is?"

"Try to avoid talking to cops."

"Figures," said Begay, "but, hey, I'll pretend you have a point and give him a call, how's that?"

"Go ahead," said K.

"How 'bout you go to the men's room or something? You cramp my style."

K shrugged, got up, picked up the crumpled-up Kleenex, deposited it in the trash basket and left Begay's office.

He looked up and down the corridor and could see no sign for restrooms. But then he did not need the restroom anyway. He leant against the wall opposite Begay's door and dimly heard a phone being dialed and Begay's muffled voice.

A door opened further down the corridor and K heard someone coming toward him. He peeled away from the wall and straightened up.

"You waiting for somebody?"

The woman standing before him was severe looking, her hair in a salt and pepper bob, the corners of her mouth turned down—permanent testimony to a life lived in bitterness—deep grooves crisscrossing her forehead and cheeks, black shadows under her eyes. K hoped very much that this was how Sheryleah would look some years hence.

"The restroom," mumbled K.

"You are waiting here in case someone comes by who you can ask about the restroom?" the woman asked. "Where'd you come from?"

K pointed his chin at Begay's door.

"Why didn't you go back in and ask him?" asked the woman.

"Phone call," said K.

The woman clicked her tongue. "Across reception. Second door left," she said and walked on.

"Thank you," K whispered.

He heard the sound of the phone receiver being replaced and re-entered the office without knocking.

"Made some friends?" asked Begay.

"A lady just gave me the third degree. Sweet Lord Jesus I'd hate to be a suspect here."

"A lady?"

"An older lady with a mouth that would intimidate a rattlesnake."

"Prudence."

"Name kind of fits."

"She's real sick, you know," said Begay. "They say terminal. Of course she don't talk about it. And I have no business telling you that, I guess. But any hardship you can think of, Prudence has had in her life. And now this. Damn well hope that those Christians have it right and suffering in this life makes for an afterlife making whoopee."

"Is she a Christian?"

"With a name like Prudence? Of course."

"So what's the haps with our man Vince?"

"You're sounding like a gang-banger around, uh, the time the Sam Wellies were founded."

"Thanks," said K.

"He said: 'Sure. Come over. Glad to see you. Yada yada yada.'"

"Really?"

"Pretty much. If you can sound clean over the phone, Vince did. He'll see us over there in twenty."

"Let's walk," said K.

"Why not," said Begay.

"I'll wait outside," said K.

The air was mild and the breeze carried the musky smell of fallen leaves. Fall was here.

"What are you sniffing at?" asked Robbie.

"Don't you like the smell of falling leaves?"

"I like the smell of mutton stew and fry bread. Liking the smell of falling leaves is a very bílagáana thing. Stop sniffing, get walking, dude. We got things to do and perps to see."

THE QUALITY *of* MERCY

• • •

What was now the Adolescent Center and Community College once had been Redwater Residential School. Redwater Residential School to this day remained the very definition of an unhappy place for so many older Diné. It was many decades since they had closed Redwater Residential School and still people who had been there as children could not go into the building without getting flashbacks of the institutional fug, the smell of carbolic soap, disinfectant and misery seeping out of a myriad of student pores, the jangling keys carried by dorm supervisors like prison wardens; matrons' harsh voices calling them by numbers instead of their names. Even as adults, in that place they felt as they had as children, abandoned, confused and terrified. The Elders knew that no child that went in that place could ever leave it happy.

Today the old BIA residential school premises were divided between the Community College and the Behavioral Health Adolescent Center.

What had then been school dormitories were now Community College teaching rooms. What had been the school's old administrative quarters was now the Adolescent Unit. It would have been more practical and a damn sight cheaper to put the Adolescent Unit in the dormitory part and the Community College in the administrative part, but during the planning phase something rare happened: The People's will was heard. The planning committee had managed to talk sense into the head honchos. The sense being that no parent with living memory of Redwater Residential School would allow their child to be admitted to the Adolescent Unit if it meant sending them to the old dorms. The building had made so many people unhappy, sick— killed some even—and had given survivors a sadness that could not be cured and that not only tainted their lives but that infected the lives of their children and grandchildren too.

And so the old administrative block was converted into dorms and group rooms and offices and meeting spaces and a canteen; and the old dorms were remodeled into classrooms and became the Community College.

The Adolescent Unit was a two-story brick building. The building having been built in times when bílagáanas were in charge of the BIA and the BIA was in charge of erecting public buildings and Indians were in charge of precisely nothing, no one had told the white architects of Indian destiny that cardinal directions were kind of a big deal in Navajo life and cosmology, and that a proper building promoting harmony should be oriented east, always east. And so the old residential school had been built in the shape of a horseshoe with a central building framed by a south and a north wing and the main entrance facing west. Nowadays cardinal directions were not such a big deal—in fact most folks hardly knew what cardinal direction stood for anymore, which meant that practically the entire Navajo philosophy of life was being forgotten, gone with the wind.

K and Begay walked along the gravel path toward the main entrance. Somebody had created the structure for flowerbeds and then given up struggling against the forces of nature. Now there was goatweed, thistles and the type of wild grass that thrived anywhere.

The entrance door was closed. Begay pressed the intercom. Nothing happened. Well, it was a busy unit. They waited some more, then Begay pressed the bell again. Zip. Nothing stirred inside.

"Your turn," Begay said to K.

K obediently pressed the bell and had his finger still on it when the door was flung open from the inside. A very short woman stood in the doorway.

"Yáadilá!" she said accusingly to K. "I heard you the first time!" Out of the corner of his eye K saw Begay smirk.

K knew how it looked to the short lady: here was another bílagáana with an Anglo attitude to time; those bílagáana: always in a hurry; always trying to press their priorities on other people; still thinking they ruled everything; even when they were on the Rez, especially when they were on the Rez. Show those Injuns what efficiency is.

"Sorry," said K.

He contemplated telling the short woman that it had been Begay who had rung the bell the first two times, but couldn't find a way to say it that did not make him appear even more of an ass.

"Next time you'll know," said the woman, as if she was expecting them to visit every day from now on. Or maybe she merely talked to the cops as she talked to the young people. She really was a very short lady and almost as broad as she was high. She was dressed in a tent-like silky blouse with a large multicolored check pattern that made her look like an unresolved Rubik's Cube.

"Yá'át'ééh," said Robbie Begay, "we are here to see Vince Benally."

"Go round the corner through to reception. I was just leaving. Shí k'ad," said the woman. She stepped aside to let them walk past her into the building.

"I thought she'd come out to open the door for us," whispered K to Begay.

"Why would they need a manual door opener when they've got an intercom?"

"Manual door opener?" echoed K.

The reception area was a large open space with three doors: one center, one to the right, presumably leading to the north wing, one to the left, presumably leading to the south wing. At the far right corner of the reception area a staircase lead to the upper story. The lobby's walls were hung with posters. One wall was given over to the promotion of the values of traditional Navajo life. There was the ubiquitous "Sheep Is Life" poster. There were posters on the Wisdom of Elders, the Value of K'é, Diné Bikéyah; a Kináalda poster that showed a young girl running through a scene of pastoral idyll. The posters on the other wall dealt with the vicissitudes of contemporary Reservation life: alcohol, meth, gangs, DWI.

The meth posters were particularly impressive in terms of artistic aspiration. They looked like posters advertising classic French films in the days of yore, all artful monochrome, little light, lots of shadow and blurred silhouettes. The lobby was a literal face-off between

quaintly depicted traditional values on one wall and stylishly presented contemporary corruption on the other.

"Why is it 'Sheep is Life'?" K asked.

"Because sheep are our life—used to be," said Begay, "in the
old days we Diné got everything we needed from sheep. You should
know that."

"You said 'sheep are,'" said K. "Why does it say 'sheep is'?"

Begay shook his head and shrugged. "Better bother yourself with
how we are going to find someone that can get that Vince Benally for
us." He looked around. "Ain't nobody here."

"Trusting of that lady to let us in unsupervised," mused K.

"Nope, she was just a good reader of character. Could see we are
Good Guys,"

K raised his eyebrows.

"I'm getting pissed waiting around," said Begay. "I was planning for us to hunt down the two other Sam Wellie dudes today." He
looked at his watch.

"How 'bout I stand in the doorway and keep open the door and
you try the intercom again?" asked Begay.

"How 'bout the other way round?" asked K.

Begay smirked. "There's no way you come out of this looking good.
Either you are the pushy bílagáana or you are the intruder bílagáana."

"OK then, if we are talking about historical reparation, tell me
what to do."

"Done tole you, bro," said Begay. "Go be the pushy bílagáana.
That's what you never see on those cop movies—the heaps of time
that you are just standing around and nothing happens."

"And all the paperwork neither," said K.

"You still got paperwork?" asked Begay.

"I call it paperwork, all the admin crap we've got to do. Actually
I wish it was still on paper. Paper can get lost, or your handwriting can
be that lousy that nobody can read it, and then they're not even going
to bother asking you for your reports because they are too frightened of
being made to read them."

"Sounds like you put some thought into your strategies there. What's up with you and admin?"

K shrugged.

"You can lose computer files too, you know," said Begay after a pause.

"Yeah. Or you can say they didn't save right, or you can't find them, or they were corrupted or overwritten."

"Boy, you really put some energy into this, huh? Helped you any?"

"They are helping me by sending me to remedial classes in computer literacy."

Begay spluttered, whinnied and proceeded to something that sounded like a full-blown hysterical fit.

"You need the Heimlich?" K said grimly.

He thought of asking Begay what was so funny anyway, but didn't because he knew damn well that this was Begay's way of releasing the tension that had lain between them since that morning.

"Can I help you?" asked a crisp voice.

They turned around.

It seemed that the adolescent unit chose their staff by physical contrast. Maybe, considering the arrangement of posters, they were into juxtapositions. This was one tall, thin lady, dressed in a severely cut charcoal grey suit that made her look like an upright knife blade. By her looks, she did not present much reason for mirth, which was probably an advantage in terms of keeping discipline among adolescents.

"We called earlier," said Begay, though the woman was looking at K. "We are here to meet with Vince Benally."

"What does it concern?" asked the woman, still addressing K.

"Collating information," said Begay crisply.

The woman nodded as if that clarified matters and said pleasantly to K, "He's in his office. Up the stairs, second door left."

"Ahehe," said Begay.

Thin Woman nodded graciously at K.

K felt like a ventriloquist's dummy.

149

They climbed the stairs.

"Do you know that lady?" asked K.

"Did it seem like I did?" asked Begay.

"I thought maybe you'd had a falling out with her," said K when 'thin ice' shot through his head.

"Shí'kis," said Begay, very patiently, "where there is a choice between a bílagáana and a Native, you always talk to the bílagáana, even if you yourself are Native."

"Oh," said K sheepishly.

"That's one advantage of growing up Native; you get plenty of time to get used to all this."

"I know," said K, "but this was kind of blatant."

"Maybe she had the hots for you," said Begay.

"That makes sense," said K. "Was it second door to the left?"

"Didn't listen. She was talking to you, remember?" said Begay and knocked on the door.

"Yah aninááh!"

Begay opened the door and K followed him in. Two boys and a man were sitting around a table. They were stretching leather over a circular frame.

"Hi," said the man, "we'll be done in a minute. We are at a critical point here.

"Hold this," he instructed one adolescent, "and LeRoy, you push this here, see? Great. I'll fix this here. Hold it, don't let go. Great. Done. Couple of hours to dry and settle into shape, then we get it ready, right?"

The adolescents nodded, got up and left. They did not show much curiosity about the visitors. Vince Benally took up the large disc-shaped object and propped it up carefully on the windowsill.

"Drum," Benally said by way of explanation. "We are making our own drum for the Appleton powwow drum circle."

Vince Benally was broad shouldered, muscular and athletic looking. He wore his hair in a braid the thickness of a ship's rope that almost reached to his waist. He was wearing a faded Cardinals T-shirt, washed-out jeans and sneakers. He was in fact, thought K, dressed quite similarly to how Noah George had been dressed when his body was found. But then this was pretty much the regional uniform for men between fifteen and fifty. Out of working hours K did not dress that differently either, except that he didn't give a shit about the NFL and as a matter of principle avoided wearing logos.

"Care to sit down?" Benally asked.

He brushed the clutter that littered the table to one side, sat down, hooked his legs around the chair, tilted the chair's back toward the wall and gently rocked back and forth. He said nothing, his face smooth and untroubled, the face of an innocent man—or a seasoned poker player.

Left to his own devices K would have sat it out and waited for who'd crack first. As far as low-input techniques went, sitting it out was pretty effective. Most people apparently experienced a few seconds of silence as cruel and unusual punishment and started to sing like canaries, just to hear some sound, any sound. The silent treatment was not just a good way of making people talk; it was interesting to see how long various folk could bear the quiet.

Through the years K had become pretty good at predicting how long people would last before they broke the silence. It was an opportunity to put the stop-watch function on his watch to good use. The longest silence, as K remembered, was forty-seven seconds, an interminable stretch that K himself had been close to breaking. That perp though had turned out to be hard of hearing, which explained his unusual ability to keep shtum. It did not explain however what had made him start talking after forty-seven seconds.

Begay said conversationally, "Nice place to work in."

"Yeah," said Benally.

"How long you been here?"

Benally turned his head to the ceiling, narrowed his eyes. "About six."

"Where'd you go to school?"

"Got my certificate over there in Albuquerque."

"Great place, Albuquerque," mused Begay.

"Sure is," Benally said.

K started to feel like he was trapped in a Pinter play. He wondered if this was a version of good-cop/bad cop where he was meant to be the tough bílagáana cop telling the Indians to get down to business or else.

Fuck you, Robbie, he thought and kept silent.

He looked around the office. His attention started to drift. Benally's and Begay's formulaic exchange faded to background hum.

Vince Benally had hung the walls with what were probably the adolescents' artistic offerings, competent pencil drawings that were somewhat limited in subject matter. There were emblems of Goth sensibility that looked like samples in showrooms of provincial tattoo parlors: snakes, skulls, crosses, bones and RIPs in various permutations and constellations. There was one shelf with Action Man figures in different costumes. Male role models for those bereft of paternal influences? Over the desk hung a pin board with photos, official notices and affirmations. A bundle of dried sage, tied with red wool and hung upside down. A stone mortar with ash in it.

Hearing 'Noah George' jolted K out of his reverie.

"Noah? Sure," Benally was saying. "We grew up together for a while."

"When was that?" asked Begay.

Benally turned his eyes to the ceiling as if he'd find a date there. "Ten years? Fifteen years? I lose track."

"You still in contact?"

"We run across each other once in a while," said Benally.

"Did you make plans to meet?" asked K.

"That's not how it works around here," said Benally, the lightest hint of contempt in his voice.

"How does it work here?" asked K with the guileless interest of an ethnographer on field research.

K thought he heard Robbie Begay sigh.

Benally shrugged. "As I say, you run across folks once in a while."

"Ah," said K. "When did you last run across Noah?"

Benally did another looking at the ceiling calculation.

His eyes returned to K. "Can't remember," he said blandly.

This would be around the usual time in an interview when people would ask: "What is this about?" or "Has Noah done something?"

Not Benally. Cool customer.

"What is this about?" asked Benally.

Wrong once more, thought K.

"You don't know?" asked Begay.

"Know what?" asked Benally.

"Noah George was found dead."

"Noah is dead?"

"He is dead," confirmed Begay.

Benally tilted his chair forward. The chair landed on the floor with a crash. Benally shook his head. His hands grabbed the edge of the table. "Dead?"

The cops nodded.

"How?"

"He was found," said Robbie Begay evasively. "Haven't you heard? It was in the Navajo Times just now."

"I haven't heard," said Benally.

His face looked as if an invisible hand was marking it. Rarely had K seen the process of painful knowledge sinking in so clearly. "It is bad news. We are sorry," he said.

Benally looked up and nodded. His face was pale, his eyes burning black.

"Why did he die?"

"It is an open case," said Begay.

"Do you mean he was—killed?"

"We are working on it."

Benally stared at Begay.

Begay looked away.

"If you are here to find out if I killed him, I didn't," Benally said fiercely, as if he too was getting tired of the ponderous pace of the inquiry. "We were buddies when we were kids. Until all that stuff happened with his folks and he moved away to live with a relative."

"Anything you can tell us, anything you remember that could be of significance to our inquiry?" Begay asked.

K risked a sideways glance. Fuck knew what cop procedural script Begay was reciting from. Begay was keeping his visage frozen in an expression that, as per genre, would be described as "impassive." Vince Benally held his own. Working with adolescents he'd probably had plenty of opportunity to practice the thousand-yard stare.

"Nope. Just a regular childhood. Just a regular Rez-childhood."

"Does being members of the Sam Wellies count as that?" asked K.

"Ahhh," said Benally.

"Yes?" asked K.

"What?" asked Benally.

"Anything you can tell us will be helpful," K said. Some folks you had to prod, poke and corner, others fared better when you left them some space and let them think that it was them in the driving seat. K figured Benally belonged to that category. Benally shook his head. He was quite good at playing it cool.

"We ran around together when we were kids. We hung out; got out there," he pointed his chin toward Redwater, "did what kids do— Rez-kids do—take our BB guns and have a pop at rabbits and prairie dogs; hitch to Appleton and get one of those gláaniís to buy us a beer; smoke some weed; try to hook up with girls. . . ."

"Was there a group of you?"

"You getting at the Sam Wellies thing?"

"Yes," said K firmly.

"It was just a phase. A short phase—when things were not working out so good for any of us. It was a way of feeling important, scary."

"Were you scary?"

"We liked to think we were."

"How'd you make yourselves scary?"

"Easy," said Benally. There was an edge to his voice. "Our elderlies are folk that have been oppressed for centuries. They had their land taken away. They had their children taken away. They were put in a concentration camp. They had their livestock destroyed. And now they are losing their tradition and their language." He glared at K. "They got a word for it now: trauma. I'm saying these folk are traumatized. They are scared all the time. They are scared of everything. Mostly they are scared of their own kids. They see everything that the dominant society has done to them represented by their own children. How do you scare the older generation? Easy: you wear black. You get a tat. You say that the old ways are b/s. Take your pick. Anything that young people do is scary to the old people. Anything at all."

"Meth?" asked K conversationally, "witchcraft?"

"There are some that do. Some that don't."

"What about Noah and your—group?"

"You wanna say gang?"

"What about your gang?"

Benally snorted. "Even back then you'd have trouble finding kids that were not in gangs. EVERYONE has a phase when they run with a gang."

"There are gangs and there are gangs."

"Just tell us about the Sam Wellies," said Begay tiredly.

"The Sam Wellies have always been around. Most of the guys around here have been members of the Sam Wellies at some point. They're still going."

"Some say that the initiation rites . . . uh, very, very bad stuff."

"What are you saying?"

Watching Benally K began to think that the man did not have such a poker face after all. All color had drained from his skin, his face looked ashen. He swallowed repeatedly. Vince Benally looked as if he wasn't far from being sick.

"I think you know what we are saying." K spoke quietly, kept his eyes on Benally's.

Benally opened his mouth, thought better of it and closed it again.

"It is not just words that speak, you know," K said. "Faces speak too."

Sometimes you had to play the shrink to smoke out a guilty conscience.

Benally stared at him with narrowed eyes and curled his lips: "Yeah? What do they say?"

Wrong fucking tactic, thought K and smiled benignly.

"Yours said BAD CONSCIENCE," said Begay in a cut-the-crap-or-else voice.

We could be here until nightfall, thought K, watching Benally's face beset by troubling thoughts like clouds racing across the sky before a hurricane.

"I had nothing to do with it," Benally said, sounding like a drowning man.

It occurred to K that if Benally was working up to a confession of some heinous crime it would be really bad timing. For a start Benally hadn't been read his Carmen Miranda, which meant that anything that Benally chose to tell them would be null and void. Anyways, they weren't here to solve cold cases, they were here purely because they hadn't got a lot on Noah George's life, which made it that much harder to solve the case of his death. And what if Benally decided to confess now to something that had happened a decade ago? Who was it going to help? Certainly not the kids Benally was teaching to build drums and who brought him their artwork to hang on the walls of his office.

"You've had a shock," he said softly, "you've just heard that your old friend has died."

Benally blinked—and stepped back from the brink.

"Yeah," he said. "It's hard to take in."

He looked relieved, though not any happier.

K did his best to avoid looking at Begay.

"We are here to ask Noah's friends if they can think of anyone that may have wanted to do him harm. Any old enemies? Any outstanding scores? Difficulties with the family? Relationships? Drugs?"

"Probably a bit of all of this. You grow up here," Benally made a sweeping movement with his arm, "that's how it rolls."

"Are there any other friends around from that time?"

K saw a nerve jump under Benally's left eye. Could be accumulated tension, then again could be a nervous reaction to this specific question.

"How many friends are still around?"

Benally stared at the table as if he had seen a ghost. "There's been a death. A recent death."

"Who's that?"

Benally mumbled a name.

"How did he die?"

"They found him out in the boonies, way out over that way. Close to Sage Canyon. They said he froze to death."

"They said he froze to death?"

"That's what they said."

"Who is they?"

"Newspapers, cops, folk."

"When did he die?"

"Couple of months back."

"Froze to death? What month are we talking about?"

"June, I think."

"Froze to death in June?"

"That's what they said."

"That's a bunch of times you've said 'they said.' Doesn't sound as if you believe them."

"As you said, who dies of cold in June?"

"That's not quite what we said. We just asked. But don't mind me saying—you sound as if you have some theories going?"

"No," said Benally, "no theories. Just fears."

"Fears?"

"Look," said Benally wearily, "you don't have to be involved in some bad shit. It's enough if you witness something, or you know about something. The Law calls you an accessory, but that's not the main problem. You dig?"

"It's a bit cryptic for me," said K.

"Most of the kids who get involved in that kind of thing, they're alright. It's just a phase. They want thrills, mainly they want other kids to believe they're real hardass. They grow out of it. There are some, just a real tiny minority, they are the real deal, they are evil. I mean real evil. And you really want to try to avoid running into them."

There was a knock. Benally got up, strode to the door and flung it open. K and Begay could see the startled face of an adolescent.

"Come on in, Jackson," Benally said in a hearty voice.

When he turned to the policemen there was not a trace of joviality in his face. He made a minute nod toward the door. "Got to work, folks. Duty's calling."

The slight-built Jackson hovered shyly in the doorway.

"Thank you," said K simultaneously with Begay's ice-cold, "We may be back soon."

"Sure," said Benally.

It was hard to tell who he was answering.

CHAPTER THIRTEEN

"Here, you hold on to this." Begay passed the piece of paper to K.

K glanced at it. "You're kidding me. I'm supposed to read that? In a moving car? Looks like it's moving all on its own."

He stared at Begay's spidery scrawl and had an idea for a parlor game: Match the Handwriting. No way would he have guessed that Robbie Begay, solid, easygoing, affable (mostly), wrote like a superannuated spinster after too many swigs of Southern Comfort.

"You can thank me for giving you some opportunity for skills training," hissed Begay. He shook his head as if there was a hornet buzzing around it. "Shashlííyááde, what do they teach you up there? You damn near told the guy to zip it—just as he's about to spill. Jesus H.! Care to tell me what's going on?"

K sighed and told him.

"Who gives a shit about Carmen Miranda?" thundered Begay. "Piece of bílagáana crap! Down here we believe that you pay for what you done!"

He sounded not unlike a Tea Party brother.

Though K could see how Begay might be pissed at having to witness a potential perp bailed out by a fellow cop. So he tried once more.

"Yeah," said Begay, "Far-sighted Mr. Social Conscience thinking of all those kids that look up to Benally."

K's contrition was beginning to wear thin. "OK. YOU tell me."

"Easy," said Begay. "Benally spills. We book him. We hunt down the other perps. They get sent to Federal and do sweet time, an example to all those folks doing things and thinking they got away with it, 'coz they've been able to lie low for a bunch of time. This here would've been a chance to show 'em loud and clear, to *demonstrate* that justice sure has a long memory."

"Show 'em loud and clear," mused K.

"Screw you!" Begay said.

•   •   •

South of Redwater the land opened up. The jagged rock, the feeder pipe of what had once been a larger volcanic landmass, rose out of the plain like a knuckled fist raised at the sky. They drove past a group of men in cowboy gear riding white-and-brown-flecked pintos, Stetsons set far back, coiled lassos suspended from their saddles.

"Look at those Indians playing cowboys," Begay said.

At the intersection K said, "Mind if we stop here?"

Begay shrugged. He pulled over and parked near the solitary food stall that had pitched up there.

"How about fry bread and coffee?" asked K.

"You buying?" said Begay.

"Sure."

"Don't kid yourself that I'm that cheap to buy off."

"I did not think so for a moment," K assured him, "but I'm hoping that fat and carbs will have a soporific effect on you."

"You want me to fall asleep at the wheel?"

"No, just something to cushion that anger that's sitting in your belly."

Begay grinned. "Cushion the anger that's sitting in my belly? Go ahead, bro'. Get me some cushion."

K walked over to the stall. It was a metal folding table, a two-ringed cooker connected to a propane bottle; on it sat a frying pan and a coffee-pot.

"Hi," said K. "Two fry bread and two coffees please."

The girl nodded, took a lid from a red plastic bowl, tore off a piece of dough that she held between her palms, turning, stretching and patting it until the dough had the approximate thickness and diameter of a Frisbee. She dropped the bread into the hot oil. It sizzled and puffed up, doubling in size. The girl repeated the kneading process with a second piece of dough. She turned the bread in the frying pan, shook it, so that the oil sizzled over the edges and pooled in the middle. The pale dough was now a golden brown and the hot oil had turned air pockets in the dough to crispy bubbles. The girl took out the bread with a perforated spatula, dropped the second disc of dough into the pan, set the cooked bread on a tray covered with paper-towels. The oil drenched the paper. She poured coffee into two Styrofoam cups and pointed her chin at a tray that held sugar, creamer and wooden stirrers. She wrapped one bread in grease-proof paper, took the second out of the pan and set it on fresh paper towels.

"Five dollars," the girl said.

He handed her a $5 bill, she handed him the neatly wrapped stack of fry breads, and K maneuvered his hand around the coffees, thanked her and slowly walked back to the car. He handed Begay a fry bread and coffee.

Begay took a large bite. "Hey, not bad, this bread. Just right, matter of fact." He smacked his lips.

"What's up? Aren't you eating?"

"Hmm," said K. "That girl over there. She's . . . beautiful."

"And she makes a mean fry bread too," Begay said and took another bite. "Hey, fry bread needs to be eaten hot, dude. What are you waiting for?"

"My appetite's gone."

Begay shook his head. "Gone where?"

He followed K's gaze. "Are you kidding me?"

"Why would I?" said K, "It's not that funny, is it?"

"Funny? Nope. But weird. I gotta see for myself." Begay said, crumpled up the greasy paper, tossed it on the backseat and hopped out of the car.

K sighed and took a sip of coffee, which was bitter and strong.

He smelled the bread, pressed a finger against it and watched the dough dimple and spring back.

The car shook as Begay opened the door and levered himself into the driving seat.

"And?" said K.

"I still got my appetite," said Begay. "Yeah. I guess she is beautiful."

He stretched and retrieved a grey rag from the floor on which he wiped his hands. "But not in a fun way, you get what I'm saying?"

Not like your ogre, you fucking opportunist, thought K.

"I guess she's like an artwork . . . or a statue or something. She's beautiful alright, but when I look at her I don't feel like I want to jump her bones, yeh?"

"Neither do I."

"But she ruined your appetite?"

K waved his half-eaten fry bread at Begay. "Don't you ever see someone that's beautiful so it hits you like a yearning—like home-sickness, or mourning? Have you never felt that?"

"Boy, you sure make it sound like a bunch of fun." Begay frowned. "Have I felt like that? Not when I'm getting an eyeful of the laydeez. Do you know when I feel like that though? That feeling, you know when I do get it? Sometimes during a ceremony I have that. When it feels like your soul is stretching beyond itself. That what you talking about?"

"That's it," K said.

"OK," said Begay. He stretched out his hand, took K's fry bread and sank his teeth into it. He finished it in no time, gulped down the coffee, stuffed the greasy paper into the Styrofoam cup, threw it over his shoulder to the back. He revved up the motor, pulled out into the road and accelerated.

"You are still weird though," he said.

• • •

"This is the day of waiting around for nothing," Begay said.

THE QUALITY *of* MERCY

They were standing outside a single-wide that had seen better days. Paint peeling, window frames crumbling, stairs sagging. But somebody here sure liked their squash. Around the trailer were carefully tended raised beds crowded with yellow squash, some so big they could serve as murder weapons. K remembered some story where a leg of lamb that had killed a husband had been served to investigating detectives by the victim's murderous wife.

Across the yard a dog was chained to the fence. The chain was iron and much too short. The dog looked menacing. It was a bulldog mongrel, stocky, with short, white, matted fur. The dog's ears were cropped in the DIY mutilation that you often saw around here.

"You try," said Begay.

K obediently rapped his knuckles on the door. And hey presto! It opened. Maybe the universe was predictable after all. A gust of wind smattered dust against the trailer and into their faces. They blinked, eyes watering.

"Come in," the dark-clad creature in the doorway said.

They followed the silhouette into cavernous gloom.

"Sit."

They lowered themselves on what they took to be the sofa and rubbed their streaming, sand-filled eyes.

"Always rub toward your nose," the creature said.

When their vision had cleared somewhat and their eyes adapted to the dark, they saw that their host was a teenage Goth of indeterminate gender.

"Really?" said Begay. "I been told it's toward the corner of your eyes so it comes out there."

"No, to your nose, for sure," the kid said firmly and pressed something soggy into their hands.

"Wet Kleenex. It will help you get the sand out."

They obediently rubbed the moistened tissue toward their noses. It seemed to work. When K's eyes had adjusted to the dimness he saw there was not just the one, but three more androgynous teenagers, curled up in seats, silent as cats.

"Thank you," K said.

"Howdee," Begay said. "We want to talk to Philbert Tsosie."

The eye-doctor kid hesitated. "He's not here."

"He's out?"

"I guess," the kid said.

"You're not sure?"

"No, I guess that's what you say: he's out."

"Where is he?"

"Out."

K looked at the kid thoughtfully. "There's out, like being away and there is out, like being flat out."

"I guess," said the kid.

"Is he here?" K asked gently.

The kid nodded.

"It's not what you think," the kid said.

"What is it?" said Begay.

"He takes stuff to sleep. He don't sleep real well. He only sleeps when he takes those pills. They are real strong. He don't take them all the time—just sometimes."

"Why all that trouble sleeping?" Begay asked.

"It's those dreams."

"Dreams?"

"Just bad dreams. I guess they must be pretty bad, coz' he's real afraid of going to sleep and getting those dreams."

"What are the dreams?"

"Sounds pretty tough," K cut across Begay. He made sure he kept his eyes on the goth-kid. At the periphery of K's vision hovered an impression of Begay's ferocious scowl.

"Yeah," said the kid, "he tries not to sleep at all as long as he can, and when he gets real, real tired he takes a pill."

"Is he not afraid of dreaming when he takes the pills?"

"You don't dream on pills," the kid informed them. "They just knock you out."

"How long is he going to be . . . knocked out, do you think?"

"It's gonna be a long while. He took them a couple of hours ago. When they start working there's nothing that can wake him."

"Nothing?"

"Nothing at all."

"We'd like to ask him about somebody he used to know. Do you think he'd talk to us?"

"I guess," said the kid.

"Your dad have a cell?"

"Sure."

"Can we phone him?"

"I guess." The kid scribbled something on a torn piece of paper.

"Thank you. When your dad wakes up tell him we were here."

They nodded at the trio of silent youngsters cowering in the gloom and got up. The kid opened the door and accompanied them outside. They walked toward the patrol car.

"I have a mind just leaving you here, you know? Might do you some good to take a hike and clear your damn head," Begay growled as K was adjusting his seatbelt. "You think you're in the right job, Mister?"

"Probably not," said K.

There was a rap on the window. Begay let down the window.

"Hey." The Goth kid was holding up a couple of squash the size of baseball bats. "Take some squash. We got plenty."

"Neat! Home-grown produce." said Begay. "Nizhóní!"

"Thank you!" K received the squash from the kid and laid them across his lap.

"I guess I could claim provocation if I club you over the head with one of those right now," Begay said.

He accelerated over washboard ridges and kept his foot on the gas.

Begay only slowed down when there were dogs at the roadside, because you never knew what they would do. Sometimes it looked as if they were just sitting there, and then they'd jump out, clean in front of the car. K was grateful that Robbie's anger did not extend to innocent creatures. Else a bunch of run over dogs would have littered their trail.

He was unwise enough to say as much to Begay.

"You know the meaning of professional liability? 'Coz that's what you are. That's the second time today—the SECOND TIME IN ONE DAY!—that you screw up our inquiry. What's WRONG with you, man?"

The car shot over a crater-deep pothole. A rain of loose gravel landed on the windshield.

K flinched.

"Got anything to say for yourself?"

"The kid," K said.

"What about the kid?"

"Whoever his dad is, whatever he did. . . ."

"So you do think he did something?"

"I don't know. But we do think he was involved in something. That's why we went there, right?"

"You said it. So why. . . ?"

"Because," K drew a big breath, "the guy did a real good job raising his kid. Great kid."

Begay slapped a flat palm against his forehead. "Damn the kid. The guy has to whack himself out to sleep. Why can't he sleep? What's he dreaming about that's so bad? Huh? You want to fraternize with scumbags, you should've gone and become a social worker. Make like those three monkeys: see nothing, hear nothing, say nothing."

"Yep," said K.

They drove in silence, passing solitary hogans, flocks of sheep, horses grazing amongst shrub.

"You still got my notes?" asked Begay.

"Right here." said K. "I think it says we take a right at the Chapter House and drive past the Elderly Center and take another right."

"Hold your horses," said Begay. "One thing at a time. You tell me again when we are at the Chapter House."

The road led toward the sandstone ridge that snaked along the plain's western border. The ridge was perfectly smooth, as if it had been sanded down. Its undulating curves looked almost erotic, if it was possible for inorganic matter to look erotic. Perhaps there was such a thing as petrophilia. And if there wasn't yet, maybe there was an opportunity to found a whole new movement.

"Are you paying attention?" asked Begay.

"Sure," said K.

"You sure looked as if you were drifting," observed Begay. "Anything you care to share?"

"Petrophilia," said K.

"Sorry I asked," said Begay without a trace of curiosity. "Don't think I can take it on an empty stomach."

"Empty stomach? You just had about 4000 calories worth of fry bread."

"That was a while ago now."

"Care for some squash?" asked K.

"I hate squash. Sure hate it."

"Poor innocent squash," said K.

"Damn squash," said Begay, "that was all we saw as kids. I mean the only vegetable. Corn . . . I don't really count corn as a vegetable. Beans neither. Potatoes neither. You get some comfort from those."

"Carbs," said K.

"Squash. Jeez. We used to have to eat it every day. In summer. That was all that would grow. And they'd get bigger, and paler, and tougher. Yikes. Damn squash. In spring we'd go and forage for wild onions sometimes. My grandma, shíma sani, used to take us. We'd walk for miles and miles. We sure were happy when we found some. We'd pick 'em and take them home and grandma would make a soup for us. We'd pick Navajo tea. But that's easy to find. Even now you hardly have to get out of your ride—it's just there by the roadside. I guess I should maybe take some time and pick Navajo tea—reconnect with my culture. What do you think?"

I think: how the hell did we get from petrophilia to Navajo tea? thought K, and said: "Sure. Sounds a good idea. Back to your roots."

Begay chuckled. "Literally."

The road ahead was straight and there was not a dwelling in sight.

"Not very populated," K observed.

"Not now," said Begay.

"Were there people living here?" asked K.

"Never heard of Black Sands?"

"Not that I recall," said K.

"Here's me thinking you are a diligent student of Diné history."

"So did I."

"How are your nerves? Feeling strong?"

"Depends."

"Never mind your nerves. I feel like telling you a story. A real-life story. The story how this place came to be called Black Sands. You ready?"

"I got a feeling you're going to tell me anyway."

"Too true. Here we go: Back in the days when the People had returned from Hwéeldi—they were just beginning to settle back down to the old ways, though some things had changed—the BIA came and took away the kids and put them in the residential schools, so there are no kids to help herding the sheep and all that, and the mothers are grieving, because they are missing their yazzies, and the kids only get out of school once or twice a year; it's too far to travel and who's going to pick 'em up?

And anyways, the elders think maybe they've got it so good over there in those bílagáana outfits that they won't like it back home, so they are kind of shy—that's how our People are, you know? They don't like to pressurize, they just hang back and wait. And the kids, they don't want to upset the elders and tell 'em like it is—a real horror-show over there in those residential schools. So it's a . . . mutual misunderstanding I guess you could say. A generational rift kind of deal: they all keep silent not to hurt the other. And this resentment builds up, you know? 'You should know how I feel. You should read my mind.' And so it goes on and they keep silent and each carries this burden, this sorrow. And it is like a kettle on a very low flame . . . it heats up, but real slow and then eventually its red-hot and there's no way of getting ahold of it and taking it off the fire, you dig?"

"Hmm," said K. The kettle metaphor did not quite cut it for him.

But Begay was too far away to notice. "There's the tuberculosis too at the schools. Overcrowding, not a lot of hygiene, malnutrition. All that makes for low immunity. Some of the kids catch tuberculosis. Some of them don't make it. They die at the school, in the infirmary. And guess what? Those school administrators don't think to inform the parents that their kids have died. They just leave it. They wait to tell parents that their kid has died until there is an opportunity. The opportunity is when the relatives turn up to pick up their kids. 'Sorry, Mrs Tsosie. Your son died in November. Would you care to see his grave? Don't worry. We gave him a nice Christian burial.' Jeez! I nearly hit that sucker!"

Begay swerved to avoid a matted-haired dog limping across the road.

"I'm giving you the background, OK? Just so you can make sense of why it happened."

K felt a chill creep up his spine.

"This kid comes back. Thomas. Thomas Tsosie in fact. He's fifteen or sixteen I guess. His little brother has died over at the school. And his sister also doesn't make it. Though it wasn't tuberculosis— she runs away one day and nobody knows what's happened to her, until one day, the next spring, this old Medicine Man is out there gathering herbs for a ceremony and he finds her . . . what is left of her. Looks like the coyotes, all kind of creatures have been at her bones. So it's two down, one to go."

"That seems like a weird way of putting it," said K.

"That's how it was," said Begay. "Thomas stays at the school as long as they keep him. Until they decide that he's had enough education; that he's now civilized enough; that they have taken all of the Indian that was in him out of him."

"Kill the Indian, Save the Man," said K.

"Precisely. So Thomas Tsosie is discharged from school. By all

accounts he's no trouble. A quiet boy—but then most Indians are quiet. That's what they think over there at the school. Sure, they know
that Indians are kind of family fixated, all that clan business and
so forth. But they also think that these Indians have large families.
And they are real poor, right? With bad health and all that? So surely
they're used to family dying, right? It's the Indian way of life, losing
people. So it's no biggie, right? To lose a couple of siblings. All water
under the bridge, bro', all water under the bridge."

"You know a lot about this," K said.

"Sure do," said Begay, "sure do. Take a good hard look over
there. Black Sands. That's where Thomas Tsosie comes back to.
Thomas Tsosie, a quiet boy. Those Anglos running the schools gave
all the Indian kids bílagáana names. Proper Christian names. Cut off
their hair too. The first steps toward civilization. Short hair and a for-
eign name. So here's Thomas. He comes back. He fits right back in.
As if he's not been away for ten years. Never talks about the school.
Never mentions it. And his folks think, 'well, he must be alright.
Maybe it was good for him over there.' Even though his little brother
died. And his sister died. Maybe, they think, he's now a Christian.
The Christians don't think about death like the People do. For us it is
taboo. I mean, for a traditional it is not weird not to mention someone
that has passed. In fact you are not supposed to. You are supposed to
avoid everything that has to do with death and the dead. But for the
Christians death is a good thing, right?"

"I wouldn't know," said K, "being Jewish."

"All the same thing."

"What?"

"Well . . . Jews and Christians is more the same thing than Navajo and Christians, or Navajo and Jews, you dig?"

"Don't know that I do," said K. "I guess you are trying to say
everything is relative."

"Yeah, I guess that's what I'm saying. Back to Thomas Tsosie."

K winced.

"You don't want to hear about Thomas Tsosie?"

K stayed silent.

"Hey! You don't want to hear about Thomas Tsosie?"

No, thought K, I don't. I think I can see where this is going, where Thomas Tsosie is going to end up. Gets taken away from his family; loses two siblings; has to cope without support; returns home where nobody speaks about all that suffering. Yes, I can guess where Thomas Tsosie is going. And I can guess why this place is called Black Sands. And why there is nobody left and nobody lives there anymore.

"Got it in one, bro'," Begay said.

K realized that he had said out loud what he thought he had only thought.

"I'm sorry," he said, "I didn't mean to say that. Really. I thought I was thinking it in my head. Go ahead and tell me. The least I can do."

"The least you can do is listen to a gory story as an act of reparation, is what you're saying?" asked Begay.

"No," said K, and, "yes . . . I guess you are right. Sorry. Go ahead. Please."

"You kind of took the fun out of telling it," said Begay. "I'd have preferred to see the full impact."

"Well, you can still tell me—if it helps. I don't really know what happened."

"You have a damn good clue when you're guessing why it is called Black Sands."

"I was hoping that it wasn't true."

"It is. That's precisely why this place is called Black Sands."

"Are you pissed?" asked K.

"Pissed at what?"

"That I am blocking you from telling me the story."

"Dunno. Don't even know why I was so keen to tell you the story in the first place. Maybe it's 'making a bílagáana feel bad' day."

"I guess there's more to it."

"Yeah, shrink man. I guess we should leave it there. Anyways,

I got some of it out of my system. Besides I could see that it got to you. That kind of helps. Seeing someone else made miserable by this helps. What do you suppose that is? Sadism?"

"No," said K firmly, "it is not sadism. It is because people are essentially social and relational beings."

"Social and relational? Boy, I need a drink."

"See? Drinking is a very social activity. And relational."

"Who says I want to drink with you? Maybe I'm just wishing I had a quart and could sit somewhere under a juniper tree and drink myself happy."

"Drink yourself happy or into oblivion?"

"What's the difference?"

But it didn't sound like a question that Begay wanted answered, so K stayed silent. Despite afternoon sun and mild air he felt cold, despondent, filled with dread. As if traveling on a hearse through a land of death. A bit like the film where Death plays chess with the knight who has just returned to a homeland ravaged by the plague.

Robbie Begay cleared his throat: "They made us go to this training about Historical Trauma, you know?"

"Uhu."

"They taught us they first used it for the Jewish people who, you know, who'd come out of those camps . . . and their relatives."

"Yes," said K.

"I guess you know about some stuff too." Begay broke off and kept his eyes on the long straight stretch of road before them. The landscape drifted past, a blur of ochre and rusty red, scattered boulders and sagebrush. Far ahead the sky met the earth. It looked as if the road was leading toward the edge of the world.

"My grandfather," said K, "was the wisest, the most benign, the most . . . philosophical man. All through my childhood, he was the one who was there. He was always there for us."

"Your cheí or your nalí?" asked Begay.

"My nalí. My father's father. Grandpapa was proof that you can stay a good person no matter what happened to you."

K felt Begay's eyes on him.

"Keep looking at the road and I'll tell you," he said. "Actually I can't tell you that much. The only thing I can tell you is that one summer's day Grandpapa took us out on Gower beach to look for hermit crabs."

For a moment K saw before his inner eye the wide expanse of sand curving toward Worm's Head, the jagged wooden skeleton of the old boat sticking out of the sand, hermit crabs with their acquired shells scurrying toward the sea. He felt a stab of something that almost could have been homesickness.

"It was warm. He had his sleeves rolled up. That was the only time I ever saw him with his sleeves rolled up."

Begay turned his head.

"Just here," K pointed to his left forearm, "was this tattoo."

"A tattoo?"

"All numbers. I didn't understand it then. I only understood that Grandpapa wished I hadn't seen it—and so I didn't mention it. And so we never spoke about it."

K sensed Begay's puzzled frown.

"Auschwitz was a concentration camp where they tattooed their prisoners. It was a kind of registration. So what I know is that my grandfather survived Auschwitz and that he was a good person. The best."

"What about your parents?" asked Begay.

"They died."

"They passed?" Begay's voice was hoarse.

"One of life's ironies," K said. "Carbon monoxide poisoning."

"Did they. . . ?"

"No. No, they had a good death. As good as can be. They went to sleep on their houseboat and didn't wake up. They wouldn't have known anything—at least that's what we were told."

"We?"

"My twin sister and I."

"Houseboat?"

"They had just moved on this houseboat. It's like a barge that you live on. They were these . . . hippies I guess you'd call them."

"Why did you say 'one of life's ironies?'"

"Because my grandfather survived the gas chambers to see his son and daughter-in-law die of gas poisoning."

Begay drew his shoulders together and coughed.

Here's to you, Thomas Tsosie. Here's to me. Here's to us all and our patches of black sand, thought K.

CHAPTER FOURTEEN

"How far are we going?" asked K. "It feels like we are halfway to the Mexican border."

"Some road trip," said Begay. He turned on the radio and began to scan through stations: about 103 that were playing country music; approximately 55 that were advertising motors; 97 that were pushing Awesome Chickin' Lickin', American Homeburgers, Ai!Burrito! and Golden Phoenix Wok franchises. Eventually Begay settled on a station broadcasting a hectoring-bordering-on-hysterical-bordering-on-psychotic-breakdown tirade on Mexican Rapists, Liberal Sponsors of Terrorism and Baby Murdering Enemies of Freedom—or the other way round.

"Jesus!" said K.

"Not your thing?" asked Begay.

"I didn't figure you for a guy who went with the program."

"I don't. Anytime I am hypoglycemic or need to raise my blood pressure I switch to that station. You didn't think I'm GOP, did ya? Tell me right now and you can hitch home."

"Who knows these days?"

"There are a lot of Democrats on the Rez."

"There *were* a lot of Democrats. Now it's Tea Party time, I hear."

"There's always some turkeys voting for Thanksgiving. You still looking at the map, right?"

K looked down and saw that he had crumpled and twisted the map into a crooked tube. He hastily tried to restore it to some semblance of its original state.

"You destroyed my map? That's all we need. Dude! It's the only directions we got. We are on uncharted territory. Christsakes, what have you done? You can't be that tense?"

"Guess I must be." K looked at the creased piece of paper. There was no way to smooth out the creases unless he ran an iron over it. On the plus side, Begay's spidery handwriting crisscrossed by and embedded in creases now looked like a piece of art.

"How come you don't have GPS?"

"Only the big guys have GPS. I guess they don't mind if us low-lifes get lost. Frees up more jobs for the big guys' relatives," Begay said. "Besides GPS don't work out here anyways."

"Surely you remember the way anyway," K said feebly, "oral tradition and memory and all that."

"Careful, my man, with the cultural references. But, matter of fact, I do. We are still a ways from the intersection. The Chapter House is where we got to turn."

"It's hard to believe there's a Chapter House here, never mind an Elderly Center. Where are all the people?"

"Over there." Begay pointed. "The road climbs up the ridge and drops down over Sheep Pass. And there's lots of outfits over there. Our Behind the Mountain People. There's some longstanding issues between this side of the ridge and the other side."

"There are always issues. Remind me: who is it we are going to visit?"

"The third dude."

"I know it's the third dude—just can't remember who he is or what he does."

"I don't think we know what he does. Just what he's done. He's been in trouble."

"So have the others."

"Sure, but with gangs there's always a ringleader. A boss man. Someone who tells the others what to do."

"And you think this one's the man?"

"No idea. How would I know? All we can do is go by process

of elimination. Also, you know that here on the Rez crimes don't get solved? We just go through the motions. Visit some suspects, cruise along, question a few dudes that are cooperative, write some reports, put it all into 'open files' and let 'em lie until they have matured into 'cold cases' and stow 'em way in the attic."

"We are just going through the motions?"

"Sure. Else you bet your ass I wouldn't be sitting here talking to you. What did you think? Didn't I just let you screw up Benally's confession and prevent a promising line of inquiry, bro'?"

"Let me? Seems you were pretty pissed at me."

"Trust me, bro'. If I had been really pissed at you, I would have handcuffed you, and gagged you, and thrown you in the trunk. Left you there for a couple of hours with nothing but Save the Wretched Radio's Last Chance Hour for company," said Begay dreamily.

"You do have a pretty sick mind."

"You think?" Begay said proudly. "There's way more where that came from. Anyways, surely even you understand that if we really wanted to solve anything we'd have to be more—systematic?"

"How'd you be more 'systematic?'"

"Uhhh, not like this."

"So all you know about being systematic is that this isn't systematic?"

"Yeah, what's wrong with that?"

"It's self-defeating, that's all."

"I don't catch you. You been screwing up at every turn of the 'investigation' and now you're complaining we ain't going nowhere?"

"There was a reason for not going along with Benally's confession."

"Sure. And Philbert Tsosie is Wonderdad."

"It would've been unethical to make the kid grass on his dad."

"Unethical? Give me a break."

"All I'm saying is," explained K, "before you start criticizing, better have a clear idea of what we could be doing differently."

"I have a clear idea. It's you that hasn't," scoffed Begay. "How about this: If we wanted to solve this crime how come we don't have a plan?"

"If we don't have a plan, what are we doing driving along, looking for a turn-off at the Chapter House?"

"Fry bread quality control. Justifying next year's fiscal wotsit."

"You don't believe we'll get this solved?"

"No chance. We got no plan, no backup—no skills neither, as you've demonstrated all day."

"I'm good at hunches though," protested K.

"Hunches? Bunch of bull crap."

"You never had a hunch?"

"Sure. What's that got to do with anything?"

"Sometimes following a hunch works out."

"Let me tell you about my deal with hunches: you start waiting for a hunch, you ain't gonna get one. What you do get is wishful thinking that's going to get you making wrongful arrests. Don't get me wrong: there ain't nothing wrong with making wrongful arrests. They're just more work making the paperwork work out."

"Nothing wrong with wasting time, public money, resources, expectations?"

"Nope. There's worse ways of wasting, believe me. Who are we hurting? How about a couple more breaks for coffee and fry bread? You buy. Damn Tribe hardly coughs up enough for toothpicks. Hey, what's the matter? You in a mood?"

"I told Noah George's bimá yazzie that we would find out what happened to him. I promised. I'm not going back on that."

Begay shrugged.

"You know his father was the victim of a hate crime?" K asked

"Noah George's dad? What happened?"

"Noah's bimá says he was beaten to death by a bunch of high school kids when he was sleeping off a drunk."

"Bet the kids got a couple of months in juvie?"

"Something like that."

"And now you feel you owe bimá yazzie?"

"Yep."

"That's just to soothe your bílagáana conscience, brother."

"Screw you."

"You want to tell me about your hunch? I'm just letting you get it off your chest, so you can't say 'told you so,' understand? Shoot."

"*Hunches*. One is that Vince Benally is clean. Sure, he may know something, but I believe what he said: he's afraid because he witnessed something bad happen. Same with Philbert Tsosie."

"So your hunch is there's some bad guys we ain't gonna get to, coz' the reformed guys are too chicken to talk?"

K considered. "I had a hunch back there at Chimney Rock when I saw Noah George."

"Yeah?"

"Whoever did that to Noah George cared about him."

"Sure had a special way of showing it," said Begay disinterestedly. "Let's find us some nice place, have us some fry bread and figure what to put in our reports, eh?'"

"Maybe you've been in the job too long. Scrap the 'maybe.' You have been in the job too long."

"Right now it looks like being in any job is too long."

"That bad?"

"I told you the other day, remember?"

"I thought maybe that has changed," K said carefully, "I thought maybe you found some consolation in the job,"

"What?" Begay spat. "I know what you are getting at," he said. "It's taken you a whole day to work up to let me have it? Don't tell me you never fooled around with anybody just because you had opportunity?"

"I have."

"So what is the problem?"

"The problem is you are fooling around with someone that you don't respect or trust, in a job that you don't like, in a system that you feel is exploiting you. Too many negatives."

"Don't you think I got sense enough to know I made a damn mistake? Hardly know how I'm supposed to go back into work. You want the honest truth? THAT's why I'm cruising along here. Just so I don't have to walk through that door."

"Well, well. But that's not why I am cruising along. I'm really hoping something will come out of this. Why not try to do a job rather than just pretending to do it? Takes about the same amount of energy."

Begay chuckled. "Hey, you got something there. Makes way more sense than that Motivational Training they forced on us some weeks back."

Franz Kafka, Motivational Life Coach, thought K. Lili'd be proud of him—if she was the type to be proud of anyone, which she wasn't. So she wouldn't. It remained to be seen how long his motivational boost worked on Begay.

"Are we on?" he asked Begay.

"I guess so," conceded Begay. "What do we do if we find anything? We got no warrants. Today's not a good day for a shoot-out. And you don't dig shoot-outs anyways. Ever used your gun?"

"Except for training? No. Praise the Lord," K said.

"You are an atheist, remember? You still their best shot over there?"

"I guess," K said reluctantly.

"How come you're so good if you don't like shooting?"

"That's probably why."

Begay yawned. "Weird. Anyways, you got no jurisdiction round here. It's me who's got to get the warrant. Let's hope none of the chief's relatives are involved. If it's his relatives they could be running a meth-lab right in front of the station and jack shit would happen."

They drove past a building with a corrugated roof. As Chapter Houses went, this was one was pretty basic. K squinted at the map.

"Quit pretending," said Begay. "I know where we're supposed to be heading. See the turn-off? That building over there is the Elderly Center."

They bucked and jolted over washboard.

"Pretty rough road," said K. "Must be hard getting here for the elderly."

"And the relatives that are supposed to bring them here. That's why I'm so pissed. They open this Center—Elderly Care, Diné tradition is Respect your Elders, yada yada yada. Big opening ceremony; blessing; Prez shows up from Window Rock to cut ribbons. They could've done something about the road, you know, there's money to spend when they want to. But they're not bothered about the elderlies staying away because of the road."

"Aren't they used to rough roads? Most of the old people live out there with ungraded roads."

"Sure they do. And they do the trips that they need to: haul water; look after their sheep; visit with relatives. But the Elderly Center? That's not a necessity, that's self-indulgence."

"How come they built the center?"

"Fiscal Operating Focus on Elderly Care wotsit—there's some money that's sitting around that needs spending so that more money gets allocated next year."

"Spend it or lose it?"

"Yep. There's been money spent on worse things, believe me. It's good they built a center for them out here. It's not good that they did not think it through. But that's how it rolls."

"What about the Chapter meetings? Anyone speak up for grading the road?"

"It is the Rez Mafia. They got it all stitched up. There's some folk that have a say and many that won't be listened to when they speak up. So they'll be attending maybe once or a couple of times, until they realize how the cookie crumbles—and then they'll give up and stay away. So these meetings are another good ole boy outfit. We sure learnt from the bílagáana."

"Don't you ever speak up?" K asked.

"Me? I been to a couple of meetings. I tried."

"So you are one of those that attend a couple of times and then give up?"

"Yeah. And don't give me any more of your motivational crap. I know what you are going to say: why give up participation when you still feel the frustration?"

"Was I going to say that? Boy, I am good. And a poet."

"Whoa! Was that my idea? Not bad, eh? What did I say again?"

"Why give up participation when you still feel the frustration," said K.

"Why give up participation when you still feel the frustration?" mused Begay. "I've got to chew it over, but . . . it kind of makes sense, doesn't it? It's kind of an Indian value—see things through, don't give up. OK, bud, let's try to do good, motivated cop work."

The car's juddering was beginning to give K a headache. They bumped past the Elderly Center. A small herd of wild horses were dining on roses and shrubs that had been planted around the building.

"I bet some of the elderlies are planning to bring their sheep here—so much free food. It'd be like a five star sheep buffet. They hardly get nothing out there, just thorns and weeds and tough grasses. Just figure you are a sheep and you get to eat a rose for the first time in your life. Yum yum."

"Are you hungry again?" asked K.

"A little snack wouldn't hurt."

"Let's just wait until we've done this last visit, this last interview. Is there anything you care to brief me on?"

"This guy: Jesus Nez."

"Jesus?"

"I guess there could be some Hispanic in his family? Don't they call their boys Jesus?"

"Guess they do. Jesús. Khe-sus."

"Maybe it's given him an inflated ego—good eh? 'Inflated ego'? Sometimes I surprise myself. Got that from Dr. Phil. I mean, maybe he's started to think that he is the Messiah or something."

"Wasn't there supposed to be a turnoff after the Elderly Center?" K asked.

There was sandstone ridge and shrubland, an occasional pinion and nothing else as far as the eye could see.

"Don't worry," said Begay, who could be pretty perceptive,

"there's some camps not that far away. Our people have had long practice hiding. Cool, huh? There's nothing that you can see."

"Maybe because there's nothing to see."

"Who's negative now?" scolded Begay.

Begay suddenly turned right. There was nothing in terms of road, path or tracks that K could see. He hoped that Begay wasn't about to drive them into a canyon or an arroyo.

Begay switched to four-wheel mode. The terrain was uneven, perforated by ditches and banks, large boulders scattered here and there, thickets suddenly looming. K hoped that Robbie Begay, in contrast to himself, still had all his powers of concentration.

Begay certainly seemed to enjoy himself. He was humming something under his breath, his voice rising when he negotiated a dip, and dropping when the car climbed an incline—quite the boy racer. As far as K could see they were in the middle of absolute No Man's land, nothing to the East, West, North or South, nothing but shrubs, boulders and the sky above.

"Did you bring any water?" asked K.

"Don't worry, Sunshine," yodeled Begay, "Daddy's gonna take good care of you."

K snorted. That Begay was enjoying the drive was fine and dandy, but elevating himself to "Daddy" was one level of exuberance too far. Begay roguishly waggled his eyebrows at K and narrowly missed a jagged boulder.

"Cool, Daddy," hissed K. He looked into the rearview mirror. Wilderness and nothing but. Begay swerved, turned the wheel sharply to the right. Now they were on terrain that, if anything, felt even rougher than what had come before.

"If we get out of this alive I am going to consult Occupational Health regarding early retirement due to chronic whiplash," said K rubbing his neck.

"Good one! Me too," said Begay.

"It is you who is driving!" .

"So? I can still get whiplash, can't I?"

"You could minimize the risk by not driving like a lunatic," K suggested.

"Come on now. It ain't that bad."

Begay swerved and swore softly as he missed another boulder by a hair's breadth and came to a sudden stop. "Well lookee here," he said.

K looked.

"I'll be darned," said Begay. He opened the door. K took off his seatbelt and followed Begay out of the car.

They were looking at the remnants of what might have been a hogan or a shed or shelter. It was burnt almost to the ground, reduced to a pile of charred planks, rubble. The harsh smell of burning still filled the air.

They walked around rubble and debris. There was what looked like bits of a pipe or hose leading away from the burnt-out ruin. They followed it to a ditch where it ended. The ditch looked as if the ground had been doused in acid. There was not one plant left, nor weed, shrub or brush. A few withered and dead roots stuck out of the dirt. They walked back to the charred ruin. Begay picked up a stick and used it to turn over debris. There were the remains of bowls, colanders, containers, molten pieces of a gas-burner, bent cutlery.

"Meth lab?" asked K.

"Sure looks like it," said Begay. He took out his cell and began to take photos.

"Must have been used until a short while ago. Still stinks like hell, that's for sure."

"You're calling it in?" asked K.

"Dream on. Look at this here." He held his cell up to K. No reception.

"Hmmm," said K.

Begay scraped his shoe over the dirt. "I'm thinking we should turn back," he said. "Turn back, get a warrant, come back with some backup."

"That bad?" asked K.

"Let's go," said Begay. "We'll chew it over in the car, OK?"

He turned and walked briskly toward the car. K followed.

"Come on! Chop-chop!" Begay commanded.

K had barely closed the door when the patrol car shot off. Begay wasn't singing now. To K it looked as if Begay was driving a different route, but seeing his tense face and white knuckles as he gripped the wheel he didn't comment. Instead he focused on pre-empting dips in the terrain. He'd already smashed his head against the roof a couple of times and his skull felt sore. His eyes burned from trying to spot obstacles on the way. He glanced into the rear-view mirror and saw a dust cloud. It was too squat and broad for a dust-devil.

Begay increased speed. K could appreciate why, though he couldn't see much advantage in hitting a boulder, breaking the axle, being stranded in a broken-down car here in the middle of the boon-docks, at the mercy of all kinds of hostile entities. But neither could he see the sunny side of being chased down in the wilderness by a bunch of irate meth merchants—who were gaining on them pretty fast.

K kept his eyes on the rearview mirror. "Better slow down."

Begay huffed. He wasn't bothering to reduce speed. He swerved. Another boulder narrowly avoided.

"Slow the fuck down!" boomed K.

Begay slowed down. "OK," he said, "you take it from here."

"Fine," said K. Whatever 'it' was and whatever 'here' was. Here was here, nowhere, where a vehicle carrying persons unknown was coming closer and closer.

It was a pickup with a cabin that sat high above ground. The truck looked pretty beat up. Tinted windows made it hard to see into the vehicle. The truck now was no more than a couple of hundred yards behind them.

"Always look at the bright side of life," K sang in a low voice.

"Are you kidding?" asked Begay, "or are you losing it?"

"Ever heard of Monty Python? A British comedy outfit?"

"Sure," said Begay "Spam! Spam! Spam!"

"That's a weird thing to know."

"Why?"

"Just seems a bit out there. Have you ever had spam?"

"Why do I need to? Believe me bro' I know damn well how it is when you eat the same thing every damn day. I could do you a song with 'Squash! Squash! Squash!'"

"Doesn't have quite the same ring to it."

The pickup was now just fifty yards or so behind them. What if they were shot while singing Monty Python's spam song? Cops dying in shoot-out and nobody'd ever know that the last thing they'd done before they croaked was sing "Spam."

"Screw this," Begay said and stopped the car.

"Did you just switch on the lightshow?" asked K.

"What the hell. May as well have fun," said Begay.

The car behind them had stopped too. Nothing was moving behind the smoke-colored wind-screen.

"Is it worth asking you to cover me?"

"Sure," said K and hooked his thumb through his holster. "Or how about you cover me and I do the footwork?"

"Maybe," said Begay. "At least I don't have a thing about shooting. I more have a thing about not shooting."

"If everyone gets out of this with no shooting, I'd be good with that. I might even buy you a beer."

Begay took his gun out of the holster and slid back the safety catch.

"Ready? If you croak I'll pour a cold one on your grave. I love you so much, I'd break my tradition for you and visit a cemetery. Now beat it."

"Charming," said K and got out of the car.

He began to walk slowly toward the pickup. He imagined walking on a buttercup-strewn meadow, toward a friendly and curious cow. He liked cows. Loved them. It was because of cows that he was a vegetarian. Maybe he'd even become vegan. If he lived.

There was this lovely, innocent cow, just waiting to lick his hand. Cows had tongues like sandpaper that they wrapped around whatever they wanted to eat. They couldn't bite, so they had to wrap their long, wet, sandpapery tongues around stuff to get it into their mouths. It was a lovely feeling to be licked by a cow. Maybe he could open a Cow Spa. They had fish pedicures after all. Why not have a Cow Spa? Surely cow-tongues had healing properties? Not just the rough massage effect, but also all the enzymes and chlorophyll and free radicals or tamed radicals that cow tongues carried after chewing all that good green stuff all day. By the time K reached the pickup he was deep into the cow-land of his imagination. He stretched up his arm and tapped on the window, smiled sunnily.

The window lowered slowly, squeaking as if a nest of mice was being squeezed. Manual window. No pimped-up ride this.

"Yá'át'ééh," beamed K, looking up at the lowered window.

He was looking into the face of a hundred-year-old woman. At least a hundred. Her face was creased by a myriad wrinkles so deep you could have snorted lines of coke out of them while she was upright without worrying about losing any of the precious stuff.

K, having anticipated a showdown in the style of Breaking Bad, was having trouble adjusting from preparing to perish in the boondocks in a shoot-out with badass drug pushers to becoming a Celebrity Cow Spa owner to now beholding the Ancient Ancestor of all Diné, a woman who looked as if she had passed her prime around the epoch of the Long Walk.

He took in a lungful of air and boomed "Yá'át'ééh shíma!" while he made surreptitious beckoning motions toward Begay in the patrol car. He just hoped that Begay would not mistake his gestures for a signal to fire. K beamed some more, nodding exuberantly, while the crone looked down on him with rheumy eyes and frozen face. Begay sure was taking his time. Maybe he was assembling his assault rifle.

"Can we help, shíma?" K asked experimentally.

The Ancient One sat silent and glowered.

K heard Begay lumbering up. He stepped aside and slowly shifted to standing behind Begay's back. Begay had the gun tucked under his belt.

"Yá'át'ééh," said Begay.

If the old woman answered it was unclear. K couldn't hear anything. Also he started to feel foolish standing around behind Begay's broad back. Step by step, stealthily, he started to move away toward the patrol car, like in a game of Grandma's Footsteps—make that Great-Great-Great Grandma's footsteps.

K hoisted himself into the passenger seat. It seemed like ages that he had last sat in it. In between then and now hovered an eternity of resigning himself to mortality, with a side-order of Cow Spa. He looked into the side-mirror. It was difficult to make out what was going on. So far no shotguns were involved. Begay was standing quite still. Officer Begay was looking at the ground.

A bluebottle had found its way into the patrol car, buzzing frantically, as it crashed against the windscreen. What did bluebottles make of glass? Did they just wonder why the air hit them so hard? Maybe that's what insects called glass amongst themselves: hard air.

K opened the door and waved his hands. The bluebottle, contrary and against its better interest, flew toward the driver's side and started bombarding the window there.

"Shoo! Fly!" said K and pointed toward the open passenger door. The fly executed a mid-air turn and obediently exited through the open door. He closed the door quickly. He did not want to overuse his fly-whispering gifts. With no fly to keep him company he began to feel a little bit bored. Nothing was moving outside and that included Begay, as far as he could see. Standing there with his head hanging down Begay looked like a schoolboy. K dug in his breast-pocket for his cell and put it in camera-mode. A little souvenir, to remind Robbie Begay of his intergenerational networking skills. Still Begay was standing, looking at the tips of his boots. Maybe the old woman was chanting the Night Way. Or reciting Deuteronomy, seeing that most folk here had succumbed to the clutches of missionaries, amongst whom they seemed to favor Baptists.

Now K was feeling thirsty. They'd covered the Rez on just one coffee and a fry bread—more accurately two fry bread for Begay and one coffee for K. What had they got? Two enormous squash, and not much in terms of hunches and enquiries. Though now they also had the remains of a meth lab that they hadn't been looking for. With any luck Begay would return another day with backup and they would find and haul in the perps. Surely even Redwater PD had to yield the occasional result, despite Robbie's jaundiced assessment?

Not that apprehending the odd meth merchant would help much. Meth labs were viral. As soon as one burnt down or was busted, another five opened. When the Good Lord made this land it was meth labs hiding from the law HE had in mind. Hallelujah.

And as the day's crowning glory they had been chased through the wild boondocks by bad guys who turned out to be one ancient lady.

As it looked right now, they would spend the night right here, with Begay out there scratching the dirt with the tip of his shoe, while the Ancient One held forth on the Lord Jesus and recited God Bizaad. K felt tempted to lean on the horn. But this was not the done thing in Diné Bikéyah. Whoever had hold of the Talking Stick was free to go on for as long as they needed to. He leaned his head back against the headrest and drifted into the potpourri of associations that populated his headspace.

A sharp pain throbbed on the tip of his nose. He came to with a start, opened his eyes to Begay's bloodshot eyes hovering a couple of inches above him.

"Ouch," said K.

"You better wake up before you start snoring."

"What did you do to my nose?"

"Pinched it. Wanted to know if it works. Supposed to be real effective."

"I didn't snore."

"Nope. But you were looking as if you were fixing to start to."

"I never snore."

"That what your lady-friends tell you?" asked Begay sarcastically.

Begay fastened the seatbelt, started the engine and depressed the accelerator and they bounced off with a roar. The speed that Begay was holding was in no way appropriate for the terrain. Through all that tense passenger seat driving K forgot to look back to see what had become of the old lady, and he did not want to distract Begay from keeping his attention on the ground. He just hoped that they would make it safe and sound to the ungraded washboard road and from there to the properly paved road to Redwater and the civilized world. Begay was driving as if a medal for obstacle racing was waiting for him. He swerved so abruptly and so frequently that K started to compose a little accompanying ditty inspired by the rhythms of revving, racing and swerving. It alleviated his tension and soothed his nerves. Miraculously they made it to the road without having hit a boulder, tree stump or anything else. The car axles seemed to have survived the drive intact, and the tires too. Reasons to be cheerful.

"So, what was going on back there?" asked K.

"Going on?"

"You had quite the conversation with nima over there."

"Shíma hashké." growled Begay. "Ayóó hashké. Ayóó bá háchį'. Ch'íįdii."

"It looked as if the two of you were getting cozy over there."

"You want to watch it. I'm not in the mood," snapped Begay.

"What happened? She was a very old lady. Poor old lady."

"Poor old lady? She spent all her life practicing chewing people's asses. And boy, was she good at it."

"What did she chew your ass about? You didn't know each other, did you?"

"That was one of her points. That she did not know me. Then she went on about my Diné, yakyakyak."

"What did she say about your Diné?"

Begay looked sheepish. "Didn't understand all of it. Matter of fact I didn't understand most of it. Matter of fact I did not appreciate how little I understand. I thought I was OK with my Diné. I get that I'm not real fluent how the old folk used to be. But I thought I was doing alright. There's many that do worse. They never get past Navajo 101 at the Community College. They know it kind of like you do, you dig."

"Thank you," said K, piqued. "For a bílagáana I do alright."

"Same here," said Begay. "For one of my generation I'm doing alright. We are talking about a diminishing language after all. But boy, did the old witch give me shit."

K was shocked. "That's a bit harsh, isn't it?"

"Harsh, but true," said Begay. "Now I understand why relations between generations aren't that hot. They are always talking about elderly abuse—you seen the posters, ain't ya? But now I see there are two sides to every story."

"You are saying that the elderlies deserve to be abused?"

"There's some that do. You should have heard how she laid into me. Just because she didn't dig my pronunciation."

"She looked kind of frail," said K. "Did she just start chewing you out?"

"Pretty much," said Begay. "She just started yelling at me and wouldn't lay off."

"Yelling about your bad pronunciation?"

"Uh-huh. The part that I understood anyhow. To say the truth, I didn't catch all she said. I told you. Maybe my comprehension skills ain't as hot as I thought. But I used to get at least 80% in the tests."

"That was then," K said cruelly. "So she was right—the younger folk really have forgotten the language."

"She would have been righter if she had picked on some other body. Least I'm trying."

"So—she started yelling at you right away?"

"I told you. She pretty much started yelling right away."

K shook his head.

"What?" asked Begay.

K shrugged. "Something bothers me."

"Maybe you are feeling sorry for your old buddy here?"

"You don't feel there's anything weird about this?"

Begay shook his head:. "When you got an old woman yelling at you like that, it kind of disrupts your ability to think straight. I'm still in recovery. What you getting at?"

"Something doesn't add up. I mean . . . we are driving along in the middle of nowhere. We happen on a burnt-out meth lab. We take a look. We decide that it is safer to return with backup. We drive on and see that we are being followed by a vehicle that must be driving pretty fast; I mean it is driving at about double the speed we are making. OK, you were driving kind of slow. . . ."

"Not that slow." Begay sounded offended. "I was driving at a speed appropriate to the terrain."

"Sure you were," said K jovially. "Anyways, so whatever appropriate speed you were keeping, that car behind us was making double that. Then. . . . What happened then?"

"Then the ch'įįdii starts cussing me out."

"Not so fast. Let's go through this step by step."

"Thank the Lord for that!" said Begay. They had reached the intersection. He indicated left and pulled onto the road. "What were you saying?"

"I was saying let's look at what happened when the pickup caught up with us. Step by step."

"We agreed I'd cover you and you went out to talk to the driver and you called me over and I got yelled at and we left."

"Step by step I said. So we stopped and then?"

"The pickup behind us stops."

"And then?"

"You go out and I cover you?"

"Eventually. But first we sit there for a while and we look at the pickup and wait if something's gonna happen. And then we decide that one of us is going to check the pickup out and one of us is going to cover. Then we discuss who's going to do what. And we decide that I'm going to get shot and you are going to shoot."

"You sure got a neat way of putting this."

"Who were you expecting to be in that pickup?"

"Who was I expecting to be in that pickup? Dude! What kind of question is that?"

"Well?"

"Some hard-ass crystal pusher, I guess. A regular Rez Reservoir Dog. That what you asking?"

"Same here. I was looking at that pickup gaining on us and I was starting to feel a bit jumpy."

"No shit, Al Pacino? You were feeling jumpy?"

"Cut the crap. That's not my point."

"OK, no sweat. Tell me all about your point."

"My point is there sure was a big gap between what we expected to see and what we saw."

"Pity your Navajo's not real strong. I can just picture you with the Talking Stick going all cryptic with the elderlies. They dig this kind of crap. I'm more see, shoot, file a report."

"Ha ha. OK, listen: anything strike you about the truck?"

"Uh, old? Kind of beat up? Dark windows? That what you getting at?"

"What else?"

"What is this? Thirty questions? Three hundred questions? Just spit it out. I had a long day, man. My head's in standby mode."

"To me it seems," K began ponderously.

"If you don't want me to drop off you better hurry. I heard lullabies that had more suspense."

"OK. Here it is: The truck was very high off the ground. Practically mounted as high as a monster truck."

"So? That's what you need on this terrain."

"Yes. But a truck that high is hard to get into. If you are not tall, or kind of mobile. . . ."

"Yeah. But your relatives can hoist you up. And help you down. That's no biggie."

"OK, "conceded K, "but what about our expectations? Why were we both expecting a badass meaning business?"

"Because we are a bunch of paranoid pussies? I thought we moved on from the guessing game? Just tell me, OK?"

"I think that it is unlikely that an old lady like that is able to drive over terrain as rough as that at that speed."

"But she did."

"Did she? What if she wasn't driving?"

"It wasn't teletransportation, was it? Or skinwalking?" Begay shuddered.

"Don't act dumb. What about this: We stop at the meth lab and we get spotted. But we are too far away for them to see that it's a patrol car. They just see the dust and maybe some reflection from the sun on the vehicle. And the folk who spotted us need to find out our business, so they go after us. Because of all the dust they don't see that we are cops until they're right behind us and you switch on the flashers. So when we stop. . . . They got darkened windows, a darkened windscreen—they decide to minimize the risk of getting in a situation with us, so they give some instructions to their old grandma and they swap over. Put grandma in the driving seat, tell her to scare the policemen off. They know she can do a good job."

"Let me get this straight: you saying that all the time she's yelling at me there's someone else in the vehicle?"

"I guess that's what I'm saying."

"I didn't notice anybody."

"The cabin's too high to get a look into it. And you were being yelled at."

"Why would they take along grandma?"

"Even meth pushers need groceries. Maybe they were on their way to City Market."

"Good boys, eh? Sure makes me feel dumb."

"What now?"

"You want to go back?" Begay asked.

"Go back and try to find them out there in the boondocks? With no backup and no cell reception?" asked K. "Let's stay with Noah George. Do some proper detective thinking. How often do you get the chance to help solve a murder?"

"More often than I take it," said Begay. "I told you—we're not that hot on solving crimes. It's the principle that these eco-freaks are so keen on: you just let nature sort itself out—weeds get strangled off by other weeds—that kind of deal. You leave the bad guys to take care of each other and pretty soon their numbers go down and you've only got half the bad guys to make trouble. Then you wait some more until they get tired and reform and turn into informants, grassing up the new baddies. Kind of the traditional way of not interfering too much I guess."

They were approaching the outskirts of Redwater-Southside. Redwater-Southside was the oldest part of town. It was the first and original settlement and still consisted of the original prefabs that had been erected half a century or more ago for coal plant and uranium mine workers. They were basic prefabs, one-room dwellings clad in weather-beaten, dark-brown plywood, sitting on a concrete base. The prefabs were closer to shacks than cabins and would not have looked out of place in the urban slums of a developing country. There was not a tree, flower or other plant in sight. There were no signs of attempts to prettify the environment. There was the occasional washing-line strung from dwelling to fence or electric post. Here as elsewhere little care was given to the safety of the poor: the next crosswalk was a mile down the road and kids going to school had to cross the highway at peril.

"Bílagáana never like the Southside," observed Begay.

"It's hardly cheerful," said K.

"Let me tell you, there are folk that are still grateful every day they been moved out of the boonies to Southside. They got utilities. They don't have to haul water. They don't need to worry about the generator running down, or the roads getting so muddy that you can't pass them. There's schools, City Market, the Laundromat, KFC, Taco Bell, Burger King, the Gas station, the Chinese Buffet, the library, the hospital, the dentist, the funeral parlor . . . what more do you want?"

"There's no crosswalk."

"Huh?"

"A place where the kids can cross the road safely."

"Oh. OK. You got a point there. Maybe we should raise that at the next Chapter meeting."

"You think nobody's asked for a safe crossing point before?"

"With these folks, it's hard to say. They are mostly Jhons and have stayed Jhons. Country folk. They are not real sophisticated in asking for things. Most of them were brought up thinking that they didn't have any rights. Most of them still think that."

"And they would be right," muttered K darkly.

"I'll make a note to raise it at the next meeting," said Begay. He sounded almost official. "Are you hungry?"

"What do you have in mind?"

"We could have a working late lunch at the Chinese place. It should be nice and quiet now. We see what we got and make our plans—and then it's about time to go home."

Trying to avoid the Walk of Shame past the Ogre, thought K.

"Sure," he said, "why not?"

Begay pulled into the Chinese buffet's parking lot. It was a small square building with a red and gold Golden Palace sign on its roof. It was quiet, as Robbie had anticipated. In the far corner a couple of bearded Anglos who looked like BIA officials were forking up food while frowning at spreadsheets.

They were barely seated when a waitress by whose looks it was hard to tell whether she was Chinese or Navajo brought them hot green tea. Begay shot to the buffet and began piling his plate. K followed. Surprisingly there were a couple of appealing-looking vegetarian dishes. Begay got up twice more, falling upon the buffet like a one-man locust plague. He shoveled, gulped, grunted appreciatively, showing no inclination to stop.

"Are you done?" asked K eventually. "Should we get on with the working part of our late lunch now?"

"Sure," said Begay and burped gently. "This is where we look at what we got and where we go from here?"

"So, what have we got?"

"Two squash. That's what we definitely got. For you to take home and feast on for the next month, my vegetarian friend. We know what we still have to get: Philbert Tsosie, family man. Family man that knocks himself out on prescription drugs."

"If you are going to go after everyone that does that, you better open a whole new branch of law enforcement. This is Big Pharma La-La Land, remember?"

"You got a thing about upsetting his kid. Same thing with your man Benally," said Begay.

"When someone's turned their life around and got to the point where they do more good than harm, even if they used to be bad."

"Hold your horses and step off your pulpit, bro'. I hear you."

"I wouldn't mind pulling you in for mixing your metaphors."

"Crimes against English? Maybe you could get together with the old ch'į̇dii out there."

"That reminds me: here's something I've got." K took his cell out of his pocket and scrolled down the menu. "Here."

"What's that? Oh, I see. That's me being cussed out by the ch'į̇dii. Better lose some weight, huh? Glad you took a souvenir snap to help me not to forget my humiliation."

"You should thank me."

"Thank you? If you erase it, I will."

"Really? You don't want the truck's registration?"

Begay shrugged and pulled his cell out of his pocket. "Mail or bluetooth?"

"What happened to the art of copying down I wonder?"

"You wonder about that while I go ahead and wonder who that pickup is registered to. All that wondering get you any closer to solving your case?"

K chewed his lip. "I wouldn't say solve, but I'm getting toward somewhere where I can build up an impression of the kind of person Noah George was."

"Brother, your long sentences are giving me a headache."

"The monosodium glutamate, more like."

"No monosodium glutamate here!" The old Chinese man was standing behind their table and shaking his head emphatically. "Never! Pure food. Clean. Very healthy."

"We were only joking. It wasn't about your food."

"Golden Dragon in Appleton full of MSG. No good. Give Chinese food a bad name."

"Your food is very good."

"You tell all your friends. Come back. Bring your friends." He put a couple of fortune cookies on the table and moved away.

Begay raised his eyebrows and smirked.

"So what are your conclusions on your man there?"

"Impressions, not conclusions. My impression is that he was conflicted. He still was getting into trouble. Most of his old gang buddies went straight. Vince Benally's gone straight. Philbert Tsosie's got this nice kid."

"Does that mean he's nice? Sometimes the worst parents got great kids. Believe me, I seen it. Sure, Vince Benally's got some stuff in his life that's legit. But that don't mean there ain't no dirt—you just gotta dig down far enough."

"What is it with you? First you say that you are not interested in solving cases and now you can't wait to dig deep enough."

"That's why I'm not so much interested in solving cases. Once you start you cannot stop."

"Like Tcheezos."

"The guy who died of hypothermia—in June. The way Benally freaked. Tsosie—the dude who knocks himself out on prescription meds. Why are his dreams so bad? That's what I wanna know. Actually, forget it. I don't want to know. Leastways I got out of the office."

Begay picked up a fortune cookie and tore at the wrapping. The wrapping wouldn't give. It was painful to watch.

"What?" Begay snarled.

"I didn't say anything," K said.

"You were thinking something," Begay said menacingly.

"I can see the future and it is wordless." K took the remaining fortune cookie and ripped open the wrapper with his teeth. No sense in taking unnecessary risks with one's dignity. He cracked open the crispy cookie shell and unfurled the narrow strip of paper within.

"Sweet Lord."

"What's it say?" Begay's fingers were still worrying his fortune cookie's shiny wrapper.

"'Your ashes will nourish a tree,'" K read out sonorously.

"Wow. That's . . . uhm. Maybe they think you're a smoker?" Begay suggested.

"Smokers deserve to die?" K asked.

"Cigarettes produce ashes I was thinking." Begay fastened his incisors around his cookie wrapper, pulled at it, discarded the wrapper, put the cookie on the table and smashed his fist into it. The cookie dissolved into a morbid heap of crumbs, with the end of a paperstrip sticking out.

Begay plucked out the paperstrip and squinted. He held the paperstrip to his eyes.

"And?" K asked impatiently.

"'You will live long happy life with plenty of love and money,'" Begay said.

"Good for you," K said.

"That's making you feel worse, huh?" Begay asked.

K opened his mouth to deny, thought better of it, considered and said, "I guess it does. Why do you suppose that is?"

"Coz' people are scum," Begay said cheerfully. "I have a mind to do you a good deed today. Though Christ knows you don't deserve it." He handed his cookie message to K.

"Thank you," said K, "though I don't believe cookie fortunes are transferable."

"Read," Begay ordered.

K read: "You will sing until you die."

"Feel better now?" Begay asked.

"Just trying to figure out which one's worse."

"Yours is," Begay said mercilessly. "Leastways I'm singing when I'm alive. The only time anyone gets any benefit from you is when you're dead. Where do you suppose they get these from? A Halloween Special Edition?"

K, who suspected that these were in fact the kind of scripts he would be tempted to produce were he called upon to think up messages for fortune cookies, shrugged.

"Anyways, back to work," Begay said. "Let's see what we got and who gets what: Noah George is yours. The meth lab's mine. Easy. Everything in between we split, like regular buddies. Not like the thing with the eagle feathers where I had to go to all those Dog Blessing Ceremonies."

"It was me who had to go to the dog blessings," protested K. "You said that you couldn't bear witnessing your traditions being defiled."

"Defiled? You sure I said that? Sometimes I amaze myself."

"So what are you going to do about the meth lab?"

"I done told you Dude."

"I smell evasion in your syntax."

"What you smell is soy sauce and pork. I already told you: depends if the boss has a relative that's got a side deal in meth labs. Our meth lab policy depends on everyone and their relatives' vested interest. I just hang and wait to do what I'm told to do. Initiative never pays anyways."

"You depress me."

"What depresses you is lack of protein. Look at me: I was kind of down and now I'm real happy. Ready to sing again." Begay slapped his bulging belly. "Ain't nothing that dead pig won't cure."

"And nothing that will cure a dead pig. OK then—let's see what we come up with." K paused and tried to summon a thought from the far recesses of his mind. "The thing about Noah George. . . ."

"We just summed up all we have on Noah George, remember?" Begay interrupted.

"We just summed up all we have that fits into one category," K objected.

"Category? What's the category? " groaned Begay.

"The category of Noah George as trouble maker. Everything that fits his death with—retaliation? Revenge? Retribution?"

"You'll find that most murders fit that—if they are not about money and stuff," said Begay indifferently.

"I told you: it's about how Noah George was found," pondered K, "the way he was laid out . . . there was real tenderness in it."

"Yáadilá!" snorted Begay. "Maybe the killer repented? Maybe he got one of those illnesses, like those folk that always wash and line up their pencils? I got a relative that's like that. Whatchamacallit?"

"OCD?" said K.

"Maybe the murderer was just a neat guy."

"There's your assumption again. How come you're so sure it's a he?"

"Coz' most killing is done by men," said Begay.

"You saw two tracks. And one could be a woman's. Small feet, remember?"

"Whatever," yawned Begay. "Right now I'm done caring."

"Let's call it a day," K said. "I need to get home, feed the cat, have some downtime."

"Feed the puddy tat, eh?" Begay looked at his watch. "Yep, let's drive down to the station and pick up our vehicles."

Begay's jolly tone indicated that he was pretty confident that, today at least, he would be spared encountering his inamorata.

Talk about the fickleness of men's proclivities.

CHAPTER FIFTEEN

K hit the white-collar rush. Compacts, four-wheel drives and pick-ups of superior issue crowded the highway to Milagro. He kept to the speed limit and savored the tailback of exasperated law-abiding citizens.

Finally at home he felt as if he had been away for an age. He was hungry—Chinese food always did that to him. When he opened the refrigerator he remembered that he had forgotten the squash in Begay's patrol car. He felt bad. He'd been so moved by the Goth kid's squash, full of gratitude and paternal tenderness, and now he'd left the homegrown gift to the mercy of squash-hostile Robbie Begay who did not appreciate it at all. The squash would sit and rot on the backseat, until someone noticed the smell and decided to investigate. Or maybe a perp would spot the squash and use it to club a cop over the head. K dug in his wallet for the business cards that Robbie had given him. He'd been generous; there was a whole bunch, embossed with the seal of the Navajo Nation, with Robbie's cell and landline numbers. He texted Robbie asking to keep the squash for him. As soon as he sent the text he regretted it. He could imagine what Robbie Begay would make of his attachment to the squash.

K's eyes fell on the calendar on the refrigerator door. It took him a while to remember why he'd marked today in red. Today was the day of the gig at Delgado Micro Brewery.

He took a scalding shower, toweled his hair dry and put on ci-vilian clothes—faded Levis, T-shirt and the leather biker jacket that he had found at the Methodist Thrift shop and so could wear without feeling that he was compromising vegetarian principles.

He opened a tin of sardines for Wittgenstein and topped up the water bowl. Wittgenstein was nowhere to be seen. He was probably outside bothering the birds.

• • •

Not being vested in official authority, K merrily broke the speed limit. It was one of the perks of the job that cops did not pull each other in—speeding cops could always claim that they were on urgent deployment, though you couldn't always count on a brother's loyalty; you never knew who was pissed at you or felt like teaching a darn liberal a lesson.

The road to Delgado led up into the mountains through forest and meadows. Aspens and cottonwoods had turned color, foliage gleaming red and gold in the setting sun. On the southern foothills the charred skeletons of trees stood as grim reminders of last year's wildfire.

By the time K reached Delgado darkness had fallen. The Brewery's parking lot was almost full. At the entrance, a woman dressed Southwestern New Age style asked to see his ticket. She raised her eyebrows when K said he wanted to buy one.

"It's been sold out for weeks."

K, who wouldn't have been surprised to find himself one of three fans at the gig, was baffled. It was a weekday night after all and The Handsome Family was kind of niche.

"Are they that popular?" he asked.

"The Handsome Family are cult," said the woman. Or maybe she said "The Handsome Family are a cult."

"You need a ticket?" said a voice behind him. He turned around to see a man inappropriately dressed in pressed slacks, shirt and tie.

"Here." The man handed him a ticket.

"How much do I owe you?"

"Forget it," the man hissed and left.

K looked at the cashier.

She shrugged. "Never look a gift-horse. . . ."

"But if he changes his mind?"

"Tough doo-doo," said the woman, "he gave it to you out of his own free will. You weren't forcing him or anything?"

"Look," said K. "If he changes his mind let me know, OK? I'll come out and he can have his ticket back."

"A man with a conscience," said the woman and looked at him appraisingly. "It's been a while since I've seen that. Now you have a great time!" she called after him.

• • •

K bought himself a pretzel with mustard, a combination never heard of in Bavaria, and a bottle of Bitter & Twisted IPA. The space was filling up. Apparently there were many takers for The Handsome Family's whimsical dark alt folk. K dug the physical contrast between the Handsome couple; the man tall and broad with graying hair and untrimmed beard, his bass so powerful it reverberated in the body; the woman's wistful beauty with a touch of Our Lady of the Sorrows, her anarchic imagination. Together these two achieved a state of alchemic transformation. They were testimony to the whole being more than the sum of its parts. Magic, almost.

When the gig was over the Brewery emptied fast. K walked into the crisp night air. The sky was black and filled with stars. A shooting star swished a luminous trail across the sky.

"Did you make a wish?" asked a voice behind him.

He turned and saw the woman who had worked the ticket counter.

"Did you?" he asked back.

The woman looked at him and did not answer.

"Did you?" K repeated, not so much out of curiosity, more out of obligation.

"Yes," said the woman. "Aren't you going to ask me what it is?" she asked.

"You aren't supposed to tell. Otherwise it doesn't come true," K said.

"If I don't tell you it will definitely not be coming true."

She tilted back her head. Her neck was long, her skin smooth and creamy,

"I want you to come home with me."

•   •   •

It took them fifteen minutes from the Brewery to her condo and into her bed. She had a taut body, firm breasts, gym-honed physique. Her sexual etiquette suggested that she hailed from circumstances that furthered a sense of entitlement. She had wasted no time taking possession of him and now gasped a stream of instructions specifying depth, pace and thrust. K was beginning to feel like he was being directed operating a forklift.

At least the military-style commands minimized any risk of male pleasure pre-empting female satisfaction. It was hard work drowning out the incessant panted orders and implorations while maintaining the modicum of excitement necessary to ensure that the lady peaked. When this was at last accomplished, evidenced by an ear-splitting crescendo of ecstatic cries, she sighed deeply, stretched luxuriously, and fell asleep in an instant.

K waited until her breathing had become deep and regular. He got out of bed, collected his clothes—no mean feat in the dark—and tiptoed out. He walked into the kitchen where he pulled on his clothes. There was a pen on the kitchen table. K looked around for a piece of paper, couldn't find one. He fingered through his wallet, fished out a card-sized paper and wrote: "Thank you for a great night. I had to go home to feed the dog." He left and hit the road to Milagro.

It was at home, showered, cleansed, in his own quiet bed, churning with self-loathing with a side-order of melancholia, when it occurred to him that he had written the note he had left on the woman's table on one of Robbie Begay's business cards.

CHAPTER SIXTEEN

After the Rez odyssey it felt weird to be back at the station. The air was saturated with a mixture of the citrus-scented cleaner that Lorinda preferred and the burnt rubber tang of Weismaker's coffee. Becky was sorting messages into pigeonholes. She raised her eyebrows and said "Look who's here," as if he'd been away on extended leave.

"Was I missed?" K asked, drawing a fistful of message slips out of his pigeon-hole.

"Sure. Just look at all the love notes you got. I feel kind of under-occupied without you asking me to sort out your IT problems. Hardly knew what to do with myself," Becky said.

"Never ask if you're not prepared to hear the answer," K muttered.

"Did I hurt your feelings?"

"A friendly welcome back would have been nice."

"You're saying I'm mean?" Becky asked and then said, "Uhuh, I see. Never ask if you're not prepared to hear the answer."

"Object lesson learnt. Mission completed."

"I don't think I'm mean. I was just trying to joke with you," Becky sounded upset.

"And I was joking with you," placated K. "I'm used to meaner. Even you've been meaner than that to me."

"When?" Becky looked thunderous.

This was a one-way street leading straight to the mean streets. K couldn't even remember how they'd gotten into this. How had it started? He'd asked her if he'd been missed, and wham! And now he couldn't think of anything to say that would turn things round. He shrugged, helpless.

"You're not gonna tell me?" Becky challenged.

"How did we get into this?" K asked. "I was only joking. You know that you are one of my favorite people here."

"That's not saying much."

Oy Gevalt.

"So how've things been? Anything new while I was gone?"

"There was something . . . the sheriff . . . ." Becky turned over the pile of message slips on her desk. "Can't recall it right now. Not sure I wrote it down."

K looked at Becky. It was not like her at all to forget to relay messages.

"There was some chaos going on. We had a disturbance."

"Must have been pretty bad for you to lose things?"

"One of those domestics got out of hand. Gutierrez brought them in and I guess he thought he had them under control, and he's booking them and—wham! It got really ugly for a moment there."

"Domestics can get like that. Lifetime of hatred and frustration finding an outlet and an audience."

"These were just regular folk though. When I think about it I can't even tell you what it was that was so scary. I mean they weren't packing or anything."

"There's some folk that'll do that to you," said K sagely.

"So where did you go yesterday?" Becky asked.

K felt a weight lift. He hadn't realized how dependent he was on Becky's kindliness.

"Across the Rez with Robbie Begay."

"Y'all have a good time . . . productive time, I mean?"

"Depends how you read it. Nothing conclusive."

"Nothing conclusive, eh?" Becky looked amused.

"We didn't find anything to help us with Noah George's death."

"Murder."

"We did come across a meth lab though."

"A meth lab? Did you take it down?"

"It was burnt out."

"Did you find where they moved it to?"

"No. Who says they moved it?"

"Because that's what they do. One lab burns down or is taken down, and they move on and get working on another one right away. They are business people, those meth cookers. They got customers to supply. If they don't produce somebody else takes their place immediately. It's a dog-eat-dog kind of deal."

"Proper capitalism," said K.

"It's all business, isn't it?"

"We didn't follow it up because we had no backup," said K.

"Makes sense," said Becky. "What's the plan?"

"Robbie's going to talk to his superiors. It's their call. I guess he'll go back if they provide backup. If they don't he won't."

"No wonder there's that Crystal problem on the Rez," Becky said.

"What's he supposed to do?" K felt compelled to stand up for Begay.

"It's not just him. It's the whole outfit. None of them takes this serious. They don't care—until their kids or someone gets mixed up with the stuff. Then they do. They don't care if some Jhons out on the Rez die."

"You do."

"Sure do. You want to know where I been on Sunday? We drove to visit this relative, Wilfred, in rehab in Gallup. He's not even a kid anymore. He's not that young. Has a family. Real loving wife, cute kids. I guess it started because they needed money for something, I think some health problems with a relative or something and they needed to help out. He's a boilermaker out on the oilfields and they say sure, he can do some extra time and they start throwing all this overtime at him and he is afraid to turn them down, cause then they'll take away all the overtime from him. So some buddy takes him to one side and says: 'You want to know how I cope working twenty-four-seven? Here's how. Here's a little something that works a treat. And if you want some more, just say. I got a good supplier.' Wilfred tries the stuff and, whoa, it sure gives him wings. He's out there working on those boilers all day and all night and the next day. He doesn't feel hungry, he doesn't feel tired, he feels real good, real energetic, as if he can go on forever. Anytime he feels like he's coming down he takes some more. His wife's real happy, his relatives are happy, he's happy and proud. Everyone thinks he's superman. It goes on like this, work, meth, work, meth, big pay checks. What's not to like? Only his highs are not so high anymore and coming down's a real drag. Pretty soon he's got to take more and more just to have a fraction of the high. The comedowns get worse too. His wife notices he's real moody. She thinks he's overworked, needs a break. One day, she's trying to talk sense to him and he's not having any. Matter of fact he starts acting real mean and before she knows it he is beating up on her. He gives her a black eye. Nose fracture. Bruises all down her arm, ribs. They been together for like twenty years, he's sweet as pie all this time, real caring, a real good provider too, great solid relationship and now he's turned into a domestic abuser. She notices how he's stopped eating, he never sleeps, he's scary mean. She gets him to spend a week at home to chill out. She gets a couple of cousins over. They keep him in the house. Pretty soon he starts twitching and scratching and tearing his skin off. Then he starts acting real weird. He's sure they are after him. His family ask: 'Who is after you?' And he says: 'the Skinwalkers. They are after me and they are gonna get me.' They see this is no joke. He's in real fear for his life. They still don't appreciate how bad he is, until one of the cousins walks in on him as he's trying to strangle himself with a wire. He's trying to gauge his eye out. No-one knows why. Like something out of a horror film. That's when they get him into treatment. When we visited with him last week, I hadn't seen him for a while. To me he was this big guy, friendly, happy, strong, healthy-looking. Do you know when folk say someone changed so much they wouldn't recognize them? I get what they mean now. Wilfred—I mean, they told me it was him, they all act as if he's Wilfred—but all this time I'm visiting with him and I'm sitting there, looking at him, talking to him, I cannot recognize anything in him. There's nothing familiar about him. Nothing at all. Millie, his wife, she's trying to keep positive. She's hoping that she'll get her old Wilfred back. That he'll come out of rehab and be like he was before: happy, strong, healthy. I know that he's not. They had to pull all his teeth. Meth does that. His skin's full of scars where he's scratched himself so badly it's . . . his doctor said it's not scratching, it's more like self-mutilation. You want to know what I think? I think he's not gonna get out at all. I mean if he is, he's going to go back in. He's not going to last long outside."

K looked at Becky's bowed head. He noticed that Becky's hair was parted in a neat zigzag. It looked like skill and trouble. He wondered how she got her parting like that.

"Is there anything to help?" he asked.

"Keep folk away from the stuff," said Becky.

"There are people that get away from it and get better, you know," said K. "There was that couple in Appleton, remember? Big case. Dentists. Whatsthename. Cran . . . something. Remember? Real successful. Surgery doing great. They get into meth, have this steep fall from grace. One day they are high-achieving professionals, the next all goes to hell. They lose everything. They're struck off. Complete collapse. Don't know what happened to the husband. Divorced maybe? But I know the wife got her life back together again."

"She go back to being a dentist?" asked Becky.

"No. They were struck off for good."

"So, what does she do now?"

"She runs a dog-grooming parlor."

Becky laughed.

"Don't laugh," K said. "She's much happier now. They say she only became a dentist because of her parents' ambitions. She always preferred dog grooming."

"Just had to become a meth freak to get there, huh?" said Becky.

"The Lord moves in mysterious ways," K said.

"Whenever you start quoting scripture I know it's time to stop the conversation," Becky said. "Anyway, I was just trying to make a point why even one meth lab is one too many."

"Point taken," said K, "but we don't have jurisdiction down there. It's up to Redwater. Robbie Begay needs to tell his superiors that they need to back him in this."

"That doesn't make me feel real hopeful."

Becky's tone made K listen up.

"I think Robbie's going to do what he can."

"I think that's not that much," Becky said. "Don't look at me like that. Robbie's a relative. I know how he feels about working down there. He was sounding me out about getting a job here. Look, I'm not being disloyal. I figure it's alright to talk to you, coz you . . . you aren't real judgmental. And we all need to let off steam from time to time, right?"

K felt absurdly pleased at this unforeseen conversational trajectory that had led them from fractious confrontation to statement of trust. He considered appropriate responses, something not too heavy, not too effusive, not too serious. Hell, communication was an art.

"I'm honored," K said.

Becky smiled.

"When's the sheriff due back?"

"Could be awhile. You have plenty of time to get on with your favorite occupation. ARGUS."

And he'd thought they were friends. Warm, fuzzy feelings rarely outlasted the duration of a soap-bubble.

The Number One Law of Human Relations.

• • •

K checked his schedule. He hadn't been allotted any extraneous duties as yet. No massaging the NRA's gonads by pandering to their mantra that the epitome of upright American citizenship lay in the possession of armory; no instructing the privileged few, parasites on the backs of the masses, how to defend themselves against the great unwashed; no explaining the rules of the road and safe driving to a motley assortment of rank egomaniacs and rank-smelling inebriates.

He shuffled the message slips together and was about to shove them under the plant pot when one caught his attention. It was from the BLM and concerned a vehicle found in the drained reservoir. No number plates, no identifiers; it looked as if it had been dumped in the reservoir. Maybe whoever had dumped it there had not known the reservoir was drained every fall. Dumping a vehicle was an offence in itself, but there was a possibility too that the vehicle had been dumped for a reason. All they had to go on was year, make and color. It was an old car, a common make, but at least the color was unusual. It was just the kind of case that helped pass working hours and justify the paycheck.

K rang San Matteo County Motor Vehicle Tax and Licensing Department and requested a vehicle registration search.

"We'll see what we can do," said an unseasonably cheerful voice. "Don't hold your breath though."

K dialed Robbie Begay's cell. It rang and rang, until K terminated the call. Right now his mind was stuck. There was no progress in any direction. No success with any of the enquiries they had attempted, so far. Noah George was still lying in a refrigerated drawer at the mortuary. Ella King was still waiting for news.

Forget the purposefulness that reigned in the police procedurals so avidly consumed by the civilian public where cops inexorably zipped toward perps like ferromagnetic metal to magnet. You practically never saw how it really was, how everybody was just tiny dots in a vast landscape, with no pointers, no pointers at all. Where finding your perps was mostly about arbitrary strokes of luck. Right at this moment, from where he was sitting, the case looked about as likely to be solved as winning the Powerball.

Maybe it was just Milagro PD's general ineptitude. Maybe it was his very own specific ineptitude.

Maybe it was time, after a decade of playing-at-being-a-boondocks-cop hiatus, to return to academia, where the unsystematic sampling of motley matters and inconsequential moot points that was his preferred style of rigorous inquiry at least did not threaten to obstruct an investigation that mattered to anyone else but his narcissistic little old self.

Maybe there was not that much wrong with just going through the motions and enjoying drawing a regular salary, as Robbie Begay advised. But Robbie Begay had not met Ella King. He had not met Dinky Sapps, who probably would think that giving up on the case was no more than Noah George deserved. Hopeless in life; hopeless in death.

The antagonism K felt toward Noah's social worker put the wind back in his sails. Onward ho! He drew a sheet of paper toward him and began doodling.

What exactly had Benally said? Something about witnessing bad things happening? Being at risk through witnessing bad things happening?

What had Ella King said? She had told them about Noah's father's death, Noah's father's murder; about his attackers who basically got off, who were still around. She had mentioned Noah's drug taking, his mood swings, his temper. She said that he was a good and loyal friend. What else? She had mentioned bílagáana who were a bad influence on him. She had not mentioned the Sam Wellies. Dinky Sapps had mentioned them, in the file. Maybe this was a symptom of race relations: the Anglo thought that Indian gangs were a bad influence on Noah George and the Indian thought that it was the bílagáana who caused trouble for Noah.

All these leads that hadn't been followed up—they weren't leads, just strands, the miscellany of a life, a life cut short, that they hadn't managed to weave together. Had not *attempted* to weave together. But where to learn, when Milagro PD's experience of homicides were those caused by domestics that had escalated and where perps would usually be apprehended right next to vics, conveniently covered in evidence, and in possession of the murder weapon, which usually was a kitchen knife, a gun or, occasionally, a kitchen implement or a pair of fists.

Then there were incidents of vehicular homicide, plentiful and equally facile to solve; and hate crimes of the kind that Noah George's father had fallen victim to.

The short of it was that there was no one in the squad whom K could think of, Sheriff included, who knew much about solving murders. But come to think of it, neither did their fictitious rivals, the protagonists of police procedurals: what solved murders, there as here, were lucky breaks.

He redialed Robbie Begay's cell, letting it ring until it cut out. He did not feel he could stomach Sheryleah right now. He tried the cell again, listened to the metallic burr and started to revise his conceit about the therapeutic value of unanswered ringing.

He retrieved the heap of message slips Becky had written out in her precise handwriting from under the plant pot. He'd been away for just one day and all his favorite customers were here: two calls from the Elks and no less than three from Chuck Woodward, chairman of San Matteo NRA. Woodward who had the pick of McCabe, Young, Dilger, Myers for that matter and Smithson too, card-carrying members of the NRA one and all, ready and proud to stand up for the freedom of citizens to carry arms. K wasn't in the mood for any of the upstanding pillars of the Milagro brotherhood.

The telephone rang. It was Becky: "I just remembered what I was gonna tell you. Lewis King's here. He's with the sheriff. Wanted to see you too. OK if I send him over when he's done talking to the sheriff?"

"Sure." K took advantage of the ideal window presented to him for a game of Mahjong.

He was into his fourth game with a 1:4 win to loss ratio when there was a knock on his door.

"I heard that," Lewis King said. "Solitaire?"

"Mahjong."

"They tell me that's a real good game. Never tried it myself," said King.

"Don't start," said K. "Sit down. Make yourself comfortable. How are you?"

King looked tired and glum. "You got time for a coffee?"

"Sure," said K. "How about the Conifer Coffee House? It's just two minutes' walk from here."

"Sure," said King. He perked up as they walked along Anasazi under trees gleaming with red and golden foliage.

"Always makes me feel better, being outside," said King.

"Me too," said K. "Fall here is beautiful."

"What is fall like over there in England?" asked King.

"We call it 'autumn,'" K said. "Haven't been for a while. Mostly it's rainy. Unless, of course, global warming has changed that."

"You believe in global warming?"

"Without doubt," said K firmly.

King looked around. "Me too," he whispered.

"Have things gotten so bad you have to make sure no one's listening when you say you believe in climate change?" K asked.

"Yes," King said.

The Conifer Coffee House offered a reassuringly hippy ambience to Zeitgeist refugees who wanted to pretend that change was possible, common sense still stood a chance and communitarian ethos would eventually triumph over egomaniacal narcissism. It was a place where "fair trade" had positive connotations and did not just stand for "suckers' deal."

They took their steaming mugs of fair trade dark roasted Ethiopian Arabica to a room at the back of the labyrinthine coffee shop decked out in a whimsical array of musty-smelling bric-a-brac. Daylight filtered through yellowed lace curtains and turned the room the color of honey.

Lewis King lifted his cup and inhaled deeply. He took a sip. "Hits the spot."

K savored the coffee's rich and pleasantly bitter aroma and wondered what the sheriff would make of it. He stole a look at King. King was staring into his cup. K decided to keep to Navajo etiquette and wait it out. Give King all the time he needed.

"Did you hear?" King asked eventually.

"Hear what?"

"I guess you didn't hear," said King. "We got the Ridgeback perp."

"You got who committed the Ridgeback homicides?"

King began to nod, then changed midway and shook his head. "It wasn't us who found him. He handed himself in. So I guess we didn't get him."

There was no triumph in King's manner at all. K nodded and took a sip of coffee.

King frowned. "It's this kid—Dale Jackson." He fell silent and peered into his mug as if expecting Pythia to rise from it.

"You don't sound that happy you got him," K said eventually.

"Guess not," Lewis King said, "Dale's one of life's losers. One of those where things always go wrong for them, you know? All his life."

"All his life?" asked K.

"Pretty much," King said. "Dale's dad was a real troublemaker, hardcore domestic abuser. Beat up on his wife, his kids, even the grandma . . . anyone who crossed him. But you couldn't get them to file a complaint. I was out there a heap of times myself. Everybody knew what was going down, but there was nothing we could do.

You know how it goes, abuse: it's like a smell that sticks to you. You're a victim, chances are people pick up on that and abuse you too. Dale had a real bad time. So bad they made him change school a bunch of times. They hoped things would get better for him. They didn't. Finally Rose, his mom, got away. Took some classes, got some certificates. Got herself a job over there at the Day Center, you know the mental health place? Great lady, Rose—helped a heap of people. Not her own son though. Maybe it's harder to help your own folks than helping strangers?"

"Possibly," K said.

King shrugged and took a long draught of coffee. "Anyways, I wanted to tell you. Because you saw how it was at Ridgeback: the case has been solved."

"Not solved perhaps," said K gently.

"You're right," King said, "we know who did it. But nothing is solved. It seems to me things are even worse now than when we didn't know."

"They are?" K asked.

"It's like a bad dream," King said, "where everybody's a loser. They talk about justice and tough justice and deserved punishment and all that, and here's this kid who's been pushed so far he kills just to show that he is someone. He didn't even know those kids. He doesn't know why he did it." King traced a finger along the smooth wooden edge of the table. "With many that say that I know they're just saying it to get themselves out of trouble. With Dale—I believe him. I believe that everything in his life was running together and burning him up."

It occurred to K that Lewis King was talking like one of those social workers who Robbie Begay had scoffed at. Making like those monkeys. . . .

"There are always different sides to every story," K said.

"I guess I should be thinking of the victims," King said, "but all I can think of is Rose and how she deals with it. All the folk she helped, all her skills. She's got a big heart, that lady."

If King hadn't been married, a family man, father and grandfather. . . .

"I reckon Rose Jackson's career is over. No one's going to believe in the mother of a murderer," Lewis King said.

Put like that it sounded shocking. Merciless.

"You don't think that people will understand what her son did is not Rose's fault?"

"No," said King simply. "Even the folks at her church won't want to know her."

"They should," said K heatedly. "After all they forgive God for the world he's created."

"God created the world. It's people that create the mess in it," King said quietly.

"Sorry," said K, "I didn't know you are a Christian."

"I don't know if I am. The older I get the less I am of anything. Funny, with some folks it goes the opposite way—the older they get the more they believe."

"What'll happen now?" asked K. He thought of the freshly elected state Senator who had begun to carve his niche with rabid fire and brimstone views that rivaled any of the raised decibel diatribe that passed for legitimate discourse in these days of political hyperbole. The Senator had, predictably, made the generous application of the death penalty his special calling.

King shrugged. "Hard to say which way it'll go. Could be they'll push for the death penalty. But there's many who think the kids had it coming because they were there for a drug deal. You heard Ernie Tso. There's many like him who are not bothered about lowlifes dying."

K found he couldn't bring himself to ask about the murdered kids' families. It was one complicating view too many.

King looked at his watch. "Guess I better go."

They walked across the park, a carpet of fallen leaves rustling under their feet. K saw King to his car.

"It kind of helped, getting things off my chest," King said. "Thank you."

K waved after King's car and went into the station.

His own chest felt tight, as if squeezed by a suit of armor several sizes too small.

• • •

"There's an envelope just arrived from the Vehicle Licensing Department," Becky said.

"Wow," said K, "it took them about a nano-second."

"Maybe they got nothing to do," said Becky, "How was your break?"

K shrugged, took the envelope and made for his office. The vehicle licensing people had enclosed a bunch of photocopies: car registration, tax, car owners' names and addresses.

The car had last been registered to a Muriel Kowalski. The name rang a bell. Then K remembered his wordless encounter with the hostile girl and the self-harming boy at Magnusson's bar.

His memory moved in mysterious ways. Oftentimes he would forget a name as soon as he'd heard it or a face as soon as he'd seen it.

He had no problem recalling Muriel Kowalski's flinty eyes and emaciated body and her companion's disquieting beauty. Maybe it was that Muriel Kowalski's name was fairly rare in these parts. Or that K appreciated coincidences. Or that K's encyclopedic knowledge of his alter ego Philip Marlowe's exploits had conjured up an association of Muriel + Lake = Trouble.

K skimmed through the papers.

According to the vehicle registration Muriel Kowalski was resident of 18 Cottonwood Trailer Park.

The first law of police work: there are no coincidences.

CHAPTER SEVENTEEN

K drove up Main Street past Camilla Archibeque's liquor store. A highly polished Toyota pickup was parked in front of the Main Street Liquors. K turned the patrol car around, doubled up and drove into Camilla's parking lot.

The doorbell jingled. The store was empty. Camilla Archibeque emerged out of the back room, dragging on a cigarette. She was wearing jeans, a fitted white T-shirt and a broad brown leather belt with a turquoise inlay buckle.

"You're looking happy," K said.

She looked radiant in fact.

"Radiant in fact," he said.

Camilla ground out her cigarette in the ashtray on the counter. "One of the things I like about you is your fancy way of talking."

"Just came by to see how everything's going."

"Oh darn. Guess I forgot. I said I would call you, huh?"

K could not recall her saying any such thing. Ever since he'd screwed up with Camilla he'd felt this persistent unease gnawing at him. Now it seemed that Camilla was not bearing a grudge. The feeling of unease ebbed away.

K began to feel light with relief and gratitude.

Camilla said, "He returned. With my car. And guess what: had it detailed for me too. Truck came back cleaner than it's ever been since I got it. I think he wanted to make it up to me."

"Great," said K and did not say what he was thinking: who is "he"?

He asked casually, "So where did he take your truck?"

"Just went driving around, I guess. Cabin fever."

"Talking about a vague destination," K mused.

"You know: 'Don't ask, don't get told.'"

"Do I? Is all resolved then?" he asked, and took care to keep his tone neutral.

"As much as it's ever going to be, I guess," said Camilla.

Her mood seemed to have shifted.

K was silent; waited.

Camilla smoothed back a strand of hair, smiled and said, "Don't be a stranger now, hear? Drop by anytime. Actually, better make it soon. I got some fancy IPAs coming in."

The doorbell jingled. Two men entered the store. They looked a bit worse for wear. K left. He didn't want to disrupt Camilla's mojo dealing with her customers.

Once outside, he began to feel worried about leaving Camilla to deal on her own with the shitfaced dudes, though he was pretty sure she knew how to handle customers in any state. Still, as a police officer it was his duty to ensure that citizens were safe from harm.

He decided to kick around and wait until the men left the store.

He strolled around the parking lot, doubled back to check out Camilla's truck. It was a white Toyota pickup, a recent model. Somebody sure had done a first-rate job with the detailing. The vehicle sparkled in the sunlight, the chrome trimming gleamed. K peered inside the truck and checked out the interior. The dashboard was clean, the cabin spotless, no trash anywhere. The vehicle looked as if it had come straight from the assembly line.

K circled the Toyota in reverie. He wouldn't mind owning a truck like this. Camilla's ride looked as if she did not drive it very much. The tire profile was still really good, hardly worn at all. K stuck out his hand and ran it over the tire. And stopped.

He bent down, brought his face close to the tire, traced the pattern with his index finger. He looked around, took out his cell, pointed it at the tire, zoomed in, took a sequence of photos. He flicked through the photos, enlarged some, looked at them and chewed his lip. Then he got into the patrol car.

He had quite forgotten his intention of waiting around for the two drunks to leave Camilla's store.

CHAPTER EIGHTEEN

"No need to look that worried," Weismaker said. The coffee machine hissed and spluttered as he topped up water. Steam rose and formed a fuggy shroud around the sheriff, like Beelzebub rising.

"I think there is."

The sheriff scrutinized K's face and motioned toward a chair.

"Sit."

K sat.

"I can see you are having difficulties starting, if that's any consolation," the sheriff said. "I hate to tell you: there's a time limit on this. I got a meeting. So shoot."

"I dropped by Main Street Liquors. I attended a callout to Camilla Archibeque couple of days ago and went to check on her. I mean . . . follow it up."

Weismaker nodded blandly.

K pulled the phone out of his pocket and scrolled down to the photos. He put it on the desk and pushed it in Weismaker's direction. Weismaker lifted it carefully.

"Camilla Archibeque's truck was parked in front of the store. White Toyota. And when I looked at the tires, I saw this." K gestured toward the screen.

Weismaker held the screen in front of his eyes and peered at it.

"Might help if you told me what I'm supposed to see."

"There's damage to the tire profile—damage to the right rear tire profile. When I went out to Chimney Rock with Robbie Begay what he found was tire tracks from a pickup with some damage to the profile. Rear right tire. Begay called it a unique identification point. When I interviewed Dom Benally's family, one of the kids said she'd been awake in the night and she'd seen a white or light-colored pickup driving in the direction where the body was found."

"What were you doing, checking out Camilla Archibeque's tires?" said Weismaker. "Did you suspect her? Just being curious."

"I spotted the damage by accident. I was checking out the truck—out of personal interest. If ever my truck's done . . . Camilla's truck looks pretty good. Almost new. As if it's not been driven much. Tire profile's real good. And then I saw the damage. I recognized it right away, because Robbie Begay spent awhile explaining the significance of certain things to pay attention to."

He looked up and saw Weismaker scrutinizing him.

"So you think Camilla Archibeque has something to do with Noah George? Noah George's death?"

K shrugged. "I can't really see it. But I do think her truck could be involved."

"So you're saying it was Camilla's truck, but not Camilla?" asked Weismaker.

"That would be my guess."

"Care to share your hypothesis?"

"A couple of days ago there was a callout on an auto theft. I took the call. 1741 Main. Main Street Liquors. When I got there Camilla said it was nothing. I got the impression she wanted me to forget about the auto theft. But it was pretty clear she had something on her mind. There was something troubling her. Today I drove past Main Street Liquors and saw the truck parked out there. I dropped in to see how she was keeping. Camilla was in a real good mood, almost euphoric. She said that 'he' had brought the vehicle back; 'he' had taken it for a drive. She was especially happy that 'he' had had the car detailed before 'he' brought it back. When I was there last time she did not mention anyone. I think she called in the auto theft when she noticed her truck was gone and regretted it as soon as she had."

"Something happened while the truck was gone?"

"I'm kind of curious about the fact that the truck was thoroughly detailed when it was returned. There wasn't a speck on it. Camilla took it as a caring gesture. I got the feeling that was one of the reasons why she was so happy."

"You know who that 'he' is?"

K shrugged. "I didn't feel it was my business to ask her."

"Hmmm," said Weismaker. "Camilla losing her head. . . ." He sounded regretful.

"Don't we all," said K.

"Speak for yourself," said the sheriff. "What I need now's those photos you've taken."

K obediently went to work on his phone.

Sending photo files from his phone was a skill he had recently acquired. In fact he had been surprised at how little skill there was to acquire. It was simple, basically. But then people said that everything was simple. And maybe it was, once you knew how to do it. It was just how difficult things were when you did not know how to do them that was the problem.

"Need some help?" the sheriff asked.

Damn. Lost in self-congratulatory reverie, K had squandered a rare opportunity to show off technical dexterity.

"Here they are," said the sheriff. "Let's just see how they look blown up. Yep. It's pretty clear. We'll just check that it matches what we have from forensics. Then we get a warrant from the DA. Then we bring in the truck."

Weismaker looked at K's tortured face. "How about we send somebody else to pick up the truck?"

"No," said K. "I owe it to Camilla."

Weismaker nodded. "Keep on standby. I want you to bring in the truck as soon as we get the warrant, OK? "

"Yes, Sir," said K.

"It ain't easy, Son," Weismaker said.

"It never is," said K.

•   •   •

K caught in himself a hankering for a cup of Weismaker's coffee. Wherefrom that longing for the sheriff's brew? Wasn't the day bad enough without an excursion into the pits of sensory endurance? And then he remembered the Bedouin way of pulling teeth. According to Grandpapa, to pull a tooth Bedouins would heat up a stone. Then someone would press the hot stone against the patient's bare sole and at that exact moment the tooth would be pulled. Because the patient had been distracted by the burning pain on his foot he did not notice the tooth being pulled.

Like many of the things Grandpapa had told him, K had carried this story along as gospel, until, far into adulthood, he thought the Bedouin method through and began to have some doubts. He could see that feeling one pain might distract from feeling another. But surely there was still pain? Was the pain of burning soles better or worse than the pain of having teeth pulled? Had Grandpapa's story been a lesson about everything being relative or a lesson about pain being inevitable?

•   •   •

K had barely entered his office when the phone rang and Becky announced that the tow truck was ready and waiting. A couple of minutes on the sheriff called. The warrant was ready.

The tow truck's driver was Darren, a young, round-faced Navajo with a bristling crew cut that looked as if it could pierce balloons. Darren was one happy dude. He was one of the few people K had ever met who had succeeded in getting precisely the job he had dreamt of as a kid. Rarer still, the attainment of his childhood dream had not jaded Darren's enthusiasm one bit. Every day that Darren was operating the tow truck to him was a good day. Darren loved everything about the truck: the design, the color, the rumbling engine, the screechy brakes, and he especially loved the truck's towing mechanism 'like a giant fishing reel.'

226

"And I like fishing too," Darren had once informed K, as if it was a matter of divine providence.

Behind the wheel of his truck Darren beamed. His grin almost made K feel OK for a moment. Sometimes it was good to be reminded that there were exceptions to the truism that most of humankind's tears are spilled over answered prayers. The boy's passion was a thin ray of light squeezing through the dark cynicism that shuttered K's soul, a soothing balm on his scabbed psyche.

"Hey, Darren," he said warmly.

"You the one that asked for the truck?" asked Darren enthusiastically. "Cool. Great day, huh?"

"Well. . . ," said K.

K's contrary brain produced a response once given by a great writer known for his bleak view of the human condition. When on a particularly balmy spring morning the man's companion exclaimed, "On a day like this aren't you glad to be alive?" the great man had given his considered verdict: "I wouldn't go quite as far as that."

"Happy Days," said K.

"Sure is," Darren agreed.

K gave Darren the address and asked for fifteen minutes' head start. Then he corrected himself. "Make that ten."

Ten minutes alone in the company of someone who felt betrayed and angry was quite enough.

CHAPTER NINETEEN

Camilla was behind the counter, writing out current offers with a broad-tipped red felt pen.

She looked up and smiled. "Strictly DIY—that's me. Howdee? Did they relax rules on drinking on the job?"

She studied K's face and put down the pen. "Can I help you, Officer?"

"Yes, you can," K said.

Camilla stood silent.

"We've come to take in your truck." He heard his voice, the tone impersonal and flat.

"My truck?"

"The white Toyota in your parking lot. That is your truck?"

"You don't know if it's my truck or not and you want to take it in?"

"Yes."

"Care to tell me why?"

"We need to eliminate it from a current inquiry."

"Ain't that what you do with suspects?"

"Yes," said K, "and with anything that may have been involved in a case too."

K waited. He waited for Camilla to ask about the incident from which her truck needed to be eliminated.

How dark Camilla's eyes were. It was rare to see irises that dark. Or maybe it was just the pupils that made her eyes look damn near black. Camilla did not ask anything.

K handed over the warrant. "You got another ride?"

"How long's it gonna be?"

"Depends," said K. That was the honest answer.

It would depend on what Delgado Forensics found. Camilla could have asked K to clarify. But she didn't. Outside an engine rumbled. Darren was pulling his tow truck into the parking lot.

"I'm sorry," K said.

"Aren't you supposed to give me something to sign?"

If Camilla had not reminded him he would have forgotten the paperwork.

"I sign where the crosses are?"

"Yes, please."

Camilla signed the forms and opened the drawer under the counter. He saw the black handle of a gun half hidden by a stack of receipts. Camilla slid her hand underneath the receipts and felt around. K laid both of his hands on the counter. Camilla looked up and put a keychain with a car key on the counter. The keychain had a tiny roulette wheel suspended from it.

"Thank you," said K.

"You bet," said Camilla without emphasis.

• • •

Back at the station K made straight for Weismaker's office. He heard Becky calling after him. He did not bother to stop. He rapped on the sheriff's door. In the silence of the corridor the knock sounded louder than he had intended. K opened the door.

Weismaker, behind the desk, raised his eyebrows. "Officer Kafka."

K looked on a burly back, stuffed into a burgundy-colored shirt, meaty neck spilling over tight collar. Weismaker's guest arduously shifted his bulk around and eyed K with no discernable trace of friendliness.

"How do, Mr. Watson," said K.

Watson responded with a noise that sounded like a snort.

"Better get going, I think," Watson announced.

"Thank you for dropping by," said Weismaker and got up to escort his guest out the door.

Watson tilted his chin at K and left.

"Coffee?" asked Weismaker menacingly when he had closed the door behind him.

"Yes, please Sir," said K.

"You want a coffee?" asked Weismaker.

"Yes," said K bravely.

"Milk? Sugar?"

"Just black, thank you," said K.

"Just black?" Weismaker echoed.

K nodded. Weismaker shrugged and filled a mug. K was conscious of Weismaker watching as he took a first sip.

"I guess you know who that was?" asked Weismaker.

"I do, Sir," said K and added "Burt Watson, Elks chairman," in case Weismaker planned to take up some more time asking him some more rhetorical questions.

"Care to know why he came to see me?" Weismaker asked. He did not pause to wait for K's answer.

"You don't think that all this," Weismaker swept his arm in an expansive gesture that encompassed the dust-ridden shelves, perilously balanced stacks of files and his office door, "isn't enough to keep me busy? Just been spending one hour of my precious day with Watson, trying to talk him down. One hour! Trying to reassure the chairman that Milagro PD is not infiltrated by commies and liberals fixing for a revolution. You met. Remember? When you did your 'Information Session on Burglary and Home Safety' at the Elks? How often do I have to tell you: NO POLITICS? No, I don't want to hear anything from you. No buts and onlys, OK? I am telling you: no more jokes, remarks, comments that can be misconstrued, OK?"

"Yes, Sir,"

"You may go," Weismaker said imperiously.

"Just wanted to let you know, we took in Camilla Archibeque's truck."

"How did it go?"

"OK, I guess."

"OK?" asked the sheriff.

"She didn't raise any objections. She did not ask any questions. She signed all the paperwork."

"Don't'cha wish everyone was that easy?"

"Yes, Sir," said K.

•   •   •

Outside his office window K saw people who looked like aliens in hazmat suits and visors stalking across shrub land opposite the station. Some were connecting hose pipes to tanks mounted on trucks; some were leading hose pipes to spots marked by orange flags, others were threading hosepipes into the burrows.

K pulled down the shades. He stared at the computer screen and thought of a film scene where someone wrote a sentence over and over, before going on a killing spree. Better than thinking of the prairie dogs who were sitting right there, right now, in their burrows waiting for danger to pass, not knowing that they'd never again leave their burrows alive.

CHAPTER TWENTY

K said, "I'd like them here, on my arm. Kind of a sprinkle, know what I mean?"

He was surprised that there was no pain at all. He had heard that it could be excruciating. But this was OK. You could have tattoos done and not feel a thing and forget about them. So he forgot about them. Until he happened to look at his arm. Saw that the tattooist had covered it from biceps to wrist in ants. He looked at his other arm and saw there two life-sized crustaceans—malformed lobsters or crabs—marching toward his knuckle. In between the crabsters there was joined-up writing, lots of it, more like scribbling. He couldn't read any of it. He saw with horror that the writing did not stop at his wrist; it covered the back of his hand. Even long sleeves would not hide the tattoos. He'd have to wear gloves. There were so many tattoos that it would take years to remove them by laser surgery. It would cost thousands. He did not think that he could stand living with them for that long.

K sat bolt upright. He was covered in sweat. He blinked, switched on the bedside lamp, looked at his right arm. He knew then that he did not have to look at his left arm too, but he did anyway.

Usually he was a light sleeper. When he dreamt he generally knew that he was dreaming. He had been really caught up in this one. When he had been trying to come to terms with the tattoos, when he had calculated how much laser surgery he'd need, he had felt like a man condemned to a life sentence.

• • •

"Good morning. Looks as if you could use one," Becky said when K entered the station.

"Ha ha," said K mirthlessly, "make my day."

"At some point today you'll probably be wishing you'd never said that," Becky said, cryptically, wisely or menacingly. K could not decide which.

"I wouldn't be surprised," he said, opting for an answer that suited all three possibilities.

He schlepped along the corridor, cast a cursory glance into the staff kitchen, which at this hour looked halfway usable, briefly considered brewing himself a cup of coffee, dismissed the idea and went into his office.

How dim it was; how dusty. He switched on the computer, logged on. Then he pulled up the shades, and, opening them, remembered why he had closed them. The municipal pest control trucks had gone. So had the exterminators in their hazmat suits. So had the prairie dogs.

He wondered if the tattoo dream was somehow linked to the extermination of the prairie dogs, but found his patience did not stretch to analyzing the symbolism. Besides, he couldn't really see how tattoos and prairie dogs were related.

• • •

"You just might be interested who's all in the Interview Suite," Becky said significantly.

K just couldn't get used to 'Interview Suite.' On some days it irritated him more than on others. 'Interview Suite' sounded like the type of over-styled hotel room with panoramic views from which Hollywood A-listers trotted out trite observations and insipid sentiments re whatever trite and insipid insult to intelligence they were contractually obligated to promote. He preferred the good old term 'Interrogation Room' with its whiff of truncheon and unconstitutional displays of power.

Not that the transition from Interrogation Room to Interview Suite had generally effected a civilizing process in terms of interrogation habits. These depended, then as now, first and foremost on a suspect's ethnicity—and the cops' degree of antipathy toward said ethnicity. He wondered who it was whose interrogation Becky thought would interest him; unless she thought that his interviewing technique would benefit from observing say McCabe or Young doing their shtick on a 'Spic.

Though Weismaker never tired of assuring his officers that the partitioning mirror really was one-way and hi-spec at that, so that they could turn on the lights in the Observation Suite and not be spied by perps, the squad by and large preferred to watch from the dark. And though the Observation Suite was less soundproof than it was lightproof, the cops were markedly less inhibited when it came to having lively conversations while "observing." Indeed McCabe and Young had once run their mouths so loudly that the sheriff had been obliged to apologize to the suspect, interrupt the interview and go over to the observation room to tell McCabe and Young in a hoarse whisper to shut the fuck up or else. In the meanwhile the suspect had had time to reconsider his options and had smartly stepped back from the verge of making a confession. Weismaker, philosophical as ever, had scrutinized the suspect's sheet and expressed certainty that they'd see him again. The sheriff had been right. And this time it had been within two weeks rather than the perp's customary three-month interval between misdemeanors. He'd possibly felt that he had some credit to spend.

K opened the door slowly and quietly stepped into darkness. It was so dark he could not see if there was anyone else observing. A hint of scent, clean, citrussy with musky notes of sandalwood hit his nose—Juanita Córdoba. He inhaled her fragrance and allowed himself a brief indulgence in a vision of coupling with Juanita against the wall in the dark Observation Suite, his hand clamped over her mouth, to stifle her pre-climactic moans. His loins tightened. Maybe there was something oedipal about his fantasy of congress with Córdoba while the sheriff was interrogating a suspect on the other side of a glass wall?

"Hi there," K said softly.

"Uhu," said Juanita Córdoba.

And there he was, the sheriff, his solid frame planted on the chair opposite the suspect, exuding calm and benign serenity, a Buddha of the Southwest. And on the other side on the table, straight-backed and very still: Camilla Archibeque. K sharply drew in air.

"They just started."

Córdoba was sitting in the far corner. She had drawn her chair close to the wall. K placed his chair next to her and sat down.

Camilla's face was that of a marble statue, pale, motionless, unreadable.

"She is very upset," whispered K.

"How do you figure that?" asked Córdoba. She didn't sound challenging, just factual, as if she was trying to learn from him.

"Don't you think she looks upset?" whispered K. He wasn't particularly keen on elaborating on his interpretation of Camilla's body language.

"I've got Asperger's," said Córdoba.

"Oh, I didn't know that," In his surprise he forgot to keep his voice down.

"I didn't either," said Córdoba.

"How did you find out?"

Strangely, his lusty fantasies regarding Juanita Córdoba had taken flight, though, as far as he knew, having Asperger's did not usually affect an individual's sexual prowess.

"I did one of those tests," whispered Córdoba.

"Did you see a psychologist?" asked K.

"No," said Córdoba, "I did it online."

"I didn't know psychologists did online assessments."

"It was one of those online tests," Córdoba explained, "you know—those free tests that you can take?"

"So you took a free online test that told you that you have Asperger's syndrome?" asked K. Too late he noticed that his voice had risen again. "Sorry," he mumbled.

"Well, my friend took it and said I should have a go too, you know."

"Let me guess, your friend is Asperger's also and did not know it," said K.

"Yes," said Juanita Córdoba "How did you guess?"

Maybe she was Asperger's after all.

"I once took one of those tests to see if I was a sociopath and it turns out, yes, I'm around 99% sociopath."

"Really?" said Juanita. Her voice had cooled a couple of degrees.

"No," said K, "I just meant to say those tests don't mean anything at all."

Although it was in fact true, as it was that the sociopath test result had unsettled him, despite his skepticism. He remembered looking into the mirror and thinking: "Here stand 99% of sociopath and 1% of—what?" It had been that 1% of undefined psychic matter that had eventually reassured him that psychometric testing was, for the most, so much bull crap. Not bull crap enough though for Juanita Córdoba's Asperger's diagnosis to have significantly dampened, if not entirely exorcised, his erotic desire for her. Temporarily, he hoped. He needed something to perk him up on drab days at the station.

"These days, everyone is something," he whispered reassuringly. "They invent new diagnoses every day."

"Invent or discover?" asked Córdoba.

Eureka! The question was nuanced enough to rekindle his fancy. He shrugged and his sleeve brushed against her arm. Córdoba left her arm where it was, which could be a good sign, meaning she welcomed body contact between them; or a bad sign, meaning she had not noticed because she wasn't interested in him at all; or a very bad sign, meaning she did have Asperger's and generally wasn't aware of other people, but instead knew all the engine sizes of all the car types in the world. Or was that autism?

"I can't see that she looks upset," said Juanita.

"Look how still she is . . . her face . . . there's no expression at all in her face."

"But how do you know she's upset?" insisted Juanita "She could be real angry. Or defiant. Or guilty."

"You haven't got Asperger's," said K.

"How come you're starting on *that* again?" said Córdoba, as if they had been discussing her online diagnosis for hours.

Juanita Córdoba of course had a point. He had taken his assumption—his projection—as gospel. What's more, he felt guilty, burdened by having been instrumental in the process that had brought Camilla here to be interrogated.

He looked at Camilla's face. True, it could just as well be read as angry or defiant. Guilty? Not so much. He could see no guilt, but something else. . . . As she sat silent and still, he could see Camilla's beauty clearly: her proud features; her poise; her charisma; her face that of a tragic heroine. That's what he could see: hurt. Camilla looked tortured. But surely she would know, she would understand that they were just doing their job, that he had done what it was his duty to do; that the sheriff was doing what he had to do? Surely she could not hold it against them that they had taken her in?

"You think she did it?" whispered Juanita.

"Did what?"

"Killed the guy . . . the . . . uh . . . Chimney Rock John Doe?"

"Noah George? No, she didn't."

"I mean . . . did she help. . . ? Forensics said there were two."

"No, I don't think she did," said K.

"How come you're so sure?" asked Juanita

"I know her," said K.

"Oh." said Juanita.

Did Juanita Córdoba sound frosty or was he just imagining it?

• • •

In the Interview Suite the sheriff and Camilla sat in silence. The sheriff sat as if he had all the time in the world: seconds building to minutes and minutes to hours, hours to days. Maybe it was his fisherman's experience that had honed his patience. Maybe it wasn't patience as much as fatalism: qué será será. Maybe fatalism was what made the sheriff a true listener—someone who could listen without agenda, without second-guessing, just letting it roll. Weismaker sat, quietly, serenely, as if anything that Camilla said or did not say was OK by him. This was just as well, because Camilla did not say anything, just sat, silent and motionless, apparently as unfazed by the sheriff's silence as he was by hers. K in one of those bizarre conjectures that almost felt like a hallucination saw how suited they were to each other, Camilla and the sheriff. Or would be, in another life, maybe.

"And miles to go before I sleep," Juanita murmured.

Hurray! Welcome back, Juanita Córdoba, to Kafka's Inventory of Worthy Sexual Objects.

"Nothing's going to come out of this," Juanita said, unaware of the honor that had just been restored to her. It took K a beat to compute that Juanita had not just rejected his erotic desire for her, but was assessing the scenario in the Interview Suite.

"Ah," said Juanita.

Weismaker had signaled, by a subtle shift in body posture, the end of the interview. Weismaker got up. Camilla rose from her chair, slowly, as if leaden weights were holding her down. Weismaker and Camilla left the Interview Suite. Juanita Córdoba switched on the lights and flicked various switches on the recording equipment. Only then did it occur to K that Juanita was here because she had been delegated to record the interview. It was a long time since K had last been asked on recording duty. The last time had been when he had confused Input and Output functions and had secured 135 minutes of audio snow footage. Though that mishap had occurred with the old recording equipment. This new equipment was bound to be much easier to handle.

"How're you finding the new recording equipment? Easier to operate, huh?"

"Uh . . . not so much. With this one there's so many possibilities to make mistakes. The old one was nice and simple, you know? You had to try real hard to get it wrong."

Good-bye, Juanita Dream Babe; hello Córdoba Emasculating She Devil.

The door opened and the sheriff stuck his head into the Observation Suite.

"Everything work out OK with the recording?"

"Yes, Sir," Córdoba answered.

"Thank you. Appreciate it," said the sheriff.

He beckoned to K.

"Becky said I'd find you here. You feel like running an errand?"

The sheriff held out a bunch of keys and a note.

"That's all she wants. Her purse. She left it in the store, in the back room, she said."

"Nothing else?"

"No. That's all."

"How long will you be keeping her in?"

The sheriff shrugged.

"I don't think she did anything. At all," K said.

"That doesn't mean she's got nothing to do with it," the sheriff said obliquely.

"So I go and pick up her purse from the store?"

"Don't forget to lock up after yourself."

"You're not worried I'd plant some evidence?"

"Nope," said the sheriff, "nor that you conceal any neither."

"You know me well," K said resignedly.

CHAPTER TWENTY-ONE

The Aspens on the foothills were turning golden, autumn leaves trundled in the breeze and woolly clouds drifted across the sky like languid flocks of sheep. K looked out for prairie dogs standing sentry by the side of the road, hoping against hope that some at least had been spared the municipality's euthanasia initiative. He couldn't see any. Maybe it was now hibernation time for prairie dogs. Though he knew damn well that whatever creatures hibernated would forage and fatten themselves up for at least another six weeks before they withdrew for the winter. And he wasn't even sure if prairie dogs hibernated at all.

Main Street Liquors looked shut. Presumably Camilla had not had the time to summon Rudy, ex-boiler maker, to staff the store. K drove into the forecourt and parked the patrol car in a spot that he judged was slightly more discrete, toward the side of the building, not in full view of Main Street. He contemplated the bunch of keys Weismaker had given him. There were far too many keys for comfort. Worse still, among the keys on the bunch, none looked obviously like a store key. And the keys weren't marked, tagged or labeled either. A couple looked as if they belonged to drawers or safes or filing cabinets, not doors, but there were still plenty of keys left to keep yourself occupied for half an hour trying to open the damn store door while half the city of Milagro was cruising by wondering what the cops were looking for in Camilla Archibeque's liquor store.

THE QUALITY *of* MERCY

Apart from not wanting to damage Camilla's rep, K most particularly wanted to avoid making a public spectacle of himself: "cop-too-dumb-to-open-door-lets-get-him-to-chew-gum-at-the-same-time." As things stood, neither calamity looked as if it could be avoided.

K gave the bunch of keys some more attention, braced himself and approached the door, hand clamped around the key he had determined looked most likely. He inserted the key into the keyhole. It stuck, did not move and it was a job getting it out of the keyhole again. That one did not fit then. He tried the next with much the same effect. Then the next. No luck. After trying the first three or four keys he gave up going by order of likeliness and started shoving any old key into the keyhole. Having to return to the station and ask McCabe or Young to come along and open the door was starting to look like a distinct possibility. K took hold of the door handle. He turned the handle. The door gave.

For one moment K thought that a small miracle had taken place, that the right key had been the key that looked wrongest, another life-lesson, another potential self-help book in the making.

Then he realized that the door had been open all along.

He pushed the door open slowly, quietly. He stepped into the darkness of the store and felt for his holster. Outside, on Main Street, cars and trucks rumbled by.

The lights at the junction turned red. Traffic ebbed and silence fell.

The silence in Camilla's store had that cotton wool quality particular to the silences of unhappy spaces. It wrapped itself around the brain, blunted the senses, carried within it the ominous current of ultrasonic frequency.

The muffled sound cutting through the oppressive stillness almost came as a relief.

K stood motionless, his entire body focused in the direction of the sound. There it was again. It was coming from the back room.

K began to move cautiously, stepping carefully toward the rear of the store, toward the door that led to the back room.

The source of the sound was obvious now. It was the sound of someone moving about in the back room. Someone treading softly and moving freely.

K felt the bunch of keys digging into his palm. At least having his hand full with a bunch of keys made kvetching on whether to draw his gun redundant. He hated drawing his gun anyway. Though in the dog-eat-dog deal that was the here and now, there was a chance that a gun would outperform a bunch of keys.

Cop wisdom had it that catching intruders unawares was about as advisable as surprising feeding mama bears: neither species took particularly well to it. Creep up on either and be prepared for show-down time. That's why National Parks made good revenue out of bear bells.

K laid his fingertips on the door and slowly pushed it open. In the dim room he made out a silhouetted shape.

"Police," he said quietly, "arms above your head."

The figure halted, then did as instructed, slowly, almost languidly.

K ran one hand over the wall until he felt the light-switch. He flipped the switch and heard the clack-clack moth-wings-batting sound of antiquated neon-lighting flickering into life. The lights came on and doused the room in a hepatic hue.

K saw a man who, even with arms raised over his head, looked sanguine. A young man, tall, slender, dark haired, in long-sleeved navy T-shirt and washed-out jeans. The man's body language did not suggest that he intended to use a gun. His demeanor did not seem like that of someone who had a gun, though appearances of course could be deceptive.

"You can lower your arms now," said K. "What are you doing here?"

"I was thinking of asking you the same thing," the young man said.

There was something about his voice that struck K.

"You go first," said K. "I'm the cop."

The young man smiled, as if appreciating a joke. "I'm staying here," he said.

For a moment K thought that the young man was issuing a challenge to him.

"Who are you staying with?" K asked.

"Camilla. Camilla Archibeque," said the young man.

"You're a relative?"

"A relative?" the man said, as if he was considering it. "No. No, I am not."

K spotted a purse that matched Weismaker's description on a chair, walked over and picked it up.

The young man watched. "Help yourself," he said.

"You'll have to leave the store, until I've verified with Camilla Archibeque that she's aware of your presence."

"Aware of my presence," said the young man.

He did not sound sarcastic, but rather as if the words held another meaning for him.

"No problem. I'll leave with you," he said. "OK if I take this?" He lifted a sketchbook from the table.

"It is yours?" asked K. The young man nodded.

K switched off the light. The young man produced a key-ring from which dangled three keys. He pulled the store door shut, locked it and handed over the keys.

"I guess you want those."

"Thank you," K said.

"Where is Camilla?" the young man asked.

"She is helping us with an enquiry."

"We met before," said the young man abruptly.

K looked at the young man, his dark almost black hair, his strange, amber-colored eyes—the eyes that held a challenge that K could not quite define—long sleeves covering wrists. . . .

"We have," K said neutrally.

"What is the enquiry about? That Camilla is helping you with?"

"Her truck," said K, looking into the young man's amber eyes.

"The truck," the young man said.

He was looking straight back at K; looking into K's eyes as if he was looking for something.

K nodded and began walking toward the patrol car.

Behind him the young man said, "Maybe we'll meet again," without particular emphasis.

K turned and watched him walk away holding his sketchbook. He walked with the fluid grace of a swimmer moving through water.

CHAPTER TWENTY-TWO

K tended to forget that the holding cells were now housed in the annex; another idiotic arrangement added to the gazillion idiotic arrangements brought in when the station had been refurbished.

Housing holding cells away from the main building in terms of the perpetually short-staffed Milagro PD translated into one lone cop in the annex guarding however many miscreants needed to be contained in police custody at any given time.

Granted, usually that wasn't that many, except during Demolition Derby—and the Devil Rose Biker Rally—and the 4th of July—and Labor Day—and the Livestock Auction—and the Rodeo and anytime the Casino put on a special event—and the first of every month—and on any given weekend. Usually it was drunks occupying the holding cells; or perps apprehended on open warrants; domestic abusers; a motley collection of what cops considered the annoying and hapless arbiters of minor social misdemeanor and delinquency.

But K remembered well a night in the annex, alone with a man suspected of a series of murders of uncommon and chillingly calculated cruelty. The suspect had spent just one night in the cell before his transfer over to a maximum security federal penitentiary. After that one night K had been left in no doubt of that man's capacity for depravity and sadism, although the extent of his contact with the prisoner had been limited to innocuous small talk.

K walked over to the annex with Camilla's purse. Behind the duty desk sat, or more precisely lay, McCabe, feet propped on desk, greasy head pasted against the wall, watching a game on the wall-mounted TV. At least he wasn't chewing on a toothpick.

Another idiotic arrangement was that the wall-mounted TV and the monitoring screen for the cells had been placed on opposite walls, probably due to some consideration regarding the Feng Shui implications of aligned screens. K, who was not much into watching TV, wasn't too bothered by this, but he knew that the more conscientious cops, who liked to catch a game now and then while on jail duty, were. No such worries though for McCabe, who had his priorities firmly sorted. McCabe's eyes, narrow slits deeply recessed in folds of fat, did not stray from the TV.

"I got to take this purse to Camilla Archibeque."

"Nope," said McCabe, without taking his eyes off the screen.

"Oh yes, I do," said K.

"Who says?" McCabe drawled, still watching the screen.

McCabe probably imagined that he was channeling Clint Eastwood, though K made him more for one of the less sympathetic protagonists of *Animal Farm*.

"Sheriff."

"Sheriff says you gotta hand over the purse to...?"

"Yes Sir," said K.

"I gonnerhafta search it," said McCabe and stretched out his arm.

K nodded cooperatively and placed Camilla's purse on the desk, just a couple of inches out of McCabe's reach. McCabe peered at the purse, squinted at K, exhaled noisily, shifted his legs from the table. The chair's front legs crashed to the floor with a deafening thud.

"Hope you didn't hurt yourself," K said cordially.

McCabe flared his nostrils, snorted and drew the purse toward him.

"Better get the paperwork too," K said.

He went over to the filing cabinet, where he managed to find the appropriate form, in triplicate. Oh lucky day. There were around 150 sections to fill in, all in about a size three font. McCabe glanced over the form.

"Aw," he said nonchalantly, "can't imagine Camilla Archibeque carrying anything that'd concern us, eh?"

McCabe pushed the purse toward K, heaved his legs, one after the other, back on the desk and turned his eyes toward the TV screen.

You had to hand it to the man. He was dependable. Sloth won over pride, every time.

•   •   •

They had put Camilla in Cell 6 at the far end of the annex, a cell reserved for the better class of detainees. It was one of two cells at either end of the annex that had a window, though the windows were barred and too high up on the wall to afford any views. At least the windows let in some natural light, and the walls were mostly free of sketches of primary and secondary reproductive organs. Cells 1 and 6 also had proper doors with inset viewing windows that gave prisoners a modicum of privacy. Through the viewing window K saw Camilla. She was sitting on a berth covered with a grey jail-issue blanket. K knocked and unlocked the door.

"Here's your purse," he said.

His voice was not at all as he had intended. It sounded cold and official, where he merely had wanted to sound neutral.

"How are you doing?" he asked.

Now he sounded cloying, over-familiar, borderline patronizing.

"I'm sorry," he said.

Now he sounded genuine.

"Don't worry," said Camilla.

Camilla sounded neutral. So neutral that any response became redundant. K understood then that there was nothing to say. That there was nothing he could say. Unless he was willing to prostrate himself before Camilla—which he wasn't. He felt a sting of anger. After all he had merely done his duty. Did Camilla really expect him to look the other way when her truck was implicated in a murder enquiry?

"No," said Camilla, "I know you were just doing your job."

K wondered if not being able to distinguish internal monologue

247

from articulated speech was a precursor of early onset Alzheimer's. It seemed to happen to him more and more.

Camilla stretched out her hand for her purse and K handed it over. There was nothing more to say, so K said nothing, left the cell and locked up.

• • •

McCabe was still watching the game, his feet planted on the desk, only now he was chewing on a large pink sausage. A photo taken of McCabe now would make terrific blackmail material.

On the monitor he saw Camilla sitting as she had before, as if no one had been there at all. He placed the cell keys on the desk. McCabe grunted, spraying the desk with half-masticated bits of sausage. K worked on suppressing his gag reflex and exited the annex.

He looked at his watch. Just under an hour until the end of the shift.

• • •

"Didn't I tell you I'd make your day?" Becky crowed when K entered Reception.

His heart sank.

"Good," Becky said, "I can see that you can see what's coming."

"Why so chirpy?" K asked irritably. "You got a date?"

He could see right away that he'd gone too far, but he was damned if he'd apologize. Not today. Today was the day to make dames into enemies.

"What?" he asked.

"Gutierrez has an emergency, so you'll have to pull his shift. He's due to be on until midnight. You're on with Young and Myers. Young's on Reception 5 to 7:45; you are on 7:45 to 10:00; Myers 10:00 to 12:00, OK?"

How come Myers had been given the shortest stint? Well, at least it wasn't the night shift, just a couple of hours. Two hours and a quarter, to be precise. These too would pass.

"No problem," K said into Becky's incredulous face.

• • •

The kitchen looked as disgusting as was to be anticipated anytime Mc-
Cabe was on shift. K gathered sponge, wire-pad, cloth, cream-clean-
er, degreaser and antibacterial spray and drew a deep breath. Twenty
minutes in he realized that cleaning up after the inconsiderate, anti-
social scum that were entrusted with keeping order amongst the cit-
izenry had a therapeutic effect. He scrubbed the dishes vigorously,
rinsed them and inspected them, holding each one toward the light, to
make sure he hadn't overlooked any smears. With each shining plate,
each sparkling glass, he felt better. Washing dishes was like rinsing
the soul. Surprising really that no one had yet launched Dishwashing
Mindfulness, dishwashing being Low Resource: High Impact; Acces-
sible to a Broad Demographic—and rife with allegories applicable
to psyche and soul. He held his forearms under the hot water tap and
splashed lustily, whistling Schubert's Trout Quintet.

"You'll make someone a mighty fine wife someday." It was
Young bearing provisions.

"You'd make a great exhibit in the Dinosaur section at the Smith-
sonian," K returned the compliment.

"I don't get you," grunted Young.

"No worries. You will not have me."

K pulled the plug and watched the water gurgle down the drain.
He rinsed suds out of the sink, wiped dry stainless steel, washed out
sponge and cloth, and advised Young, in mellifluously honeyed tones:

"Make sure to leave a mess, hear? I need something to pass the
time."

No response from Young.

But then Young had his head stuck deep in the refrigerator, a hog
snuffling for truffles.

• • •

In his office K continued with his cleaning therapy. He dusted surfaces, dead-headed plants and sorted out papers for shredding. Then he lost a few games of Spider Solitaire, quite a few actually, and when Spider Solitaire had lost its appeal, set off on a virtual Odyssey through the World's media. By the time he was due at Reception his eyes were burning and he had the beginnings of a headache.

He gathered all he had on Noah George, then reconsidered and took along Walter Benjamin's Arcade Project as well, in case he needed light relief. Besides, K had discovered that an impassioned lecture on the wondrous insights offered by Benjamin had the miraculous power to cut short unbidden conversations and inexplicably drive people into flight.

Book in hand and file under arm K made a detour to the kitchen, where he discovered that Young had indeed obliged him by leaving it in a God-awful mess. He laid down book and file on the corridor floor—in the kitchen there was no inch left unsoiled—shut down his peripheral vision, wandered through the desolation like a Zombie and brewed himself a coffee. He left, shutting the door behind him. Somehow he doubted that he would have the energy to clean this hellhole again tonight.

•   •   •

Young hunkered behind the Reception desk chewing on a large pink sausage.

Perhaps McCabe and Young shared each other's provisions. But it was also possible that Young had just helped himself to one of McCabe's sausages. Young had a reputation. Though K—so far—had not had any trouble from Young regarding his tubs of hummus. Young stuffed six inches of sausage into his mouth, wiped his kisser with the back of his hand, wiped his hands on his shirt, raised his head and significantly looked at the clock.

"Oh my, 7:47 already! I am so sorry! I do hope I have not inconvenienced you," K said effusively.

Young, his cheeks bulging with sausage, narrowed his eyes. He placed his fat fingers on the keyboard and logged off.

"Anyways, away you go! I'm here now," K trilled, and he waved an airy hand toward the corridor. Young's expression was that of one discovering a tarantula squatting in the plughole. Faggot-liberal channeling Scarlett O'Hara. Chew on that, buddy.

• • •

Young's Reception shift had apparently passed uneventfully. He had left nothing but sausage scraps and a small pile of chewed matchsticks behind. It made sense that Becky kept a stash of cleaning products in her bottom drawer. K sprayed the desk with antibacterial degreaser and wiped the surface with a wad of Kleenex. Not exactly environmentally friendly, but hey.

Then he logged on. He wondered what Young had been doing on there. Ogling titties? Ordering guns via mail order? Posting hate mail on bigot forums? K went to Start and opened Mahjong. After a dozen or so games out of which he won precisely three, he started to feel depressed. He got up, stretched himself and felt the need for some fresh air.

The streets were dark and deserted. There was barely any traffic. There was the kind of chill in the air that came just before the first night frost. The first night frosts made K think of the Yeíbicheí— the Nightway Ceremony. He could almost hear the rhythmic high-pitched chants, smell the wood fires, visualize the masked dancers' eerie procession. Maybe he would find time to go this year. He'd go on the last night, the culmination of the ceremony, and stay all night until sunrise.

He looked at the lights in the annex. Over there was Camilla. Would they remember to turn the light off for her? Probably not, if it was McCabe pulling a double shift.

The flickering light of the TV screen projected moving patterns onto the dark parking lot. A couple of blocks up Main Street Taco Bell's malfunctioning neon signage created a hectic red glimmer that looked like emergency services lights. The star-spangled sky could not compete with Taco Bell's faulty neon. K sighed and went inside.

He picked up Noah George's file and leafed through it. So little left of a life. There was the Delgado pathologist's report, the Benally family's statements, Noah George's dental records, a short synopsis probably compiled for probation services, Dinky Sapp's impersonal case-notes—there was a loose handwritten page—his own attempts at drawing together what they had so far. If the clues to Noah's death lay in his past there was scant chance that it would ever be solved.

So vast was the Rez, so easy it was to disappear, to never be found again, alive or dead. Easy for those who knew how to live according to the old ways, but possible even for outsiders: outlaws from other tribes, even Anglo fugitives managed to live out their days in Diné Bikéyah.

K read over what he had written. He had missed out the one factor of any significance to the enquiry: Camilla Archibeque's truck. So now they had something that connected Noah George's death to Milagro.

K's mind was shrouded in a brain-fog that he recognized as resistance. He stared at the page and had not a glimmer of an idea, absolutely no hunch, just a woolen emptiness that filled his skull.

In a few days, no more, the police enquiry into Noah George's death would be relegated to low priority, then to "cold case." Which was OK. In terms of professional pride he could live with that. They were provincial cops, not detectives. They knew how to spot and apprehend DWIs and DUIs; they could catch a shoplifter; find a lost dog; at a pinch they knew how to break up a domestic. Burglaries were borderline—whenever a perp was not found in situ it got complicated. Unless the perp had a highly individualized style of committing his crimes, and a rap sheet that went back to the Pleistocene, and had been considerate enough to leave plenty of clues and a business card with current contact details.

Yes, in terms of professional pride he could live with being a methodologically challenged small-town cop. After all, deciding on this life had been his informed choice. He had had other options. Options that anyone who knew him believed were preferable to burying himself alive in a provincial police station in the redneck boondocks.

But K liked this life, as much as he was able to like a life.

He liked the mountains, the plains, the desert, the vastness, the proximity to the Rez. He liked his home. Where else could he have afforded thirty-five acres of land, a mature orchard, a pond? K even kind of liked being exasperated by Young and Co. It was all grist for the mill.

But the lack of progress in this case he did not like. Because there was Noah's Aunt Ella King and all the other people who had lost someone to a hate-crime or else to a cause of death that remained unsolved because the death of an Indian still was low priority in the Enemy's land. K wanted very much to show Ella King that her nephew had mattered.

And perhaps what he also wanted was to atone for the neglect of the cops who had failed Noah George's father, whose murderers had been free for these past twenty years, conceivably bestriding the community without remorse, quite possibly raising sons in their own image—and of their convictions.

K looked at the clock. It was 9:10 pm. Time dragged.

He closed the file and opened "The Arcades Project." It occurred to him that there were some parallels to how Walter B. had gone about his monumental project and the Milagro PD's detecting methodology:

It was all about traveling in order to get to know one's geography.

CHAPTER TWENTY-THREE

K felt a rush of cold air and looked up from Walter Benjamin's tome. Somebody, a man, had come through the door. Had it not been for the draught, K would not have noticed him. He closed his book and watched the man cross the dim Reception.

The man was tall. He walked with an easy grace. There was something familiar about him.

It was the young man with the amber eyes; Camilla Archibeque's guest/not relative. Their short meeting this afternoon seemed light years ago.

"It's you," said the young man.

"It's you," K said.

"About Camilla," said the young man.

"There are no visiting rights," said K.

"This isn't about visiting rights," said the young man.

He rested his hands on the counter. K looked at the hands. What perfect balance of force and grace. What a splendid specimen.

"Can I talk to you?" asked the young man.

"Go ahead," said K.

"I am here to make a confession—is that what you say? Make a confession?"

"What is it you'd like to confess to?"

"Camilla Archibeque's truck," said the young man.

"The truck is implicated in a current enquiry," K said.

"I know," said the young man.

"You know?"

"I know. I drove the truck."

"Drove the truck when?"

"I drove the truck at the time your enquiry pertains to," the young man said.

If every confession was expressed as concisely a whole lot of fun would be drained out of the interrogation process.

Maybe, K thought, this was a case of answered prayers—with all the twisted trappings. There he was, pulling a late shift at Reception, bellyaching about the impossibility of solving this case and his personal failures and shortcomings; envying the fictional Alpha Cops in police procedurals who always managed to solve their cases by hook or crook, or sometimes both, worrying about disappointing Ella King, and what happens? The door opens and in walks the perp volunteering a confession.

Small drawback though: it is night time. There's no one to go through the constitutional rights spiel, monitor the interrogation, witness the confession, never mind helping the dumbass technophobe cop set up the Interrogation Suite. And the dumbass technophobe cop who's on Reception duty means to handle this confession. He knows that the other cops on shift, namely Young, Myers and McCabe, pinnacles of team spirit every one of them, are certain to insist on K completing the shift wherever the rota says he should be: that is, Reception. And Reception being a kind of wide open thoroughfare is not conducive to the confessional process, which needs intimacy and/or intimidation. Not that K favored untoward methods. McCabe and Young though, who belonged to the "Hang 'em Now, Ask Questions Later" brigade, were sure to want a go at the interrogation.

"You've chosen your moment," K said, gesturing toward the darkened corridor.

He often found that it worked better to be candid than to pretend he had everything under control.

"I have," said the young man.

He had a way of talking as if to himself, as if everything that he said worked on a different level that only he was aware of.

"Don't worry," said the young man, "I don't mind about all the constitutional stuff."

"Unfortunately I have to," said K.

"Unfortunately?" the young man looked as if he anticipated a reasoned statement on the merits of disregarding citizens' rights.

"I was being flippant," K said.

The young man lifted his shoulders to the hint of a shrug.

"If I do not mind all the 'constitutional stuff' your confession becomes void."

If ever there was a dumb way of briefing a possible perp on the get-out clause. . . .

"I am going to confess," the young man said evenly, "and sign whatever I'm supposed to sign."

K looked at the clock: 9:48.

The young man followed his eyes, "I am not going to run."

K tried to look as if this possibility had not occurred to him.

"Why don't you just take a seat over there for a couple of minutes."

The young man did as asked. K couldn't decide whether he was disconcertingly detached or just very casual. He rooted around Becky's desk for the old Dictaphone that he knew she kept there for emergencies. It was about the only piece of equipment he felt comfortable handling. Never mind that someone would have to transcribe the interview. That wasn't his problem. And here were statement forms too. He looked at the clock: 9:55.

The way the young man was sitting reminded K of how he had seen Camilla sitting on the berth in her cell. Camilla and the young man both had an aura of someone looking into an internal abyss, though the young man looked as if he had long since gotten used to the view.

Myers appeared on the dot of 10:00, glanced at the young man, asked disinterestedly if anything had happened, to which K said he didn't know yet. Myers shrugged and hissed that one day he'd stuff one of Young's sausages down his throat so far that it'd come out of his ass. "You don't believe the goddamn mess this mother's made in the kitchenette—I couldn't stand being in there long enough to make myself a cup of coffee, would you believe that?" He looked at K dolefully.

"Oh yes, I do," K said curtly.

He knew Myers' chutzpah. Myers was hoping that he'd offer to make him a coffee.

K gathered Dictaphone and statement forms, went over to the young man and motioned toward the corridor. The young man did not wait to be instructed. He rose swiftly and followed K.

The hair at the back of K's neck pricked, the way it had, when hiking, he'd crossed fresh cougar tracks. He looked over his shoulder. The young man had kept a conventional distance. K opened the door to his office, turned on the lights and beckoned the young man to a chair. He held up the Dictaphone and said, "Our conversation will be recorded."

"My confession," said the young man.

"What is your name?" asked K.

"Jared Beausoleil."

K pressed record, spoke date, time and their names into the machine, recited the Miranda and reminded Beausoleil of his right to legal representation. Beausoleil shook his head and K told the Dictaphone that Jared Beausoleil had declined the right to legal representation. Beausoleil, speaking in the direction of the Dictaphone, confirmed this.

So far, so collaborative. Now only the vast stretch of legalistic black ice that was contemporary custodial interrogation procedure lay between him and a legally valid confession.

"You presented at Milagro Police Station tonight and said you wanted to make a confession, is this accurate?"

"Yes," said Beausoleil.

"Can you confirm that you have come of your own accord and that you have not been pressured by anyone to make this statement?"

"I confirm," said Beausoleil.

"Over to you," said K.

He was beginning to feel the effects of the double shift. Pretty soon he'd be caring more about going home than being interested in collecting syllables from this opaque individual.

"I took Camilla Archibeque's truck without her knowledge or consent to transport Noah."

Jared Beausoleil certainly had a gift for concision.

"You do know Noah's last name?"

Beausoleil shook his head. "No."

"How did you come to dispose of Noah's body?"

"Repose."

"Repose? How did you come to 'repose' his body?"

"I concluded his life."

"How did you—conclude his life?"

"I helped him stop breathing."

"You helped him stop breathing? How?"

"I held a pillow over him until his breath stopped."

K looked at Beausoleil, tried to read his expression. He had not been able to get anything from Beausoleil's voice.

"How do you feel about . . . that?" K could not bring himself to repeat Beausoleil's words. He could not stop himself asking Beausoleil about his motives. It was as if the young man was dragging him way off course.

"How do I feel?" Beausoleil echoed as if this opened a completely new perspective. His amber eyes looked into the distance. K waited and listened to the whirring of the Dictaphone. It sounded like a distant wind tunnel.

"I feel I did him a kindness."

"You feel that by suffocating Noah George you did him a favor." K kept his voice neutral.

"Noah George," said Beausoleil.

"Noah George. So you did him a favor? Could you tell me why it is that you feel you did him a favor?"

258

Beausoleil lifted his shoulders. "I did not do him a favor," he said clearly.

"You did not do him a favor?" echoed K, "Did you not just state. . . ?"

"I said: kindness."

K felt that peculiar chill rising in his bones that he sometimes got when he was about to witness something truly terrible. He tensed and waited. The Dictaphone whirred. And Beausoleil said nothing. K waited some more. When he felt that he had waited long enough, he said: "Tell me how come you suffocated Noah George."

"There was an accident. He hit his head. He was unconscious."

"You could have taken him to the hospital."

"Yes," Beausoleil agreed, "But why?"

"To give Noah the chance to survive."

"Yes," said Beausoleil, "But why?"

"Why not?"

"You feel like being here all night?" asked Beausoleil wearily. "I said all I have to say. I'll write out a statement and sign it."

"You've not told me who helped you," said K.

"No one. I was alone."

K felt a rush of adrenaline, a white-hot surge from solar plexus to brain, the hunter's euphoria before a kill.

It was the moment when everything fell into place, when seedling hunch, submerged somewhere in the preconscious, sprang forth and exploded into full bloomed certainty. The first law of police work: there are no coincidences.

"Muriel Kowalski," K said.

Beausoleil said nothing.

"We know that someone helped you. We have the footprints."

Beausoleil said nothing and looked into the distance as if there he saw something of infinitely greater importance.

K said, "You, Noah and Muriel Kowalski were traveling in Muriel's vehicle. You had an accident. Noah was injured. Unconscious. You decided it would be better to kill Noah than to help him. For whatever reason. To get rid of the evidence you and Muriel dumped her car in the reservoir. The two of you took Camilla's truck to transport Noah's body. You, with Muriel's help, took Noah's body and dumped it at Chimney Rock."

"I was alone," Jared Beausoleil said, "and I did not dump him."

"Who did?"

"It wasn't dumping. I laid out his body."

"You laid out his body."

"Peace," said Beausoleil, "I put him in a position of peace."

"You put him in a position of peace? With his face in the dirt?" K asked incredulously.

"The sky's overrated." It did not sound as if Beausoleil was joking. "There's nothing up there."

K remembered the sketchbook. Beausoleil's sketches that he had looked at in Camilla's backroom. He knew what would come next as surely as if he'd seen the script: "—as opposed to down below," K said.

Beausoleil's eyes probed his.

"You put Noah George's face in the dirt because. . . ," said K.

"All of life is down below," said Beausoleil. As if he had no doubts at all about what he had done and why.

"You did him a . . . kindness." K contemplated. He looked at Beausoleil. He could see that Beausoleil had said all he was going to say.

"You did him a kindness, and you laid him out to communicate . . . with life below?"

Beausoleil's eyes widened, shone golden in the desk lamp's light. "I would do the same for you," he said gently, his eyes resting on K.

K felt an abyss open, felt as if he had been stripped of skin and flesh, stripped to the marrow of his bone.

"I'll write my statement now," Beausoleil said matter-of-factly.

K left the Dictaphone running as he watched Beausoleil write out his statement with economic precision. He heard the thud of his blood, felt it rushing, round and round through his body. He spoke date and time into the machine and announced termination of the interview. His voice sounded surprisingly normal.

"We will have to keep you in custody for now," he said.

He took Beausoleil back to Reception where Myers was busy with his newfangled phone, probably collecting a gazillion points in a game chasing worms.

Then he went back to his office and phoned through to the annex to let McCabe know about getting another guest. McCabe sounded as if had been chewing another sausage, or maybe he had just woken up.

"Let's put him in Cell 1," K suggested.

It was probably better to keep Beausoleil and Camilla as far apart as possible. K escorted Beausoleil over to the annex, where McCabe was waiting for them with a bunch of keys. McCabe looked at them without curiosity.

"Do you need anything?" K asked the boy.

"Nothing," Beausoleil said with finality.

"I'll see you tomorrow."

Beausoleil looked at him. K felt another chill. McCabe was shaking his keys at Beausoleil, cocking his head in direction of Cell 1.

Beausoleil said, "Good bye."

K stood for a moment and looked after Beausoleil being led by McCabe down the corridor to the cells.

It was midnight. Time to go home. Time to get some sleep. K collected his stuff, left the station and drove home. Finally.

CHAPTER TWENTY-FOUR

He came to with a start. Opened his eyes and stared into pitch black space. Saw nothing. Around him all black. As if he had gone blind. Felt panic. Looked around in the dark, frantically, until he located the faint glimmer of the illuminated digits of the alarm clock. Still felt terror. Groped around in his memory, tried to recall what dream had jolted him awake. He remembered no dream.

The dread was there still. Dread ran cold in his veins—a terrible, invasive dread coursing through him like a toxic river. He got up, groped his way through the dark house, went outside, stood on the porch. The air was chill-cold, the sky clear, speckled with myriad stars. In the orchard he could hear deer stalking through the long grass. From the pond the malevolent growling and snarling of fighting raccoons. In the distance the hoot of an owl, thrice repeated.

The Navajo believed that owls brought bad luck. Wearing owl feathers could drive a person crazy. Other cultures believed that the hoot of an owl was the harbinger of death.

Then he remembered what lay at the heart of his dread. He strode back inside the house. A shape flitted past, squeezed though the door before he had fully opened it.

"Aren't you supposed to spend nights outside, old man?" he asked the cat rhetorically.

He went to the phone. His heart raced as he dialed.

The phone rang. And rang.

"Huh?" grunted a sleep-sodden voice.

"McCabe? It's K here."

"What's wrong with you?" McCabe asked irritably.

"Beausoleil," K said.

"What?"

"Beausoleil. Jared Beausoleil—the guy in Cell 1."

"Buy-solly?" said McCabe. "What about him?"

"Is he OK?"

"Whaddayamean, is he OK? What dumb question is that?"

"Did you check on him?"

"Did I check on him? What is it? You are my supervisor now?"

"Is he OK?"

"Bleeding heart . . . the guy's a killer, you worry if he's alright?? Gimme a break. Sweet Lord Jesus."

"Did you check on him?"

"Got him right here on the monitor. Tucked up all nice and cozy; peaceful like a baby. Got it much better than he deserves, believe you me, buddy. That all? Jeez. . . ."

McCabe hung up before K could say any more. K went back to bed.

Dread throbbed through him like an infected wound.

•   •   •

When the phone shrilled through the darkness it came as a relief.

"Can you come in? Now?" Weismaker's voice was tight.

"Yes," K said and replaced the receiver.

It was 5:45 am.

In Reception Smithson nodded at him. "You just about missed the circus."

"Sheriff's in his office?"

"Yeah."

K went through and knocked on Weismaker's door. He didn't wait for an answer. Weismaker was standing at the desk, on the phone. "See you folks in an hour then."

He motioned toward a chair.

"I'd rather stand," said K.

"You know what this is about?"

"I can guess."

Weismaker looked at K as if he was trying to read his mind.

"Beausoleil, your arrest yesterday," Weismaker said.

"He handed himself in voluntarily."

"Anything strike you?" Weismaker asked.

"Not at the time. Just that he is a—thing apart. As if he was not quite of this world."

Weismaker exhaled, "Was."

"So something has happened," K said.

The sheriff nodded, "You don't seem surprised."

"Where's McCabe?" K asked.

"In shock. They took him to the hospital."

K found he could not bring himself to speak.

"Gutierrez came on shift at 4:45. Gutierrez and McCabe did the handover check together. Gutierrez thought that there was something strange about the way Beausoleil was lying on his berth. He was right."

Weismaker spoke rapidly.

"Seems he managed to bring something—something sharp—into the cell. He stuck it into his neck, right into his aortic vein. He knew exactly what he was doing. Lay facedown. All the blood soaked into the mattress. He made sure he wouldn't be found until it was too late."

"He's dead," K said.

"Gutierrez and McCabe called emergency right away. There was nothing they could do. Such a lot of blood . . . a lot of blood. Right now we are waiting for forensics."

The sheriff looked at K. "You are not surprised?"

"I knew something was wrong. I woke up in the night and knew."

"You didn't notice anything when you interviewed him?"

"I noticed he was—different. When he admitted—confessed—killing Noah George he said that he did him a favor; no: a kindness.

With some people that's defensive. They're trying to justify what they did. Beausoleil . . . he genuinely could not understand why saving someone's life would be a good deed."

"He said that?"

"Not in so many words. He just said 'why not?' when I asked why he suffocated Noah George."

"He didn't think he did anything wrong but he confessed?"

"I think he did it because of Camilla, for Camilla. When he found out she'd been arrested because of her truck."

"He confesses and kills himself?"

"He was more of death than of life, I think."

"Angel of Death," said Weismaker.

"He probably would have liked you saying that."

"Now he'll never hear anyone say anything ever again. What a waste, eh? There'll have to be an inquest, of course."

CHAPTER TWENTY-FIVE

"I need to talk."

"You beat me to it. I meant to call you."

"I need to talk, Lili."

"Sounds serious."

"I. . . ."

What a miracle this was. Not a miracle. A wonder of science and technology. Sound trailed by breath traveling across the continent, desert stone and grass-covered plain and mountain range, canyons and lakes, small hamlets, big cities to the coast and then a thousand leagues under the sea along the cable snaking under a hundred quadrillions of gallons of sea-salty water all the way to other side.

"Franz? What's up little brother? Tell me."

Once he started to speak he could not stop. A torrent under the sea. Sound not breath. Whys. What ifs. If onlys. Under the sea, under a hundred quadrillions of gallons of sea-salty water along the deep-sea cable all the way to the other side, until his breath ran out.

Silence.

"Lili? Are you there?"

"Yes."

"Say something."

Syllables. Waves of sound. Interrupted. The hum of transatlantic currents.

"What did you say?"

"I said that I couldn't always tell if you are speaking about your young man, Jared, or yourself." His twin's clear voice traveling all across the Atlantic under a hundred quadrillions of gallons of sea-salty water.

"Speaking about myself?"

"Yes," said Lili. "Hey? Little brother? Say something! What are you thinking?"

"What a miracle this is."

"A miracle? What is?"

"Sound traveling so far. Across all this landmass. Under the sea. Don't you think that's a miracle?" said K.

"I think you had a shock, Franz," his sister said softly.

"What did you mean when you said. . ." he couldn't say what Lili had said. He did not remember what Lili had said. "What did you say?"

"That when you spoke of Jared Beausoleil it sounded as if you were speaking about yourself?"

"What?"

"When you spoke of Jared Beausoleil it sounded to me as if you were speaking about yourself. As if you saw something of yourself in him. Didn't you?"

"I saw—I saw that he was lost and did not mind. I saw that he was lost and believed that it was not a problem. It was a solution." That sounded nothing like himself. K never had any solutions.

"That is a lot to see," said Lili. "I imagine that he saw that you saw. And that he knew not everyone would see as clearly as you did."

"He offered to do the same for me," K whispered.

"He offered to kill you?"

"Euthanize me," said K. The lump in his throat was making him hoarse. "He didn't offer. I think he was trying to reassure me: 'I would do the same for you.' There was tenderness in it."

"You sound frightened," said Lili. "What is it that is frightening you?"

"That to him I seemed so unhappy that he thought it was doing me a favor, no, a kindness to let me die."

"Aren't you?"

"I can't take your humor at the moment."

"I wasn't joking," said Lili, "but neither do I think that you need to take as gospel what a lost young man, however charismatic, says to you. I think you had one thing in common: a fantasy about saving the world. It's just your definitions of saving that differed."

"That's incredibly cynical."

"Cynical? No. Fatalistic maybe."

"If I had handled things differently. . . ."

"Maybe the outcome could have been postponed, but not avoided. Believe me. Did he give you any hint at all that he wanted help?"

"Maybe he did. Maybe his offer to help me should have made me understand that he wanted help for himself."

"He certainly did choose his moment."

"What do you mean?"

"Do you know what day it is?" asked his sister in a cool, clipped tone. "Today's the anniversary of our parents' death. Now he'll always be part of the family."

CHAPTER TWENTY-SIX

"Yeh."

It wasn't a question and it wasn't a statement. It certainly was not an encouragement. Perhaps a discouragement cloaked in a statement with an inflection that hinted at a question.

The Ogre was buffing her talons with a minute cloth. Today the Ogre wore rainbows at the tips of her fingers. Light flitted through the windows and set the Ogre's fingers aflame with color.

"Officer Begay," K said, as the Ogre, whose eyelids were weighted down with palettes of cosmetic product, opened her mouth, "—is expecting me. NOW."

The Ogre's lips twitched in an uncertain smile as she picked up the phone.

"Officer Cuffcart to see you," the Ogre said meekly into the receiver.

"Officer Begay will be with you right away," the Ogre said, face still contorted to an approximation of affability.

K nodded tersely. Seething malevolence would get you where considerate civility would not, every time.

"How about we go for a drive?" asked Robbie Begay. "I was thinking Jumping Goat Pass."

"Haven't been up there for a while," said K.

"Won't be long now 'til the first snow."

Begay stopped at Gopher's Burger Den Drive Thru and bought two large coffees.

"Did you know the value of a car depends on how many cup holders it has?" he asked, placing coffees in cup holders.

He did not wait for an answer. "It's good and hot. Here, I got you a bunch of brown sugar to sweeten it up."

At the Junction Begay took a right to Highway 288 South. K looked out the window at Needlerock, the skeleton of a volcano, its weather-ravaged core pointing skyward like a bony finger.

"It doesn't much look like a needle."

"No," said Begay.

"What do you think it looks like?"

"Depends on my mood, I guess. Sometimes I see something happy . . . like Goofy with one ear flapping, see? Sometimes, something sad, an old man bent over with pain, that's his back over there. Sometimes, something scary, like. . . . Why? What do you see?"

"I see a finger stretched into the skies . . . a skeleton finger. A warning finger."

"Good time to go up to Jumping Goat. By the time we come down you'll see something else."

"I'm putting my hope into your hands," K said.

"Good choice. Do you see a ghost?"

"I don't know what a ghost looks like. Am I supposed to?"

"Needlerock, when the bílagáana first settled they called it Ghostrock. Wanted to name the town Ghostrock too. The Elders had to raise hell, get a delegation together and petition those Anglos that us Diné don't really rate ghosts. Took a lot of campaigning to make our White friends change their minds. You know how Anglos like to go places they have no business in and naming everything they see?"

"You Name It; You Own It," said K.

"Is that why they named us Natives too?"

"I suppose so," said K.

"Needlerock is kind of a dumb name for a rock. I guess we agreed to it to keep our bílagáana friends sweet."

They passed Needlerock.

Begay took a right.

"Hey, you remember? That's where your beautiful girl made the fry bread."

The lay-by was deserted. A dust devil whirled a funnel of debris across the plain. The road was straight and stretched to the horizon. To the left mountains grew from dusty yellow foothills to craggy rock-face to a towering, forested range. Begay took a left on a road that was so perforated with potholes that it was like driving on an ungraded road—one of those infamous Rez-washboards. This road too cut in a straight line through the plain and vanished inside the forested folds of the mountain. At the foot of the mountain the road cut serpentines into red rockface.

"Did I tell you we used to spend our summers up here when I was a kid?" Begay asked.

"My cheí would bring the sheep up here the old way—walking. Even when they got themselves a truck, he still walked with the sheep. Said the sheep needed to know where they were going and so did he. Later he got rheumatism real bad. Nights got too cold for him up here. So we took over. From the time I was twelve we kids would stay up here with the sheep, all summer. They'd take the sheep up by truck though. And our provisions. Cousin Roy was a couple of years older. He was supposed to take care of us. Cook food for everybody. Make sure nothing bad happened. Cousin Roy made us bust our asses running after the sheep, hauling water, gathering wood. All the time he's sitting around working his way through the provisions. All we got to eat was potatoes. Nothing but potatoes. End of summer, Cousin Roy's real fat and we are real skinny."

K laughed. It had been so long since he'd laughed that it felt strange. "What happened to Cousin Roy?"

"He's on the Tribal Council, what else?" said Begay.

The car climbed the serpentines. Tracks led away from the road to summer pastures deep in the forest. Further up a dark, bulky shape crossed the road.

"Damn bear," said Begay.

"You don't like bears?"

"It's obvious you haven't stayed awake whole nights banging pans together to keep the damn bears from getting into your stuff. Hold on tight now," Begay said and took a sharp left.

The car bounced along the track then left it as Begay weaved through the forest, expertly avoiding tree stumps and boulders.

Begay stopped the car under a tree. "Alrighty. Let's get going. We got things to do. How 'bout you go and have a look at the view? I'll be with you in a mo."

K shrugged and walked across the clearing. The air was fresh, bitingly cool and smelt of pines. K picked up a cone sticky with resin and smelled it. What power a smell held, conjuring up the past better than any séance could.

They were on the mountain peak, a high plateau that looked out onto the plain. In the distance Needlerock was barely visible, the plain a gradient of pastel shades of red, ochre and yellow. K had not realized that Needlerock had companions. Strewn across the plain were smaller cones, once live volcanoes that wind and weather had worn down to their core funnel that ran down to and fed from the earth's red-hot center. It looked as if Needlerock was surrounded by miniature Needlerocks, infant Needlerocks, midget Needlerocks. A confederation of volcanic sleepers.

"Hózhóní," said Begay.

"Ao," K said.

"Come on, Shik'is."

K followed Begay to the clearing. Begay had been busy. He had draped a Pendleton blanket on the ground, had lit a fire in a small tin drum and had dug a hole a foot wide and a foot deep.

"I'll be your Medicine Man today," said Begay. "Sit, Shik'is. Sit."

K took off his shoes and sat on the blanket. Begay sat opposite him. Begay had piled up a pyramid of pine cones. He took the topmost one and gave it to K.

"Now you give what's got to go to our friend here. And he'll take it away with him." Begay motioned toward the fire.

K took the pinecone. "Can I not just tell you?"

"You can tell to whoever you want. But I sure as hell don't want to be stuck with this shit. And neither do you."

"Purification?"

"Yes Sir. Shoot, coz we ain't got all day."

"I probably need a Ndáá, don't you think?"

"Maybe. For now this is what you get, from your personal hataałii Begay, a custom-made ceremony developed exclusively for you."

"Is that a disclaimer in case the Diné Medicine Men's Association get after you?"

"And the Diné Hataałii Association, and the Association of Diné Medicine Men. Anyways—you should feel honored. Hataałii Begay doesn't invent a traditional ceremony for just anybody, dig?"

K looked at the cone. It looked a bit like a microphone. He held it to his nose and inhaled the bitter-green, deep resin scent.

"We went to see Ella King. The sheriff and I. It was as if she'd waited all this time for us to come and tell her what had happened to Noah. How he had died."

He saw the old woman before him again, how she had beckoned them into her trailer, bid them to sit down, how she had carefully with care and attention brewed coffee and had served it in her chipped, yard-sale souvenir mugs. This time K had got I ♥ NY. He did not ♥ NY and doubted that Ella King did. He had let the sheriff do the telling, while he looked at the old woman's stoic face, her milky eyes looking into nothingness.

He could not tell if the fact that her nephew's murderer's motive had been a mercy killing made a difference to her grief, nor how she felt that her nephew's killer had committed suicide. All she had said was "I waited for you," when they came, and "Ahehe," when they went.

They had crossed the trailer park and knocked on Muriel Kowalski's trailer. There had been no answer. Then the trailer park manager appeared and told them that Kowalski was gone and still owed rent. He looked at them hopefully, as if they had come to recover it for him. The manager did not know how Muriel Kowalski had left, whether she had a ride or if someone had picked her up, just that she had left stuff in the trailer that he intended to keep in lieu of owed rent. He looked at them as if he expected them to sanction his plan. Weismaker had advised him to adhere to statutory process rather than take the law into his own hands.

"Who knows?" he had said. "Maybe she'll come back?"

The manager had snorted. They saw he wished he hadn't told them about planning to hang onto Muriel Kowalski's things.

After the pathologist had determined suicide, and forensics had cleared the scene, they had had to get another cleaner in, a middle-aged no-nonsense Mexican woman from Ciudad Juarez, to clean Jared Beausoleil's blood out of the cell. Lorinda had refused to do it, had refused to go near the cell. Had told them if it was up to her she'd have the annex burned to the ground. But at least they should have a purification ceremony. In times of crisis it seemed that it was the belief of her ancestors that called to Lorinda.

It had been McCabe of all people who had agreed with Lorinda. Becky, who was, apart from Lorinda, the only Native on the team, had been cautious in her support of Lorinda's request.

They had had a ceremony to purify the annex, conducted by an NAC Medicine Man. The NAC weren't as concerned about ch'íidii as traditional Medicine Men. Which was why Lorinda still did not like going into the annex. Clara, the Mexican lady, had said that she didn't mind doing that job, she was legit, she had papers to prove it and besides, compared to what she'd seen in Ciudad Juarez, a bit of blood from somebody who'd voluntarily died was NADA. Weismaker was currently looking into the budget. Maybe they'd take on Clara as Designated Annex Cleaner.

Begay plucked the cone out of K's hand, threw it into the fire and handed him another one.

"Jared Beausoleil had no family," K said to the cone, "at least none that we could find."

Beausoleil's driving license had been from New Mexico. The Land of Enchantment was pretty easy that way. Almost anybody could get a license there. They could get nothing from Jared Beausoleil's

Social Security number. They had searched through the land, posted small ads in local newspapers.

Beausoleil had brought into the cell a knitting needle that he had whittled razorsharp. The Japanese had a suicide ritual perforating the neck artery.

Begay took the pinecone off K, threw it into the tin-drum and gave him another cone.

"These cones are easy to talk to," K said.

A lot of forethought and planning had gone into Jared Beausoleil's suicide.

"And I did not pick up on any of that."

He should have remembered the first time he had met Jared Beausoleil. That night at Barbie's when he had seen Beausoleil's arm.

"I should have known."

He had not spoken to Camilla Archibeque since the night of Beausoleil's death. Nor had she spoken to him. She'd been OK though with Weismaker, who'd taken on looking after Camilla for the time.

It was after Beausoleil's funeral up on the small cemetery across Milagro Mesa that things had gotten worse.

Bert Radebrecht and Coney Krohn, Milagro's municipal grave-diggers, had waited in the background, though not too far in the background. There was an icy wind blowing down from the foothills and Bert and Coney were eager to get back inside the cemetery's paraffin-stove-heated shack for a scalding cup of joe before the next funeral party was due. Camilla Archibeque stood at the grave. She stood still and tall and though she did not wear a veil or even mourning dress, just regular clothes and a warm jacket, that was what K saw: Camilla shrouded in a long black veil.

Later, when Weismaker had bidden him into his office, had pressed a cup of his special brew on him—which was when K knew for sure that Weismaker knew about the Bedouin way of pulling teeth—K had, his cold hands clamped around the cup, under the sheriff's gaze, begun to crack.

"I don't know how to live with the guilt," he had said.

The sheriff said nothing.

"If I hadn't looked at the tire, if I hadn't followed up on it. . . ."

But that was old hat. He'd been through that already.

A conflict of interests, a conflict of responsibility and ethics. Sooner or later it happened to everyone. Though perhaps not always with such drastic consequences. And maybe Lili was right. Beausoleil hadn't wanted to live. He would have done it sooner or later. K had merely been an instrument of providence, speeding Beausoleil along on his morbid trajectory.

"It is bad enough," said K, "to have caused another person's death. To know. . . ."

Weismaker's clear eyes held K's.

"Do you know what's worse though?" K asked and gulped down a draught of coffee so acrid that it felt as if he was pouring acid down his gullet. "Even worse is what I've done to Camilla. Jared Beausoleil's dead. For him all is over. But Camilla—she's got to live with it. She's got to live with the loss of her lover."

"Her son," said Weismaker.

"What?" K said. All had gone muffled and there was a whirring in his ears, like the beginnings of tinnitus.

The sheriff leant forward and gently took the cup out of K's hands. K pressed his hands against his temples. His sight was obscured by flickering, dancing sparks of light. He could not focus. "Son?" he heard himself saying into a void as hollow as an echo chamber.

The sheriff's voice rumbled like a mountain stream over rocks. K couldn't make out what he was saying.

"What?" he said.

"Breathe, Son," the sheriff said, "breathe slow. That's it. Easy now. Breathe."

"Her son," said K.

"Listen to me," said the sheriff, "it is important that you listen good, OK?"

K nodded.

"When Camilla was a young girl she got herself into trouble. That's what her folks called it—getting into trouble. They forced her to give up the child. When she went into labor, they took her to hospital and that was it. They took the baby away. She never saw her baby. Never heard it even."

"Beausoleil is Camilla's baby?" K croaked.

The sheriff shook his head. "Camilla's baby was taken away from her when she wasn't much more than a child herself. All her life her lost baby has been on Camilla's mind."

"And then she finds him and he kills himself," K whispered.

The sheriff shook his head again. "We don't know. Camilla doesn't know. She meets this strange, beautiful boy and she . . . fixes on him being her son. She wants him to be her son. There's no way of knowing if he really was her son."

"DNA," K said.

"It's a possibility," conceded the sheriff, "though I'm not sure it's a possibility for Camilla."

"Why not?" asked K.

The sheriff's expression was pensive, probing. "You live in your head a lot, don't you, Son?"

"I guess," said K. He hoped this wasn't going somewhere even worse.

"Then you'll know it's a curse and a grace, both. As long as Camilla doesn't know for sure, she has the choice. Could be that in a few years she'll be ready again to hope to find her lost baby. Or she'll keep holding on to Jared Beausoleil's memory."

"I'd prefer to know he wasn't her child," whispered K.

The sheriff got up and laid a hand on K's shoulder. "I do hope you'll forgive yourself, Son. In time."

• • •

"Oh boy," said Robbie Begay.

He took two cones and threw them into the fire. They hissed and spluttered when their seeds exploded in the heat. The burning cones' sparks mingled and whirled skywards.

Begay looked at K. "I got a feeling there's still something."

He handed a cone to K. It was a big cone, perfectly formed, oozing resin.

"Beausoleil died on the day of my parents' death."

"So he has a place in your life now," said Robbie Begay.

"Funny, that's what my sister said."

"Say good-bye to this cone," Begay instructed, gently plucking the cone out of K's hands.

The cone hissed and spluttered when it hit the flames, and the bitter-sweet forest smell of warm resin filled the air.

"Get up. Take off your shirt."

K got up and did as told.

Robbie Begay held a smoldering bundle of sage and walked around K, chanting in a low, soft voice. The burning sage smelled bitter and dusty, like the essence of this land and its soil. Begay rubbed the singed sage between his palms and smudged crushed leaves on K's back, his chest, his face, his forehead.

He emptied the burning contents of the tin drum into the hole, sprinkled sage on it and covered the hole with earth. K looked at the smoldering pile of sorrows being buried under the sod and felt tears running, as freely and easily as if someone had turned on a tap. Tears ran down his cheeks, dripped onto his chest, ran down his stomach. He rubbed his hands over his face and upper body, looked at his wet sooty streaked palms that smelled of sage-ash and sea-salty tears.

Begay came and stood before him, crushed more sage-leaves in his palms and smudged them onto K's forehead. He handed K his shirt. "This is where we leave these troubles."

K followed Robbie to the car. He felt lightheaded, spaced out, as if he'd taken drugs.

They drove down the serpentine road, down the mountain, onto the plain. Before them Needlerock rose out of the afternoon mist.

"What do you see?" asked Begay.

"I see the father. The father and his frightened children."

GLOSSARY

NAVAJO TERMS

A

Ahehe	Thank you
Ahwee nohsinish?	Would you like coffee? (2nd person plural)
AIM	American Indian Movement; group campaigning for American Indian rights; considered militant by the mainstream.
Aoo'	Yes
Aoo' yá'át'ééh	Yes, I'm good. Response to greeting yá'át'ééh
Anglo	Generic/regional: White person
Apple	"Red on the outside, white on the inside" = derogatory term for assimilated Indian
Ayóó bá háchį'	Very angry
Ayóó hashké	Very mean

B

bahadzid	Dangerous/terrible/taboo
BIA	Bureau of Indian Affairs
Bílagáana	White man/White person/Anglo
bimá yázhi	Maternal aunt (3rd person singular)

C

Cheí	Maternal grandfather
Ch'įįdii'	Devil, evil spirit

D

Diné	Navajo People
Diné Bikéyah,	Navajoland; Navajo Reservation
Diné Bizaad	Navajo language; also: Diné
Dinetáh	Navajo homeland

G

God bizaad	Bible
Gláaníis	Drunks (vernacular)

H

Háísh	Who?
Hataałii	Medicine Man
Hogan	Traditional Navajo dwelling
Hózhó	Beauty
Hwéeldi	Fort Sumner

I

IHS	Indian Health Service

J

Jhon	Rural Reservation dweller/Navajo yokel (too dumb to spell "John"; hence, Jhon)

THE QUALITY *of* MERCY

K

Kináalda	Girl's puberty rite at first menarche
k'é	Kin
Kokopelli	Southwestern Native deity, usually represented as hump-backed flute-player

M

Medicine Man	Traditional healer
Mountain-Way	Healing ceremony

N

Na'ashǫ́'ii dich'ízhii	Horned toad (Horned lizard)
Ndáá	Enemy way healing ceremony
nalí	Paternal grandfather
NAC	Native American Church; also: Peyote Church
Nima	Your mother
Nizhóní	That's great!

P

Powwow	Intertribal social gathering/ceremonial

R

Rez	Reservation; the Navajo Reservation

S

Shí k'ad	Conclusion: I'm done; I'm leaving
Shíma hashké	My angry mother
Shíma sani	My maternal grandmother

Sing	Generic: healing ceremony
Skinwalkers	Shapeshifters; malevolent witches
Shiyáázh	My little one; my son, also: my nephew (maternal aunt)
Shídeezhi biyáázh	Younger sister's son (woman speaking; first person singular)
Shí'kis	My friend

T

Traditional	Someone adhering to Navajo beliefs

Y

Yáázhe	Son (mother speaking)
Yá'át'ééh	Hello
Yá'át'ééh shíma	Hello, my mother
Yáadilá!	Exclamation
Yah anínááh!	Come in; enter
Yeíbicheí	Nightway healing ceremony

For Navajo vocabulary and spelling the following works were consulted:

Parsons Yazzie, Evangeline and Margaret Speas; *Diné Bizaad Bínáhoo'aah; Rediscovering the Navajo Language*; Flagstaff; 2007

Navajo Preparatory School, Inc.; *Diné Bizaad Bóhoo'aah: A Conversational Navajo Text for Secondary Schools, Colleges, and Adults [Vol. I and II]*; 2004

Wilson, Garth A.; *Conversational Navajo Dictionary*; Conversational Navajo Publications; 1994

ACKNOWLEDGMENTS

Thank you Jeanne Fitzgerald, for teaching me that sometimes doors do open when you most need them to. For your gracious and generous hospitality that made it so much easier to write up my PhD, which in turn facilitated writing this book.

Thank you shádí Gwen, lovely and loving company, great support and for being you: a special lady! And to Chuck and Orville Johnson.

Thank you shik'is Anita, for being a good friend, a role model of strength and kindness.

Thank you Judy Wolfe, landlady extraordinaire, mentor and tireless campaigner. Keep up the good fight!

Thank you Fernando and the Nakai family for your big-hearted hospitality and all the things I learnt on your farm.

Thank you, Charles Stacey, lively spirit and inspiring man of ideas.

Thank you Arlene and Lewis for letting me be part of the Anger Management group and for being patient and wise teachers.

Thank you June, inspiring group worker, generous, kind and perceptive spirit.

Thank you Tony Goldtooth, Alice Wagner, Lorraine Manavi and Herbert Benally who generously let me audit their courses: Baa ahééh nisin.

Thank you Larry King, for sharing your bold and inspiring thoughts and helping me understand the subtler points of intergenerational trauma.

Thank you DBHS and IHS staff, Tina, Mary-Liz, Gerald, Arminda, Rita, Abigail, Amber, Johnny, Sylvia, Bettina, Mr. Ernest B., Jerry (if you are not mentioned here it does not mean that you are not being thanked—merely that my memory for names could be a whole lot better).

A special thanks to all clients who taught me about the power of groups and the spirit of sharing. Walk in Beauty.

In gratitude to the Wenner-Gren Foundation for a Dissertation Fieldwork Grant the unplanned side-product of which is this novel.

To my PhD supervisor Professor Roland Littlewood who allowed me to go my own way.

To "Editrix" TseTse for reading—and reading again; to Bär and Corvin; to Sharon Keating, fellow-traveler, author and poet; Petra Villinger. for a forensic eye and uncompromising criticism; Beate for a patient first draft read-through; Kathryn and Rod for providing an oasis on Road T. La Comadre Consuelo, a true raconteuse. To comrades on the Artist's Way for being a creative bunch of people to warm the cockles of a sceptic's heart; Farmington Public Library, a truly awesome community resource and Will Gray of Fort Lewis College in whose class I first got the creative writing bug.

To Lisa Graziano, Managing Editor of Leapfrog Press for her patient and understanding handling of a rookie author. To Sara Pritchard, judge of Leapfrog's 2016 Fiction Contest, for enormously encouraging feedback. I felt you got it!

To friends and family—for everything.

Being thanked here does not imply agreement with sentiments and politics expressed in this book.

THE AUTHOR

Katayoun Medhat was raised in Iran in a multicultural household and experienced her first significant culture shock at a convent school in rural Germany. She studied Anthropology in Berlin and London and trained as a psychoanalytic psychotherapist. Working in the mental health field taught her to appreciate individual resilience and the healing power of humor as life force. A PhD in medical anthropology led her to the Navajo Nation, whose vast landscapes and endless skies incidentally remind her of Iran.

She lives in the south of England near the sea and is currently working on *Lacandon Dreams*, the next novel in the Milagro Mysteries, set in a culturally diverse and historically fraught rural Southwest and featuring non-conformist cop-with-a-conscience Franz Kafka (and his cat Wittgenstein).